In the Shadows

By

C.D. Gill

Copyright © 2021 C.D. Gill

All rights reserved. No part of this book may be reproduced in any form or by any electronic or mechanical means without written permission from the author, except by reviewers who may quote brief passages in a review.

ISBN: 1732534537

ISBN-13: 978-1-7325345-3-7

The characters in this book are inventions of the author's imagination. Any similarity to real persons, living or dead, is coincidental and not intended by the author.

All places and events mentioned in this work are used fictitiously.

Cover Design: Sherri Wilson Johnson

www.cdgill.com

Read more from C.D. Gill:

The Freedom's Cry Series

Behind Lead Doors
On Wings of an Avalanche
The Apricot Underground

Against All Odds Series:

Undefeated
Unprecedented

Ferra Empire:

In the Shadows

Learn to do good.
Work for justice.
Help the down-and-out.
Stand up for the homeless.
Go to bat for the defenseless.
Isaiah 1:17 (MSG)

Chapter 1

The broken-down *favelas,* perched haphazardly on the hillsides of vibrant Rio de Janeiro, never offered a limitless array of destinies to fifteen-year-old girls like Daniela Gomes, especially not for the lowest of society's members—the *catadores*. The world of promise sitting below the pristine feet of Christ the Redeemer on those sun-bleached concrete walkways seemed a universe away from the reality of her day-to-day survival.

While the city's upper class joined the tourists at Copacabana Beach to soak in the March sun and play in the ocean water, Daniela donned her heavy-soled boots, a few sizes too big, to complement her shorts and tank top. She had yet in her daily pickings to find a decent pair of boots her size.

Wearing hot boots of any size was better than contracting a disease from discarded, dirty needles like Mamãe had two years earlier. All it took was one needle piercing through Mamãe's flimsy shoe to fill her body with Hepatitis B. Mamãe quit sorting recyclables the day after she got her diagnosis and now spent morning to dusk bemoaning her fate on a stained, threadbare mattress that she shared with Daniela's father, Gerson, in the family's two-room apartment.

When Gerson came home, that is.

In the Shadows

This morning their usual route took them across an uneven cobblestoned road, bordered by newly painted graffitied walls. Men of all ages patrolled, carrying military-grade firearms. The business sector's green, orange, and blue walls portrayed a fun and carefree atmosphere. Outsiders either didn't know or chose to ignore the commonplace drug trafficking and constant corruption that tainted the streets as often as rivers of blood carved paths through the dirt.

Overhead cables sagged from window to window, weaving across alleys alongside clothes lines. Neighbors "borrowed" electricity from those who tapped into the paid electricity sources of the rich at the bottom of the hill. Brazilian flags and clothes of all sizes hung from posts and windows. They swayed in the occasional breeze that carried aromas from the bakery, taunting the pedestrians from two blocks away.

It wasn't much, but it was home.

As they walked to work, Daniela juggled and flipped the ever-present *futbol* at her feet. At the street corner, she bounced off Davi's outstretched arm, stopping without a sound. His face scrunched as his eyes stared into the sky. Distant shouts echoed off battered brick residences. Davi had an uncanny sense of danger which Daniela no longer questioned. Correct or not, his caution was never self-centered.

Davi peeked around the bullet-riddled cement wall. In her line of sight, stray dogs trotted through the streets looking for scraps. Old men on rusted bicycles carted obscenely large piles of wood behind them. Small children scampered around with cloth-strapped babies on their backs. All soldiered on as if nothing were any different today than yesterday.

There was a truth to the way they lived, and almost certainly a resignation. The only way to escape becoming a victim of fear was to avoid the open violence—to become immune.

When Davi stepped into the intersection, Daniela followed tucking her ball beneath her arm. A block away, a large crowd loitered outside the gated front entrance to a government building. They shouted and hurled whatever their hands could grasp at the building's soiled exterior.

What now?

As they approached the group, Daniela's boot snagged, plunging her forward. Davi grabbed her shoulder to keep her upright. Twisting to the side, she caught herself with her left hand in a puddle of brown goop. On her feet she glanced behind her. A bag of trash lay in the street not far from another opened bag. In fact, garbage littered the entire paved area around the protesters. Their angry feet smashed it into the road without a thought, as they shouted curses at government officials and their families and chanted phrases like "Stealing our jobs? Who are the thieves now?" and "Corrupt politicians are padding their own pockets when we can't eat."

But three blocks down and two blocks over, the noise vanished. The hostility in the air dissipated like a cloud covering the sun.

Entering the side gate of the waste management facility, they grabbed neon vests from a box and hurried inside. Cambridge sat in a broken chair nearby, sorting through a collection of books he'd salvaged already this morning. Mach, a gray-haired man with scars covering all of his visible skin, stood nearby monologuing about the easier times when a legion of troops was at his disposal. Same stories every day. He hated his life, and he especially hated being a *catadore*.

Cambridge listened in silence to Mach. When he finished up his diatribe, Cambridge jumped in. "What are you grateful for today, Mach?"

"Nothing. Not even the breath in my body." Mach spat through the toothless gaps.

"Never seen you go to the doctor, Mach. I've known you thirty years. Not many people can say they haven't had a day of

In the Shadows

bad health in the past year much less thirty. Don't let good health be wasted on you."

Mach snorted. "Bad health would give me a day off of this hellhole."

"You'd miss it." Cambridge waved to Davi and Daniela.

"Bah." Mach grumbled. He didn't like kids of any age, so Davi and Daniela were part of the lucky few Mach never complained to.

Cambridge's life pursuit was very different to Mach. His book knowledge was free-flowing and meant to be shared. The books he saved from the landfills he lent to his reading friends in the *favelas*, so they could talk and learn together.

"Did you have to detour today?" Cambridge called from his three-legged chair as his fingertips soothed the ink-laden paper stacked on his lap.

"No, but we probably should have. Why were there protesters throwing trash at the government building?" Davi asked.

They donned their vests and followed Cambridge to the pile where they'd left off yesterday.

"It's good news for us. Lawmakers passed a new bill forbidding scavengers from picking through trash in street cans. Business owners have complained for years that they were losing shoppers and tourist money because people would be sorting through bins outside their shops looking for recyclable materials. Which means…" Cambridge opened his muscled arms. His black eyes disappeared into a squint as he smiled. "Fortune has smiled upon us."

Cambridge's dimpled grin eased the severity of his crooked yellow teeth. Davi laughed as Daniela did a little celebration dance.

"Let's pick our manna before the sun wilts us," Cambridge said as he climbed the worn path to the top of the heap.

Ever since Mamãe demanded they work instead of go to school, Cambridge took it upon himself to teach her and Davi himself. Daniela spent all of last year learning how to multiply and practicing English vocabulary while Davi navigated more complicated topics like English phrases and molecular cell structure.

Whatever that was.

She didn't care that much about math. And Cambridge knew it. She needed to be smart enough to survive her future as a *catadore* and not be stuck in Mamãe's situation.

So, they talked and learned in order to pass the time. When Cambridge was positive he had imparted a sufficient amount of learning for the day, Davi and Cambridge discussed boring topics like politics, military strength, and men's sports, leaving her alone with her thoughts and dreams.

Cambridge said knowledge chased away his darkness, and its hope empowered him. She believed him, because he lived out his hope.

Mamãe hated Cambridge's perpetual sunshine. He had never let her wallow which was why Daniela and Davi were drawn to him with a magnetic force all those years ago.

"Life isn't worth living when you wake up feeling sorry for yourself every day," he said during a visit to Mamãe after she'd sputtered harsh words at him.

Her venom seemed to slide off of Cambridge like water off plastic. Daniela craved that kind of immunity. Davi called him *de pele grossa* (thick-skinned.) If knowledge and positivity could give her that gift then she would stay a *catadore* forever simply to pocket deposits from Cambridge's storehouse. As it was, criticism clung to her like the stench of decay and gnawed at her spirit no matter how much she tried to rid herself of it.

She didn't begrudge others their privilege, though. Because without it, she wouldn't survive. Without their obsession with perfection, her story would follow the path of so many of the helpless.

In the Shadows

The people who claimed that you can be anything never spent a lifetime filling their lungs with the rot-tainted air of a trash heap. They never competed with the thieves of the sky for food scraps or swallowed mouthfuls of muddied water, praying to God it wasn't liquid deception. Somehow even the soul-reapers and *garota de programa* (call girls) counted themselves a class or two above the human ants. They didn't crawl over mounds of waste with the heat blazing like wildfire most days. And that made them better, in their eyes.

They stopped to eat after four hours of sorting. Davi found an entire sack of unopened, unspoiled muffin packages. Even smashed they were a treat. Davi stashed the rest in a woven potato sack near Cambridge's books to be divided out later between them. Other *catadores* roamed the piles, but Daniela and Davi only shared their spoils with Cambridge, as he did for them.

The others must have heard the good news, because laughter could be heard over the groans of the heavy machinery. Spontaneous songs broke out throughout the scorching afternoon.

Usually, everyone would take a break for the hottest part of the day, but today was different. No one wanted to take this opportunity for granted, in case it turned out to be too good to last.

Glean and sell.

Strong backs and empty pockets.

A humble life lived with pride.

Around dinner time, Cambridge sent them home with a book each and their share of the scavenged food which they ate as they walked. They stopped by their usual buyers to unload their day's finds and get paid. Then with the money stashed in their boots, they ended their evening on the packed dirt they used for a *futbol* field.

Daniela wiggled out of her boots and tucked her money in her bra. She was the only girl that played on this field each day. The others just came to watch. Though the women's *futbol* ban was lifted in 1979, girls still hadn't adopted the sport as easily as they had volleyball.

Their loss.

Nothing beat the feel of cooling evening earth beneath your feet and a ball at your whim after a day in hot boots. A few smashed toes had inspired her to spend time perfecting her footwork, thus earning her the nickname "*monstro ágil*" (light-footed monster.) Every time she played, she pushed her tired body harder, to become stronger and faster and smarter, to see all angles. The boys had no mercy on her either. No one wanted the embarrassment of having been schooled by a girl.

Daniela hoped to change their surprise humiliation into expectation someday. No longer would boys assume they could challenge a girl and win.

They ended the evening's game with a score of five to four as dusk overtook their makeshift field. Tomorrow, they'd remix the teams and play until dark again. Holding her boots, Daniela strolled home next to Davi with a huge smile on her face. Sweat dripped down her neck. Best part of every day. They stopped at the fountains in front of the government building to clean up.

"If we can continue earning what we made today, we could afford for you to attend the *futbol* camp at the grass arena in October," Davi said, wiping the sweat from his neck with his t-shirt.

Daniela splashed water onto her face. They'd talked about this. "The one for boys?"

"There's nothing on the poster that says it's male only. Maybe there are girls waiting for others to say they are going so they can sign up."

Another wish that would get swallowed in the ocean of reality. There were a thousand other more practical things to do with the money anyway. Survival things. Her heart swelled at his belief in her skill level. "I don't know, Davi. That's a lot of money for a week of fun and no work."

In the Shadows

"It wouldn't be just fun." Davi scowled at her, propping a hand on his hip. "It'd be really demanding physically and your skills would multiply instantly. Imagine how much better you could be with real training. No one on that field tonight would be able to touch you."

"But that's it, isn't it? That's where it ends for me. That field." She plunged into her darker fears and drew them into the light. "What use is being good at *futbol*? Playing professionally is a wisp of a cloud that keeps my dreams cool at night. I'm nobody with nothing."

Davi stopped at the bottom of the stairs leading to their upstairs rooms. His dark eyes flashed with displeasure. "You're wrong. We're going to get out of here someday. You and I have big things we are supposed to do. And until we believe that, we'll be stuck surviving. Not everyone in the world lives this way and we are going to figure out how to live that life—"

A shriek echoed down to them over the competing thump of the neighbor's music and someone else's television program. Daniela sprinted up the crumbling steps behind Davi. She was a coward for sending him in first, but his presence calmed Mamãe. Stopping behind Davi in the doorway, she held her breath as Mamãe shrieked again.

Something flew across the room toward Daniela's father, Gerson who slouched at the table appearing uninterested. "Maybe I wouldn't have stepped on the needle had I not been out rummaging through trash heaps because you couldn't get your lips off the bottle. Just a handful of change would have bought me decent shoes, but now I live this death sentence while you're off doing only God knows what."

"You could have gotten shoes." Gerson's words sounded less like a protest every time he said them.

Daniela sighed and squeezed her eyes shut. They'd had versions of this conversation regularly for two years since Mamãe got sick.

"When? You drink away all our money on the day you get paid. Every week you do this. We've lived in this *favela* for fifteen years. You promised me a house with a view." Mamãe glared out the window at the grime-covered wall of the neighboring building.

Never mind a nice house. A regular food supply would be worth more, in Daniela's opinion.

Gerson grunted. "Houses are more expensive than they used to be."

"The clinic nurse said my liver is in bad shape and the trash we have to eat isn't helping. A lingering sniffle could kill me. Is that what you want? Me to be dead? After all I do for you—"

He waved his hand in her direction. "Lay in bed all day if you want. Just make sure you have dinner on the table when I return from work."

Mamãe grabbed his throat with a hiss. Terror lit Gerson's eyes. "Dinner? With what money, you sick fool? The few *reals* the kids can scrape together after working all day every day? You live in a fantasy world."

The pit of Daniela's stomach burned. She held her breath, waiting for Gerson's response. Their work wasn't enough. It never was. Mamãe had become that woman—the woman the whole *favela* hated because they could hear manic screams a mile away. She didn't seem to care anymore.

"I have been feeding the kids expired trash scraps for a decade. It's a miracle they're even alive. All so you could piss away the rotgut that makes you a shadow of the man you used to be? Such a royal waste, a breathing disappointment. You don't deserve the good family you have. You're never around to be a part of it."

"The kids are ungrateful little menaces, just like you. No one appreciates how hard I work." Gerson shrugged off his words as if they didn't mean anything to him or to anyone else, yet they

In the Shadows

stabbed a knife into Daniela's frail soul, producing a flinch. Mamãe's eyes flashed with a storm she was about to unleash.

"Get out," Mamãe seethed. "Leave and don't return until you have something worth contributing."

Gerson stood, towering over Mamãe with tightened fists. His lips twisted into a sickening smirk, the look of a mad man. Daniela squeezed Davi's arm in silence. They'd seen bruises on Mamãe but never had seen Gerson actually hit her. "Money? Is that all I'm good for to you?"

Mamãe spat in his direction. "You're not even good for that."

Gerson stalked from the room without a word. He didn't acknowledge them as he shoved past on the stairs. They saw his back more than his face these days.

Daniela watched his form disappear into the waning light of the night, wishing for an alternate life—one in which he stayed to love and provide for them as a family. They'd be better off without him, wouldn't they? A man like that around could only do more damage than good.

Davi's father, Vagner, hadn't stuck around. Why would Daniela's?

Mamãe pulled the rice and beans from the stove and wiped the wet strands of hair from her red, sweat-streaked face. "Come eat, you two." Her voice was dull and soft, no longer the sharp-toothed knife. "Let's sit and figure out a way we can stay alive for a little longer."

Chapter 2

Ronaldo Cevere tugged his apartment door closed. Flimsy was too generous of a word to describe the lack of quality of his door. Locking up was only ceremonial in nature—an illusion that made him feel better after twenty-eight years of caring. His habit made known his preference for privacy rather than a statement of wealth—which was ludicrous right outside the *favelas*. No one lived here if they had the money to live elsewhere.

Unless that person had an impossibly strong motivating factor as Ronaldo did.

Ronaldo's morning routines followed the weather patterns. His sunshine days played out differently than his rainy days which contrasted the cloudy days. Each change was structured to make his mornings equally as enjoyable by adding a defining element to the day rather than bemoaning the unpredictable temperament of nature.

Some habits, however, stayed the same day to day. Like slipping into his favorite worn loafers before leaving his home and buying a newspaper from Sven at the corner stand for twenty-five *reals*.

As usual, the paper told very little news of interest, and what it did say was politically correct so as not to offend any one member of society with a statement of truth—God forbid

In the Shadows

someone have an opinion—but rather to reduce the population's expectations of the media's responsibilities. The stories evoked no happiness or sadness but produced a sigh of longsuffering in hopes the day would come that there would be a news story to feel deep in his soul. Instead, the papers squandered the valuable attention spans of the literate by dishing on the scum of the earth in one cheap piece of pulp and ink.

He browsed the circular with an interest level garnered by the fact that he spent money to acquire it. The back page sported a lengthy column with names of local arrests and the related gangs. Police felt ambitious now and then and raided a gang-controlled *favela* to give the unconcerned public and results-oriented politicians the illusion of taking control of what they never would tame without an all-out war.

On a rare occasion, a politician's name would find its way on to the list of arrests. Not because the leaders were above reproach, but because they paid to stay off the list or the government tended to turn its head at the poor behavior of its own, always more forgiving to insiders than anyone else. That was a particular brand of favoritism that was far too common—gross corruption.

Two blocks down and ten over, he dropped his paper next to a sleeping homeless man lying in a doorway with threadbare blankets covering his filthy body. It was Ronaldo's attempt at offering the paper the chance to do some good in the world while doing some good himself. The man would use it to light a fire later if he could manage to sneak a light off someone. The man left the homeless shelter a block over in the early morning hours in order to sleep on the doorstep with his bowl out for change.

Annoyance poked into the contentment of the sunny morning routine. Yet again, the unreliable media dragged their hobbled legs on news that would hold the powerful accountable to the watchful world.

Ronaldo paused to scan his badge at the electronic keypad that protected the grass practice arena of the Brazilian men's national *futbol* team from outsiders. Three levels up enclosed in his office, he donned the required khakis and uniform polo shirt of a professional.

His street clothes didn't make him worth a second glance to anyone lying in wait near the *favelas*. His salt-and-pepper hair and tanned skin lent him an uninteresting quality to the kids. By nature of his age, they could assume that he was a force to be reckoned with if he'd survived the outskirts of the *favelas* that long.

The joke was on them for their assumptions.

"Ronaldo, good man." Lenz Pereira slapped the door frame of Ronaldo's office. "Big day today."

Not big enough. Ronaldo lifted his eyebrows, his heart thrumming an accelerated pace at the Federal *Futbol* Committee president's sudden appearance in his space. The man slinked around the office like a hunter tracking his prey.

That made Ronaldo suspicious.

"New recruits are taking the field. We don't want to miss that."

Ronaldo shoved his mobile phone into his pocket and trailed Lenz to the elevator that would deposit them on the field level. They arrived as Head Coach Rui Alves blew his whistle to call the team to huddle.

"Good morning," Coach Alves said. "I'm excited as you are to get started today. We have fresh blood joining the team—five new recruits. Make them feel welcomed without terrorizing them, please." The men chuckled, affirming it had been a common thought if not already a reality. "Observing our practice today are the esteemed president and vice president of the Federal Futbol Committee, Lenz Pereira and Ronaldo Cevere."

Coach Alves motioned in their direction and they lifted their hands in response to the curious stares of the newcomers. Humanizing the authorities made the men react one way or the

In the Shadows

other. The FFC had plenty of fans and foes camped on separate sides of the river.

Loving the Committee or hating them didn't do the players any favors when it came to their paychecks, so at most, Lenz and Ronaldo received a respectful handshake and nod from each player before being ignored for the rest of practice.

Aside from the odd comment here and there regarding the team's potential on the international stage this year, silence reigned between them for the next two hours of practice. At the break between field play and weightlifting, Lenz took the opportunity to flex his authoritative muscles in front of Alves who took the posture of a long-time admirer, appeasing Lenz's fragile ego with a well-timed laugh or compliment.

Ronaldo excused himself to find solace in the arms of his desk chair where he buried himself in his work until his computer chimed with a reminder of the evening's health care fund-raising event. After calling for a driving service to pick him up, he slid into his tuxedo and shiny black shoes that he kept hanging in a garment bag on the backside of his office door. His choice of where to keep his tuxedo baffled his coworkers and the majority of people in his life that did not know where he lived.

What they didn't understand was that he made his decisions out of logic and practicality, not laziness. If he entertained, he did so in public in the city. His private life remained his own—rare in a world far too willing to erase those boundaries without regard to the consequences.

He tucked his street clothes into his briefcase and waited for the town car just inside the gate. Arriving home after dark was already ill-advised, but to do so wearing a tuxedo would be inviting assault or worse. The driver arrived and opened his door for him. Ronaldo fidgeted with his cufflinks no less than ten times on the twenty-minute ride across town to the harbor.

Forty-seven and he still fought nerves before parties. Long ago he'd given up on the idea of outgrowing his social anxiety.

Even now, he could hear his sister Mariana laughing at his jitters as she straightened his bow tie. She'd been gone for twenty-odd years and the heaviness of her violent death still weighed on his heart. The sharp pangs of grief had dulled to the ache of nostalgia and sadness long ago. Good memories disappeared faster than time, but the horror and shock of that night never left him.

Harborside, he exited the car onto the short red carpet the host charity Saving Grace laid out for the evening. An ocean breeze tousled his jacket bringing with it a fresh inhale of beach scents and salt water.

The tension fell from his shoulders. The ocean would always be there for his escape. Elegant music accompanied by polite laughter floated out the front door that was framed with little white lights. The party only started at this level of calm. Once people relaxed, the music and drinks would get more exciting to open wallets and elicit large commitments and donations. Brazilians knew how to party. There would be no shortage of food, dancing, and drinks.

Ronaldo checked his briefcase at the door and pasted on a smile. This, as so much of what he did, was for Mariana. It had been her favorite charity. She liked to joke that they should call the fundraising events "Saving Face" since the elite of Rio only darkened the event's doorway so they wouldn't be labeled as someone who didn't care about the poverty-stricken children of the *favelas*. Public guilt worked wonders on the rich and famous.

Inside the room, all traces of the usual nautical decor had been removed. In its place was elegance with a hint of magic. In the last fifteen years of securing an invite to this event, never once had the atmosphere been less than excellent. Tonight, the sheer cloth swoops draped from the ceiling encased more small white lights and greenery as if he'd stepped into a garden party instead of a boat house by the ocean. Potted flowers with big showy blooms sat strategically placed in corners and posed nonchalantly in front of locked doors. With the greatest of ease, Saving Grace

In the Shadows

had taken their small decoration budget and transformed the place into a party space fit for millionaires.

Ronaldo snagged a drink from the table and surveyed the room while he attempted to dislodge the dryness in his throat. Almost as soon as his glass was empty, a refill appeared in his hand.

Then, there she was.

The most beautiful woman and doctor to walk through the doors of…anywhere. Her shimmering floor-length red dress fit her slim figure to perfection. Her midnight tresses had his fingers flexing in desire to touch them. Her tan skin glowed in the soft light. Nothing about her needed enhancing or subduing. Aging didn't affect that one bit.

Hers was a mystery he'd happily engage in, if given the chance.

For two years, he tended to their growing friendship as he would anything needing his gentle touch, biding his time. Tonight, he was going to risk ruining his hard work by asking her to dance with him as more than best friends. Life was too short not to ask, but it was also too short to mess up a solid relationship before she had the chance to see their potential. Ronaldo grabbed an extra glass of champagne and weaved through the crowd to Isadora Rey's side.

She beamed at him as he approached. Her smile lit his world on fire. "Isadora, you are stunning."

"Ronaldo, I'm so glad you're here. You know I can't survive these events without you."

Next year, let's come together as a couple.

The brave words shied away from his timid tongue as Isadora kissed his cheek, then accepted the offered glass. She smelled of lilacs and vanilla—an enticement that grabbed his male senses by the throat and refused to shake loose.

The gleam in her dark eyes sparkled with ferocity. "Don't think I don't notice how you never qualify your compliments."

Her wit was as sharp as her intellect. Ronaldo laughed. "It would be a huge disservice to myself for me to tell you that you are more beautiful tonight than you are every other day, because every other day your beauty is just as breathtaking. And not to acknowledge that would be self-harm."

Isadora paused. "That was so remarkably stated. And thank you. I accept your compliments with blushing humility. While we're on the topic, I've never seen a man look as at home in a tuxedo as he does his street clothes. But here you are making all the men in the room look unkempt and shabby." She slipped her hand around his arm. The warmth of her grasp shot a spark of happiness through him. It wasn't just her easy touch. It was to be known and understood by her that made him feel alive.

He placed his hand over hers and walked her from the door. "You know the director may come scold you for being seen on my arm."

Isadora grinned with her dimpled smile and straight teeth. "If the director needs the illusion of my romantic availability to woo rich men into opening their pocketbooks, then he must be grasping at thin air for a program tonight. That is a young girl's game. I am a forty-five-year-old doctor with established credentials, not a twenty-two-year-old charity showpiece." She lifted her finger in the air. "Although, I don't mind being complimented by handsome men…"

Ronaldo nodded with a broad smile. "No need to be discerning on who you accept compliments from."

"Exactly, just who I spend my time with." She patted his arm. "You understand."

"Dance with me tonight?" The words slipped from his mouth with embarrassing eagerness.

Isadora clucked her tongue. "Only if you promise to step on my feet once or twice to make it seem like you're a novice. It's not fair to the rest of the world that you be devastatingly handsome and graceful."

In the Shadows

"I can assure you that any faltered steps are not a ruse. My gracefulness extends only to the *futbol* field and even there my skills are waning."

"Hm." Isadora turned to look him in the eye, all trace of humor gone. He raised his eyebrows but never moved his gaze from her dark chocolate stare. "How is your classified project going?"

He cocked his head. "Still waiting, but I doubt you'll be able to miss the fireworks when they start."

Isadora nodded and led him toward the food table. "Just don't stand so close that you get burned." She handed him a plate, her playful grin returning. "However, if you do find yourself singed, I'll be manning our new clinic that is opening in your part of town next week. Don't go running into the arms of a *futbol* on-call physician and take away my chance at seeing the great Ronaldo Cevere in a moment of vulnerability."

Ronaldo grunted, unwilling to admit how pleased he was that she cared. "At least, I know he'd never go to the press without knowing he'd lose his license and carefully curated celebrity status."

A feigned gasp escaped Isadora's full red lips with an accompanying look of horror. "Are you suggesting that I'd out you to sharks, Sr Cevere? The very beasts who launch at me for practicing medicine in charity clinics. No, they don't deserve to snack on you." Isadora leaned in close to whisper in his ear. "I am your biggest fan, Ronaldo. Don't ever forget that what you do to rid this world of corruption and promote health among poor women and children makes all of our lives better."

She stepped away to load her plate with appetizers. Here was a woman not afraid to eat in public. Her confidence thrilled him. Once they left the serving table, she sauntered onto the deck overlooking the water and he followed. God help him, but he would always follow if she walked away. The waves competed with the increasing volume of the party. She popped a bite into her mouth and moaned. "I do love catered food."

Ronaldo stared at the water, envious of its ability to move past any obstacle in its way without great difficulty. It knew the secret to winning—unrelenting, unapologetic persistence. The same dynamic necessary to win a woman's love.

He waited until they'd finished their plates and held out his hand. "Ready to dance?"

She clutched his hand and they didn't leave the dance floor all night except to eat dinner and watch the program together.

As the night ended with a slow song, she leaned her cool cheek against his heated one. "If there was any doubt, Ronaldo, I want you to know that I'd be honored for the chance to care for a real-life superhero if he ever found himself in need of healing and comfort. I take trust very seriously."

He tugged Isadora closer although there wasn't any daylight between their swaying forms. His hand cupped her waist as he buried his nose into her flower-scented hair. "If I ever meet a superhero, I will send him your way, but in the meantime, I hope I'll be a good stand-in."

"I think you'll do just fine," Isadora whispered.

Ronaldo ended the best evening he'd had in more years than he could remember by having his town car drive Isadora to her place. He accompanied her to her door, lingering long enough to plant a good night kiss on each cheek and her forehead. Romance didn't need to be rushed. Her lips would save for another day, another perfect moment. And now that he knew with confidence that they both anticipated the kiss, he could plan on making it one to remember.

He awoke the next day to a cloudy sky and a slight chill, but he was floating in another world. He slipped into his loafers, purchased a copy of the newspaper from Sven, and slid into his booth at his favorite cloudy-day breakfast cafe. After a sip of coffee to fortify him for the drivel ahead, he unfolded the front

In the Shadows

page to unveil the full-sized picture of his boss Lenz Pereira's angry face beneath a slit-throat title.

"Federal Futbol Committee President Caught Making Illegal Payoffs to World Cup Referees"

Slowly, Ronaldo's breathing reengaged and a smile crept over his face. At last, public accountability had arrived for what some at the Committee had secretly known about for weeks. No one wanted their national team to lose over and over again, but paying off the referees to slide their team into the running for international tournaments was going too far. Now the world knew and would be watching Brazil's every move.

Ronaldo couldn't wait to give them something worthwhile to see.

His mobile phone hopped across the table on vibrate.

"*Estou*—I am here," he said into the phone.

"I'm sure you've seen the news by now," the caller said.

"I was enjoying my morning coffee until I saw Lenz's face," Ronaldo said. It was the truth, but now he enjoyed his coffee even more than before.

"Lenz is gone until the investigation comes up empty-handed or puts him away. You're the new committee president. Hope you're ready for the impending storm."

Ronaldo thanked him for calling and hit the red button on his phone with vigor. He snapped the newspaper back into place to finish reading the article and said to no one in particular, "I am the storm that's coming."

Chapter 3

Daniela woke up with the feeling that something was off. That feeling became a buzz coursing down her spine when Cambridge wasn't at the gate to meet them in the morning. The man was as faithful as the sun, never missing a day. In fact, he wasn't anywhere to be seen on the heaps. Daniela traded worried looks with Davi as they grabbed their neon vests and set to work.

Cambridge could take care of himself and had done so since his mother disappeared when he was seven. His grandmother raised him in a nice section of Rio until he was fourteen. While she gave him the best she had, hers were the feeble efforts of an aging woman whose body and mind were not meant to sustain a young one.

When his grandma died, Cambridge's aunt and uncle inherited her money and Cambridge. The money was welcomed with open and eager hands. Cambridge was not. He had been in the *favelas* working for his survival since that day. His teen years were one of the main reasons he was so concerned with Davi and Daniela's education.

Daniela and Davi worked side-by-side, combing the hills for metals, plastics, and glass. They hadn't slowed their pace since that first day and had seen a remarkable income difference because of it, along with an increase in recyclables to gather. By no means were they making close to minimum wage, but the money allowed them to purchase a fresh pineapple and some vegetables for dinner at the local market two nights after Gerson left.

Mamãe's eyes were round as *futbols*, pulling her briefly from her despondence. She couldn't believe they'd found a pineapple in the dump with no rot at all. Not one bad spot, no bugs, she had muttered over and over again. Daniela and Davi grinned but had agreed not to tell Mamãe the details yet.

The secrecy was Cambridge's idea. Admitting their good fortune would jinx them, and bring in more workers who were suddenly willing to be seen as one of the shunned *catadores* in order to survive. A small influx of treasure hunters came anyway. They weren't familiar with the layout and how things worked so they gathered at a strict disadvantage.

The rest of the *catadores* didn't take to the newcomers—the temporary imposters—so no one felt much of a need to teach them anything except to stay out of the *catadores*' way. To the newcomers' credit, they did keep to themselves but with whining and loud complaining about the smell and the heat. Soon enough, they would find out which water streams were drinkable and which were runoff from the mounds. After making that mistake, they'd never make it again.

The thought brought a smirk to Daniela's face.

Theirs wasn't a world where everyone survived. Nor was the job as simple as everyone thought. With the little formal education that *catadores* received, people assumed they were ignorant and unskilled. Very few knew the skill it took to sort through tons of waste each day with a practiced eye, never bothering with imitation items that wouldn't bring a high value.

Daniela wiped her forehead on the bottom of her tank top but didn't rest. She hummed a song to push the worry away. When she stopped to take a breath, a bird whistle sounded twice in the distance. Davi's head popped up. He looked around and lifted his bag in acknowledgment.

"Cambridge." They picked their way down the hill, stopping every little bit to snag something for their collection.

Off to the side of the gate, Cambridge organized his newest book additions in size order. Davi and Daniela crouched to sort through their bags as they waited for Cambridge to tell them why he whistled.

"Just had a meeting with the facility managers," Cambridge said in a low voice. "They're going to start charging an entry fee to get in here." Cambridge huffed out a humorless laugh.

"Pay? To get in here?" Davi stopped sorting. "Who would do that?"

Cambridge motioned to the rest of the grounds where *catadores* and trash hunters crawled over the heaps. "Newcomers over the past two weeks have inspired some ideas for revenue changes, apparently. With the new law in place, they see it less as doing us a favor and more of an opportunity for them to make money where they haven't before. If all these people know is trash, then they have no chance to decline the entrance fee. Businesses aren't leaping at the chance to hire *catadores* these days."

Daniela finished and propped her hands on her hips. "So, what do we do? Pay the fee? Find another way to make money?"

Davi shot her a glare. He assumed anytime she mentioned another job that she was referring to what some of the other *favela* girls did to survive. No way was she going to be offering her body as a good. Davi would work without sleeping so that wouldn't happen.

"Well, I had a couple ideas." Cambridge tilted his hat and glanced at the sky. "We have about a week for the fees to take effect."

"We could boycott," Davi said.

In the Shadows

"Could, but that hurts us worse than it does them. That's why the trash hunters threw a tantrum at the government building. We need options before we boycott, as well as a mountain-sized miracle." Cambridge scratched his head and looked off into the distance. "We need to canvass the area to find sources that will pay more for our goods. Then once we have a good list of buyers, we need to find ways to extract the recyclables from their trash bins before they hit the facility."

Davi cringed. "And with the trash hunting laws, that would be almost impossible."

"Might be." Cambridge shrugged. "Or we need to be more respectful than the trash hunters. We ask business owners politely, clean up after ourselves, and be discreet. We make friends with janitors, back-end restaurant help, and garbage truck workers. Anyone and everyone with access to trash, we talk to. At the end of the week, we make our decision. Do we stay on and pay the fee in hopes that we can earn back the money spent? Or do we boycott their greediness? No need for the rich to get richer and the poor to get poorer."

"When do we have time to do that? If we're working all day until late, every store front is closed. Not to mention we come in early before stores are open." Davi motioned for Cambridge and Daniela to follow him. "It's wasted time, Cambridge. We have an opportunity right now and for the next week to gather as much as we possibly can. I say we use it to work around-the-clock shifts, especially while the others go home." He snapped his fingers. "We talk to our buyers as we sell and let them know what's going on. If they're on our side, then maybe they can put pressure on the facility."

"No cheap resources for them means raising their prices which could result in less business." Cambridge tapped his forehead and winked.

"What do you think, Daniela?" Davi turned to her.

Daniela shrugged in surprise. Did they really care? What did she know about boycotts and business at fifteen? "Let's work extra hard this week and then we look at better options after that."

Davi nodded in satisfaction and wandered off with Cambridge to discuss the problem further. Daniela went back to their original spot. Working all day meant no *futbol*. No *futbol* made her crabby.

What would they do if they had to pay? They'd have no money for the *futbol* camp she'd begun daydreaming of. At least, Mamãe knew nothing of the found success, now lost opportunity. She'd worry and ruin what little health she had left. Throwing Gerson out had sapped much of her will to live.

Mamãe loved him.

Regardless of how long Gerson disappeared between coming home, he always showed up for Christmas with little treats. She had done her best to behave when he was home so that he would have a reason to stay, but he never did. Even though Mamãe blamed his drinking, Daniela couldn't help but feel his lack of interest was partially her fault. Maybe if she had been closer to him, or more interested in his job, or more grateful that he came home when he did, then he would have stayed.

But that wasn't her reality. Sorting through trash and hoping for dinner was.

Over the next week, she and Davi agreed to stay at Cambridge's small apartment next to the facility. Davi took the night shift to work under the bright security lights. When he awoke, he strategized and checked on Mamãe each day. He told her they were working extra to help make up for the loss of Gerson's income which seemed to appease her.

From dawn to dusk, Daniela worked with Cambridge nearby. She missed Davi. He was her one constant in life besides work. She'd come to rely on his steady presence and quiet care for her.

It was just one week.

In the Shadows

Cambridge tried valiantly to fill the gap Davi left. He gathered during the day and part of the night, stopping to sleep for a few hours at a time when he got too tired. The lessons stopped in favor of preserving energy for stockpiling their survival.

The first time Davi went to sell the goods to the buyers, they refused. The buyers only wanted to purchase a specific amount each day in order to meet the demand. Now the bags of excess sat outside the apartment awaiting their chance to be sold. That was their stash to sell when the drought began.

Monday morning of the next week, the facility posted a man at the gate to collect a fee for the day. Davi, Daniela, and Cambridge watched from Cambridge's apartment. A few regulars complained loudly as they paid the fee in those early morning hours, but no one else appeared. The boycott was in full swing. Cambridge gave a satisfied grunt.

Today was the first day of their new endeavor.

They started in the shops closest to their buyers, individually canvassing the street asking for the chance to take recyclables before the trucks collected each week. A few eyed Daniela and consented. Their swift words left no doubt that she'd be booted if she left a mess. She promised fervently that they'd be clean. The rest said no before she finished her request. She was a *catadore*.

Unclean.

"No respectable person asks to dig through trash," an owner sneered at her. "Get out."

And no respectable person should allow another to have to dig in order to survive.

All Daniela could do was thank him for his time and take to the street like a stray dog with its tail tucked between its legs. The next shop window caught her eye before she opened the door. There next to a variety of old dolls and antique tables sat the most beautiful glass mosaic of green pastures and blue sky. A tag propped in front of it boasted that it was handmade in the store. A thrill shot through Daniela. She yanked the door open and entered the dimly lit space.

A woman's voice called hello from somewhere towards the back. Daniela glanced around. None of it would she be able to afford much less have a use for. Collectibles and decorations were for the rich.

"Can I help you?" the woman's voice sounded closer. Then a short Brazilian woman wearing a baggy, flowered dress over her small frame appeared from around a rack of clothing.

"I noticed the mosaic in the window. It's beautiful. The sign said it is handmade."

The woman nodded while Daniela spoke. "I try my hand at art in my free time." She giggled softly as she put her hand on Daniela's arm.

Daniela liked her instantly but decided to risk the question anyway. No use in liking someone to have to not like them after they found out the real reason for your presence in their store. "Where do you get your glass? Because I sell glass, if you're interested."

"You sell glass?" The woman's eyebrows raised. "Do you make glass to sell it?"

"No, I sell what I collect."

"Ah." This was where Daniela usually lost people. "I'd love to hear more about what you have available and see some options of what you sell. There's something so magnificent about making pictures from broken glass, don't you think?"

Daniela nodded. She finally had a lead. "I can bring some by tomorrow for you to look at, if you'd like."

"My name is Gabi. I'm here every day. I'll expect you tomorrow…"

"Daniela."

Gabi curtsied and grinned. As she walked to the front of the store, Daniela paused to look at the mosaic up close.

In the Shadows

"How much does it cost for this one?" Daniela ran her fingers over the glass pieces.

"Seventy *reals*," Gabi said.

Daniela retracted her hand as if stung. Something that expensive was not for her to be touching so casually. She couldn't afford to pay for a broken one, much less a whole.

"The tourists love them. I sell three or four a week."

Daniela's jaw dropped open. "Is that true? In one week?" She tried to do the math in her head like Cambridge had been teaching her. With money like that, they could actually make closer to minimum wage between her and Davi.

Gabi grinned. "It helps when you have beautiful glass to use. Come back tomorrow with some for me?"

Daniela nodded and waved as she exited onto the street. Cambridge strode toward her from further down the street. Daniela ran to him.

"Where's Davi?"

Cambridge's brow furrowed. He grabbed her shoulders. "He will be out in a minute. Is everything okay? Did someone hurt you?" Cambridge scanned her arms and hands. She pulled away from him as Davi came out of a store shaking his head.

"Davi!"

Davi's reaction was the same as Cambridge's-- moment of panic. She waved away his concern.

"Come with me." She gripped his hand and tugged him toward Gabi's store window. Cambridge stayed beside them. Daniela stopped and motioned at the window. "What do you see?"

Davi stared with his mouth open. "Old furniture. Overpriced items that no one needs, especially not us." He shook his head. "Daniela, what?"

"That mosaic is made of glass pieces."

"Yes, and it's beautiful," Davi said with a shrug.

34

Daniela pulled him away from the store so Gabi wouldn't see or hear them from inside. "The store owner makes them by hand. Guess how much she sells them for."

"Thirty *reals*," Cambridge said.

"Seventy *reals*. She sells three or four a week." Daniela paused. "That's—"

"Two hundred and eighty *reals* a week and eleven-twenty a month," Cambridge said. Air whistled through his teeth.

Davi stared at his feet as he walked. Daniela wanted to smack his arm and tell him to think out loud.

"Our buyers don't pay us nearly that for so little glass. So that makes me think that if we were to make our own pieces from what we collect, we could sell it to tourists as handmade Brazilian art for so much more than we are making now," Daniela said.

"It's unlikely that would work," Davi said. Daniela couldn't tell if his pessimism was born from logic or a distrust of good in the world.

"But if it does, then we'll be so much better off than we were before." Why didn't he want to try it? She planted herself in front of him and grabbed his arms. "Listen to me, Davi. This is worth a try. At the end of our supply, we have nothing, right?"

Davi blinked at her. Anger boiled inside her throat at his silence.

She shook his arms. "Right? We have nothing?"

At that, he pursed his lips then sighed. "Nothing."

Her heart sank at the ripe dejection in his answer. He worked so hard for her and Mamãe. She wrapped her arms around his shoulders and tucked her chin into his neck. "I'm so sorry, Davi. I didn't mean it like that."

Davi hugged her back. "We'll try it. Just a few pieces to see how it works."

Daniela nodded. She would find a way to make it work. If it worked for Gabi, it had to work for people like them. But then again, that's not usually how things happened in their world.

Chapter 4

A flurry of interviews and requests for official statements regarding Lenz Pereira's investigation made their way onto Ronaldo's calendar and, more frustratingly, onto his now-cluttered desk. He much preferred his assistant, Katrina, to the Lenz's assistant, Mara. Katrina knew his work pattern--that he couldn't get anything done with stacks of paper on every surface. However, the hierarchy needed to remain as it was for one more day as Mara trained Katrina.

Mara had already been advised that she was going on unpaid leave. According to committee policy, someone needed to be with Mara every moment that she was in the office so files and important documentation didn't go missing. No corruption was quite as simple as it appeared on the outside. Although Mara had promised her full cooperation, Ronaldo doubted she would hang her boss out to dry. Lenz had been very good to her.

Too good.

Ronaldo grabbed his briefcase and locked his office door behind him. He waved goodbye to Katrina, signaling for her to keep an eye on Mara. Katrina smiled and nodded. Outside, the air was warm and thick with moisture. Ronaldo slid into the back seat of the waiting town car.

In the Shadows

Today was the opening of Saving Grace's newest clinic. The fundraiser finished off raising enough money to open the doors of the clinic on schedule instead of the threatened three-month delay.

Of course, a Brazilian "on schedule" already entailed a long enough wait. Time didn't march to the same drum here as in other parts of the world. Sometimes it sambaed wildly, but usually it paused to take in the view before strolling onward as if knowing this moment would never appear again.

Because time was so easygoing, Brazilians had to be, too. Not that they minded. To Ronaldo, a hurried life wasn't worth living. However, the moment Ronaldo exited the car outside the clinic couldn't have arrived fast enough today.

Isadora opened each new clinic by dedicating a week to each location until a regular rotation of doctors could be established. Very few of the doctors on the charity's list agreed to work in the *favela* clinics. The clinic locations were too dangerous and doctors claimed it was bad for their professional reputations, but Isadora didn't care about either of those things. She worried about the safety of the women and children who came to her, battered and ill. Isadora's calling was to heal and that calling didn't have a class or pay bracket attached to it. That was just another thing he deeply respected about her.

The driver dropped him off and said he would be back to pick him up later, but Ronaldo dismissed the idea. "I'll get a ride from my friend."

The truth was he planned to walk home since the clinic wasn't far from his place, but the driver didn't need to know that. The driver winked before closing himself into the car. Maybe he would take Isadora out to dinner tonight after she finished working. The thought cheered him immensely.

Ronaldo strolled into the clinic past the line that wound out the door. He glanced around the well-lit room. Isadora insisted on decent lighting if she was expected to have any success helping her patients. The stench of unwashed bodies made the place smell like a locker room and it was only the first day of being open.

"Hi, Fire Marshall," Isadora's sweet voice sang over the din of crying babies and loud talking. Ronaldo grinned and followed the sound of her voice.

Isadora waved from her post in a chair beside a teenage boy. She held the boy's wrist in her hand and pressed with her thumb. He winced and paled further. Isadora scribbled notes on her ever-present clipboard and handed the sheet to the nurse to take over. Standing off to the side of the room, Ronaldo let her come to him just this once. This was her territory.

She walked across the room to meet him. Her dark hair stuck out in a thousand directions and she was as breathtaking as she'd been the night of the fundraiser.

"Well, *Presidente*. Those were some amazing fireworks." Isadora stretched to kiss his cheek.

He inhaled silently. Lilacs and vanilla—heaven. "I told you that you wouldn't miss them."

She ran her hands down his arms sending chills across his skin and glanced him over with a smirk. "Any burns?"

"Not yet, but you'll be the first to know if I do."

Isadora tapped his chest. "See that I am. I specialize in firework trauma." Facing the crowd of patients all waiting for her gentle touch, she sighed. "Of all forms. As usual, more demand than supply."

"Don't spread yourself too thin."

"I don't know the meaning of those words, *Presidente*," Isadora said with a wink. "Pull up a chair and chat with the patients while they wait. I'm sure the charity director will be eager to hear of the local opinion of this clinic."

Ronaldo bowed. "Anything you wish."

Isadora stopped in her tracks and pinned him with a serious stare. "Anything?"

In the Shadows

A shiver ran the length of Ronaldo's spine. Such dangerous words to utter. "Anything within my power."

She paused as she reflected on those words, then tilted her head. "I'll keep that in mind."

The control she weaved over him commanded full use of his faculties. What was going on in that gorgeous head of hers when she said something like that? Could she see the sincerity in his eyes? He sighed as he debated whom he would talk to first. The director would have to wait on getting the local opinions on the clinic. He had more important things to talk about.

Ronaldo grabbed a chair and set it between two patient chairs. Both were teenage girls waiting to see Isadora. "Good afternoon, ladies. It's a beautiful day to be sitting in a chair, isn't it?"

Their wary eyes turned toward him and then to each other. They giggled. And he was in.

"So do you ladies play *futbol*?"

The girl on his left nodded. The one on his right shrugged.

"I need opinions from professional teenagers. You two look to be just that. Are you willing to give me those for free or must I give you candy as payment?" Ronaldo extracted two lollipops from his briefcase and held them out to the girls, not at all ashamed that he'd resorted to bribery before he had asked his questions.

They giggled again and took the treat.

"Okay. You first." Ronaldo turned to the girl on his right who had shrugged. "Would you try out for an all girls' *futbol* team for teen girls your age?"

The girl was hesitant. "I'm not very good, so probably not. I just like to play for fun. I don't get to play like the boys do."

His heart hurt for her, but they were the words he had expected. When it came to leisure time and sports, girls didn't get the same privileges the boys had. But that was going to change some day and Ronaldo wanted to be on the front lines of that fight. Not just for these girls, but for every single girl who never got the chance to pursue her love of a sport, or her love of anything, because of the social expectations set on her. This was for the girls like his sister, Mariana, who wouldn't have been in the wrong place if she had been allowed to play *futbol* like she really wanted.

Turning to his left, he said, "What about you? Would you try out for a team if there were tryouts nearby?"

She nodded, her eyes shining. "That would be a lot of fun. Then I wouldn't have to keep playing with the boys. It'd be nice to have other girls to play with!"

"What position would you play?" Ronaldo asked.

"Front left or front center." She answered without hesitation, a clear sign that she knew her place on the field.

Ronaldo loved her confidence. Here was a girl who had never been on a formal *futbol* team in her life, yet she knew where she fit in the scheme of the game. He could only imagine how many other girls felt the same way. Ronaldo stayed and chatted with both girls for a few minutes until a nurse interrupted them. Excusing himself from the teens, he found a mother with a young daughter sitting nearby.

"Mãe, welcome to the clinic," Ronaldo said as he sat on a bench beside her.

She nodded her thanks and grabbed the hands of the child on her lap to keep her from scratching herself. Distrust shown clear in her brown eyes as she adjusted the child on her lap. This was a woman not used to trusting strange men. Her story couldn't be an easy one to hear. The child however had no such reservations and stared at him with open curiosity. Dark curls framed her dirt-smudged cheeks that had dimples for good measure.

He extended two lollipops to the mother, unable to ask about her opinion of girls' *futbol* right off. It seemed too trite when she wore such pain in her eyes. Something about her distrust made him feel as if he could hurt her further by simply asking about the sport. "What do you think of the new clinic?"

In the Shadows

"It's close to where we live and very nice."

Ronaldo smiled. "Dr. Rey is the best doctor around. She really, really loves children so I think you'll like her."

The woman didn't return his smile. "I don't mean to be rude, but she doesn't need to like children for me to like her. I need her to tell us how to feel better so my children don't have to live on the streets with no one to care for them."

"How old are your children?"

"Taynara is fifteen. Quim is eight. And this is Eliana. She is three."

"What do they like to do?"

The woman's lips quirked upward. "Quim and Eliana play with their friends and all the children follow Taynara around the neighborhood while the parents work. She thinks she'll be a teacher someday." She huffed as if it were impossible.

Ronaldo swallowed his sharp retort about the future of Brazilian women never progressing if their parents never gave them something to hope for. "Does she play *futbol*?"

The woman shrugged. "She is always forming teams for games with children she's watching. I work all day, and other parents give me gifts for Taynara keeping their children safe. It's a good arrangement." She grabbed Eliana's hands and squeezed. "Quit scratching. You'll make it worse."

Eliana's eyes pooled with tears, but she didn't make a noise.

Ronaldo cleared his throat. "Well, you make sure she knows to come here anytime she or the other children need medical help, okay? Dr. Rey will take great care of them."

The woman nodded and Ronaldo excused himself once again. He left briefly to pick up some dinner for Isadora, leaving it with one of the nurses and a note in the bag promising her a real dinner very soon. She was the kind of woman who wouldn't wait for the chaos to be over before barging in. Her preference was to be right in the middle of it to his great relief, because he had chaos in spades at the moment.

A plan forming in his mind solidified into place as he strolled home. It was three parts insanity and two parts genius, if he could pull it off. If he couldn't, it was one hundred percent a failed government-attempted program.

All night, Ronaldo mulled over the idea. Back and forth he went, revisiting the plan from every angle he could conjure. The next morning, he was in his office waiting when Katrina came in for the day. She did a double-take at him in his chair and leaned against his doorway.

"How long have you been here?"

"Early. Couldn't sleep. We have a lot to do, Katrina."

She nodded as if she understood, but she didn't.

Not yet.

"I have an idea forming that I need budgetary numbers for. Do you have those on hand?"

Her eyebrows rose, but she disappeared. The words couldn't have been that far off from what Lenz had spoken to Mara before he took her down the bumpy path to corruption. No doubt Katrina worried about his motives.

She laid the sheets of paper in front of him. "I went over these with Mara yesterday before she left. This should be the balance of the books."

"Good, good," Ronaldo murmured, running his fingers down the columns.

There. That might be enough.

"Katrina, I'd like to visit the potential of creating a new revenue stream, but it also is going to require reworking our infrastructure a bit. Now, this is going to take a lot of energy especially on my part. But…" He left her hanging to see how invested she was in what he said. Big change after exposed corruption wasn't always the best strategy. That he knew. Katrina leaned forward in her seat. He continued. "I want to create a league of FCC-sanctioned girls' *futbol* teams that feed into our national women's *futbol* team."

In the Shadows

Katrina scribbled on the notepad in her lap. Her writing seemed to last longer than what he'd actually said.

"I'll donate my time to get a team started. We can charge fees for existing teams to join the league and we'll need organizers. However, I want this to include all girls. So, with that in mind, I'd like to set aside money in the budget for scholarships for girls from the *favelas*."

To Katrina's credit, she didn't flinch but stayed quiet, which made him highly suspicious of where her mind was taking this.

He cleared his throat. "But first, I want to run a *futbol* camp for a week in two or three different *favelas* to give the girls there more of a foundation than they have. Most of them probably wouldn't have a prayer of competing against someone who had been playing their whole life and their parents could afford to put them in a *futbol* league."

The only answer was the gliding of Katrina's pen against paper. When she stopped writing, he opened his hands, willing her to say something.

"When would you like to start the camp?" Katrina asked.

"The advertising should get started before school starts again in February. We can advertise the *favela* camps for a week or two, then hold our first camp in February, and then have tryouts the first part of March for the league."

"*Senhor*, do you think you can get budgetary approval for scholarships for these girls by then?"

"I certainly hope so. We have an abundance of funds for the men's teams and every scholarship we have goes towards them. We need to restore some national faith in our committee. What the public needs is a story to get behind and believe in. They need champions rising from the dumps to inspire them to greatness. We tried and failed with the men. They don't get the same amount of coverage, because they are men and they are expected to overcome. But for some reason, people make an exception for women as if they can and should be overrun. That needs to change in society and it needs to change in *futbol*. No more waiting for changes to trickle down to us. We need to be on the forefront and we'll start with the weakest women we have. Once we empower them, the rest of the country will follow."

Katrina grinned for the first time since she sat down. "I like your fire."

No doubt. It was the most time he'd spent talking to her since she came to work for him.

"We are going to get a lot of pushback for this, so prepare yourself mentally. The media mess we have now is nothing compared to what it might be if we start giving the girls in the *favelas* hope and a future past surviving on the streets. Let's get this nailed down firm before we let it loose in the wind. I could be sent packing right behind Lenz if I'm not careful."

Katrina tilted her head. "The women need an advocate. Once they realize their strength, there will be no returning them to their tiny little box. Even if you go down trying, your efforts won't be wasted. We'll see to that."

Chapter 5

On the second day of the boycott, six other *catadores* banged on Cambridge's hollow door at daybreak. Daniela and Davi had just arrived for their morning lessons when the group interrupted. Cambridge's broad shoulders drooped as he let the others in, whether from the lessons being put aside or the weight of carrying everyone's burden—it was hard to tell. He couldn't and wouldn't leave them to suffer on their own. They were his people, just as he was theirs.

Shielded from the downwind of the dump, they smelled of smoke and body odor—scents that were usually generously masked by the ripe stench of refuse. Each person spoke at the same time, their volume attempting to rise above the others.

"There isn't another facility nearby we can move to."

"How do you plan to survive?"

"What should we do?'

"Can we make enough to pay the fee and still live?"

No one had found any ideas of their own in the one day without work. Cambridge fielded their fears as they filled his tiny living space. With everyone gathered around and finally silent, Cambridge unfolded a district map of Rio to explain what he planned to do. In pencil, he blocked out three additional areas on the map, not far from the trash facility. Then he assigned to each

In the Shadows

block a group of two, aside from the territory he and Davi had already scoped and planned out.

Cambridge told them everything about his plan to get business owners on his side and secure their permission to have access to their recyclables before putting them out. They'd be doing what the trash hunters did, only legally because the owners would be inviting the *catadores* in to dispose of their trash for free.

As the light dawned in the others' eyes, resentment blossomed in her chest. He'd handed the others' his carefully crafted survival plan, except Daniela's idea of re-purposing what they found. That he kept to himself. Their helplessness grated on her nerves. She brushed past them to sit on the crumbling stairs.

Couldn't they for once do something for themselves? The *catadores* were resourceful, creative people, but they'd come to depend on Cambridge's advice and wisdom. It was the poor feeding the poor.

But who was she to talk? Doing something other than finding recyclables in her future was a distant wisp of a cloud.

Cambridge didn't have a foolproof scheme to share. He had crafted a survival plan that didn't have a success rate yet. His plan of finding business owner partners or paying the fee were the best options and Cambridge wasn't going to fork over a fee to work without a fight.

The air hovering above Davi and Cambridge was one of defeat when the others left, talkative and cheerful. They'd traded in their fears for hope. Now, there wasn't much hope left to hold on to.

In silence, they trudged to their block of businesses and Cambridge motioned Daniela to take her place outside in full view of the window so he could see her from inside. Davi waited with her for a few minutes while Cambridge went in to the first shop. Daniela carried an empty trash bag tucked in her pocket in case they caught a break with a shop owner.

Enough time passed for Daniela to watch all manner of life stroll by on their way to whatever important events occupied their days. It was difficult to picture a life with enough or extra. Last night's leftover rice and beans that she'd finished this morning gurgled in her stomach as if irritated at her petty imaginings. Yes, so long as they ate each day, they had enough. At last, the store door opened and a grinning Cambridge appeared, a bulging trash bag locked in his fist. He put the bag down and grabbed Daniela's face.

He kissed each of her cheeks with fervor. "Daniela-love, you are a magician! A genius! A miracle worker!" He tossed his hands in the air. "God above has smiled down on us today."

Daniela stood motionless, awaiting his explanation. Certainly no one had ever accused her of above-average intelligence before.

"Did you get the owner to give you his recyclables?" Davi asked, peering into the bag.

"All I said was that my daughter had an art project that required a variety of glass, metal, and plastic, but she was too afraid to ask. Would he mind helping me out? The owner saw Daniela through the window and told me that I was welcome to what he had and more anytime."

Davi's stance stiffened. "I don't know that I like pawning Daniela off on them like that. Her beauty could work in our favor, but what happens when we're not with her?"

Cambridge laid his hand on Davi's shoulder. "This is our territory. Daniela is not 'working' these businesses long-term. Now if she comes along while we talk to them, then we can make use of her presence. We both know that she'd be better off not coming here by herself. Okay?"

"What?" Daniela stepped closer. "What do you mean I'm not working these businesses long-term? What are you not telling me?"

Now it was Cambridge's turn to look uneasy. "We had a couple different ideas for what you could do until you're old

In the Shadows

enough, but Davi and I both agree that leaving you to wander around these districts by yourself is dangerous."

She huffed. They'd planned her future for her without telling her? "And those ideas are…"

Davi motioned for them to walk. "We think you should develop a better relationship with that lady you met yesterday. She could teach you a few things about art. Sell her your glass, but then take the opportunity to learn from her. She's an intelligent business woman. If she doesn't hire you, she may teach you more than Mamãe ever could."

Her heart dropped. "You want me to take girl lessons from this woman." It wasn't a terrible idea, but it did feel as if they were ganging up on her since the suggestion came from both men at the same time.

"Yes and no," Davi said, his hand landing on her shoulder. "We want you to learn from her, so you can pass the information on to us. By nature of her being a female, Cambridge and I thought she might be a safe place to start. She's a business owner. She knows what sells to the tourists. Since you are young and female, you can ask her questions without her getting suspicious. Watch what she does to make her art and tell us. Maybe we never sell our art in her storefront, but we will have gotten ideas from someone who uses recycled materials to make art every day."

"So, what about the girl stuff?" Daniela crossed her arms.

Davi's brown cheeks tinted pink as he shrugged. "All I'm asking is that you take some time to observe her and see if she's a nice person who might help us. If she's not, we'll move on. If she is, then maybe she can be your friend."

"How do you know she's not dangerous?" Daniela asked.

"I asked about her. They say she was a nun." Cambridge shrugged. The glint in his eyes revealed the depth of his knowledge. Cambridge didn't participate in half measures. He had no use for a life like that.

Daniela kicked her toes into the ground. She hated that they were probably right. "Nuns can be dangerous. Cambridge, you read everything you get your hands on—"

"This one isn't. She's devoted to her love of God and her work. She caught a boy stealing from her last year and instead of turning him over to the police, she let him keep the item as long as he worked for her a couple hours a day for a week. Daniela, she's a decent person." Of course, Davi would never let her walk into a situation with unknowns.

Daniela let out a frustrated grunt. If she didn't know any better, she'd think they'd orchestrated this whole fee-paying business so they could get out of the heaps and into the streets. They seemed to know everything and nothing she said could shake them.

Cambridge dug through his bag and pulled out a couple of glass bottles. He motioned for her to open her trash bag and he dumped them in when she did. He retrieved every glass item he could find and placed it in her bag. "Let's go sell some glass and see if she'll let you stick around for a bit while Davi and I talk to others."

"I don't need a babysitter," Daniela grumbled as they trudged toward Gabi's shop. She pasted a smile on her face as she walked into the store.

The bell jingled above the door. Not a sound greeted Daniela as she started toward the checkout desk, her glass bottles clanging in the quiet.

"Olá? Gabi?"

A display next to the counter caught Daniela's eye. She set her bag of bottles on the floor and stared. A beautiful array of burlap bags hung from wire stands. Bags of various sizes with fabric of assorted patterns had small handles or big shoulder straps. No one was looking for the burlap in the dump when people would pay for the glass, metal, and plastic. She turned the bag over in her hands.

In the Shadows

"Olá! Sorry to keep you waiting." A woman's voice called to her from the back.

Daniela dropped the bag into place and turned to face Gabi. Gabi's eyelashes were wet and her nose red. Daniela inhaled to ask if she was okay, but Gabi carried on first.

"My supplier for those bags just moved last week, so that's the last of my supply for a while."

Daniela gasped. The guys could be right. This could be their lucky day. "I might be able to help with that."

Gabi dabbed her eyes and smiled. "Yeah? You know someone?"

"I could ask." Daniela shrugged as if it wasn't a matter of life or death to them. Cambridge could figure it out, if anyone could. If bags and glass art sold well, then that's what they needed to make.

"I'd like that. Those bags are really popular around here." Gabi sniffed. "So did you bring me some glass?"

Daniela hefted the bag onto the counter. "I wasn't sure what kind you were looking for, but if none of this works for you, I can look specifically for what you need."

"Actually, the clears and browns will work well for my upcoming project. I am attempting a glass silhouette of a guy and girl. Or maybe it will be just a girl in a pretty dress." Gabi chuckled.

"Can I see your current project, if you have one?"

Gabi tilted her head and offered Daniela a half smile. "Sure. I bet you'd like to see what kind of things your glass is going toward."

Truthfully, Daniela cared more about the money, but Davi and Cambridge cared about the art. So by default, she cared about the work. Gabi motioned her to follow. They went down a short hallway into a back room that was lit with the most dazzling sunlight from ceiling windows.

"Wow. This is a beautiful room."

"I think so, too. It inspires me." The bell chimed on the front door. Gabi laid her hand on Daniela's arm. "Stay here for a second. Let me help whoever that is."

Gabi disappeared into the front. Her voice carried down the hall and mingled with another woman's. Daniela glanced around. Art supplies littered the room. A clay bowl lined with glass pieces glittered in the sunlight. Daniela leaned against the desk and looked down as her hand brushed a pile of papers stacked on a notepad. The top note had wet marks that smudged the ink.

Dear Gabriella Ramirez:

We regret to inform you that your appeal has been denied by Father Jose Da Rosa. We appreciate your interest; however, we have concerns about your health. We suggest you look for other ways to serve the Lord as the world is full of need and could use the pure in heart to heal it.

She was a nun just as Cambridge said. Or wanted to be one. Beneath that page was a stack of similarly stated letters that each regretted to inform Gabi she wasn't invited to this abbey or that. Her sadness for Gabi felt too invasive.

Daniela moved to the opposite side of the room to stare at a finished mosaic up close. Each piece of glass fit perfectly alongside the others. Why would someone want so badly to be a nun that they cried about not being one? The only thing she could think of that she felt that way about was *futbol,* but those two were worlds apart.

The doorbell jingled and the cheerful lilt of voices stopped, followed by a heavy coughing fit. Gagging interrupted the coughing fit. Daniela almost left her post in front of the mosaic to check on Gabi. The rejection letters were right about her health.

Daniela sighed. She shouldn't have snooped. It was none of her business. Gabi swept into the room. Gone was the rosy flush of the tears, leaving her face looking gaunt.

In the Shadows

"Are you okay?" Daniela stepped closer, then thought better of it. What if she was contagious?

Gabi waved her away. "I've had the cough for years. It's nothing."

"Your work is beautiful. I wish I could make something so beautiful." And she did. Down to her very core, she wished that she could be good at something besides being a burden.

A thoughtful look stole across Gabi's features. "I could teach you."

"I don't want to impose. I would love to watch you though, if you'd be okay with that."

Gabi's lips lifted into a smile. "I would love the company. Bring me as many colors of glass as you can find each day. I'll pay you a fair price for them. Then you can stay as long as you'd like. You would be doing me a favor. It has been too long since I have had someone around to talk to. It will be a girls' party."

Her giddiness was infectious. Daniela giggled. The guys were right. It would be nice to have a female friend.

"Well, I'm sure you have other buyers to take your glass to, so let me pick out some glass and you tell me your price," Gabi said.

She didn't really have any great options for buyers, but she didn't need to say so. She trailed Gabi to the counter. Gabi rummaged through the bag picking out bottles at random, so it seemed. She counted the bottles and opened her register. "How much for thirteen bottles?"

"Four *reals*," Daniela said.

Gabi's eyebrows shot upward. "How about seven *reals*?" Then shoved the money toward Daniela.

Daniela blinked. Had she offered her more than she asked? "You want to pay more?"

"Yes, quality supplies are worth more. I want you to bring me the best you find. The color variation and thickness of glass will make a beautiful piece of art."

It looked like regular glass bottles to her. Clamping her jaw closed, Daniela accepted the money and nodded. She glanced out the window. Cambridge and Davi stood across the street deep in discussion.

An idea struck her.

"Gabi, there's someone I want you to meet." Daniela left her bottles in the shop and ran outside. When she burst through the door, Cambridge and Davi jumped to attention.

"Come inside and meet Gabi." She grabbed Cambridge's hand. "Unless you've already met her, too."

Cambridge chuckled. "Not yet. Just heard stories."

Daniela swung the door open and pulled Cambridge through. "Gabi, this is Cambridge and my brother, Davi. This is Gabi. She's going to let me watch her do her artwork." Gabi greeted them both with a big smile. Daniela snagged a burlap bag off the display and handed one to each of the guys. "Gabi's supplier for these bags moved away. Think we could help her out?"

Cambridge turned the bag over in his hand. Davi inspected the inside, muttering about the stitching and precision.

"May we bring something by for you to look at some time soon?" Cambridge asked, as he hung the bag back on the stand.

Gabi leaned forward on the counter with a big smile. "I'd like that a lot."

"Thanks for letting Daniela observe." Cambridge's low tone drew Daniela's attention. Cambridge hadn't taken his eyes off Gabi, but she didn't seem to notice his rapt attention.

"My pleasure," Gabi said, her fingers twisting in front of her. "Hardly seems like you should thank me when I'll be grateful for her company."

Cambridge straightened his back and clapped a hand on Davi's shoulder. "Ready to get back to work?"

Daniela waved goodbye to Gabi, promising to bring some more glass options soon. Was she imagining the spark between Cambridge and Gabi? Maybe he had found out more about her

In the Shadows

than he had let on. She suppressed the hope that bubbled inside her heart. Nothing good lasted forever.

Lucky breaks didn't happen for girls like Daniela. They always came at a price. Daniela dreaded the cost for this one.

Chapter 6

Was two hundred too many copies? Or too few?

Ronaldo leaned over the laminator, debating numbers while choking on the fumes of melted plastic. Katrina stood next to him, sliding the tryout posters into plastic sleeves and then into the machine.

"Better to have too many, right?" Ronaldo mumbled and strode back to his office. The minute he logged onto his computer, his video conferencing software chimed with an incoming call. He swung his door shut with his fingertips and answered the call as the door latched into place.

"Sophia, my dear. It's great to hear from you," he said as Sophia Ferra Carter's face took over his screen.

Her dazzling smile touched every part of her face. "There's my famous cousin. I heard about the waves you were making there in Rio and had to check the source myself."

Ronaldo chuckled and ducked his head. It'd been a week since the press went live with his findings. His family had been close knit like most Brazilian families, but Sophia was the cog that connected the wheel of his extended family. She spread the important news, but kept the big secrets. She fought with every weapon in her arsenal for the ones she loved, but could be a peacemaker with the same force. And when she'd used that fight

In the Shadows

to protect him on more than one occasion, his respect for her grew exponentially.

He sat back in his seat ready for the questions to come at him. "Tell me what you've heard and I'll confirm what I can."

She waved her hand in the air nonchalantly. "Is that the illustrious office of the President of the National Futbol Committee that you are occupying?"

"It is." Ronaldo checked around him. His windows opened to a stunning view of the stadium field. "Not too shabby for an aging man like me. The altitude is nice. The air is cleaner now that I'm upwind."

"Tell me how you are changing the world. I know you wouldn't sit in that chair without having some giant aspirations for yourself."

"You know me too well." He ran a hand through his short hair which served as a reminder of how times had changed for him even though Sophia looked like she never aged.

"As a man of solid character, you make it easy for me. Your kind of men tend to be predictable in the best way, but unstoppable just the same."

Ronaldo huffed at the praise. "I think you're confusing character with corruption. Corrupt men are harder to stop. Men with character tend to get shoved to the back of the line and stomped out like a dying ember. But I'm holding out hope that the good guys get a win this time."

Sophia clucked her tongue. "I'll join you in that faith that good conquers evil."

Her words soothed a rough spot in his heart. The case against corruption needed another win after too long of a drought. "My biggest plans are for the girls' and women's teams. Our national team has good players, but we can do better. If we spend the time developing these girls from their youth onward, we'll find ourselves on an equal playing field with the top international contenders. However, our fishing pond is stocked with those girls whose parents can afford to pay for their training."

Sophia nodded and leaned in. "Doesn't always mean talent as much as it means money. You want to strike gold in the uncharted territory of the lower class."

"If anyone's going to go after it, it should be top dogs, don't you think? Truth is that those girls probably spend more time with a ball at their feet than anyone else."

"It's brilliant. How are you going to do it?"

Ronaldo barked out a laugh. "I'd like to think the board would see the investment as a valuable community tool and redirect some of the men's scholarships to the girls, but…"

"Doubtful. I'm on a dozen boards that are blind to that kind of thing." Sophia lowered her reading glasses on her nose as she wrote something on a pad of paper.

"Exactly. I need to find a way to approach them with numbers instead of charity. If we could get a small percentage of vulnerable girls off those streets and onto the *futbol* fields, I think our country would see a vast improvement in rights for women and children and a decreasing number of child prostitutes and trafficking. It's not just about *futbol*. It's about—"

"Mariana. You sounded just like her right then." Sophia grinned, her words soft. "So many years surrounding a beautiful soul, Ronaldo. I think you've done her proud. She would love this."

"She'd be beating me over the head for not getting here sooner." He scrubbed his hands over his face. "If she hadn't been trying to get girls off the street that day, Soph, she wouldn't have been there for the shooting. It's as simple as that. No one is safe. Especially not women and children. The police only make matters worse. Things can't go on like this any longer."

The silence lasted a heartbeat before Sophia jumped in. "What if our corporation sponsored a couple of girls to go to training? How much money would we be talking?"

In the Shadows

Ronaldo's jaw went slack. International sponsorships, that was genius. "Really? It would cost the price of equipment for her and part of the facility rental, if we had to pay for it. We're still working on getting deals in place and securing fields to use. I will need to get back to you on the numbers, but I would imagine that a couple hundred *reals* would go a long way for quite a few girls."

Sophia pushed her glasses on her head and typed away, mumbling about the exchange rate and international charity laws. "I will talk to our lawyers and make sure we are good to donate internationally. In the meantime, you should look into setting up a charity for these scholarships so businesses like ours have a solid place to put their money instead of floating it to the Brazilian National *Futbol* Committee. That would look pretty suspicious, I imagine."

Ronaldo's mind reeled. If Sophia's company was willing to donate, how many other organizations abroad would follow their lead and invest in the girls of Brazil?

"I'll get my assistant on that now. I'll give you better figures when we have everything set up."

"Have her reach out to my finance department, and we'll get you what you need."

"That would be a dream come true. I'll make sure we have signs and logos on the fields—"

"Don't bother. Put our name on a website if you want, but I want every cent of our money going to help those girls, and you. In fact, Xander's company is doing very well with teaching the homeless to repurpose recycled material and make money. This would be right up his alley. Find a few girls whose stories I can tell him and his board and I'll pitch it to them immediately."

Everyone had a story. Finding someone willing to tell him hers would be the hardest part.

When he ended the call with Sophia, the fire of excitement burning in his chest grew into a beach bonfire. This could really happen for him.

C.D. Gill

For them.

The girls of Brazil might actually have a fighting chance, if he could get everything together.

He called Katrina over the phone intercom and sent her chasing after information for establishing a charity for the *futbol* scholarships. She had already enlisted the help of other trustworthy assistants who would keep their mouths closed about this massive undertaking until it was time to let it out.

Meanwhile, he had posters to hang so girls would know to come to the tryouts. By lunchtime, four professional coaches jumped on board with his plan, agreeing to head up training and tryouts. He'd make more calls tomorrow.

In his best dreams, he had coaches, intervention staff—medical and psychologists, and food donations on hand at every meetup. *Futbol* was a sport, but he wanted the field to be a safe haven, a place to hide from the despicable circumstances surrounding girls. He wanted to see that each one of those girls had at least one decent meal for the day. And to get there, his team needed to consist of adults who saw the girls as children instead of problems from the *favela*. Was he crazy to hope they found him?

His experimental tryout was the one closest to his home. He posted a few himself on the outside, but paid a *favela* teen girl to post the papers where the kids liked to loiter and tell all her girlfriends who liked *futbol* to come. They were the ones his sister would have tried to rescue first.

After changing into his street clothes, Ronaldo spent the afternoon finding the perfect places for his posters on the outside of *favelas*. If there was a group of kids in the street, he walked straight up to them and asked them if they could read and where he should put the sign. The boys got excited when they saw the *futbol* until he told them it was for girls only.

"Girls playing *futbol*?" A tall boy scrunched his nose. "It'll be like watching mice fight over scraps."

In the Shadows

"You'll have to hold their babies," another boy said, causing the other boys to erupt in laughter.

His heart sank at the words. "I'll hold as many babies as I need to. Bring your sisters and cousins," he said. "See you there."

His final three posters he saved for the newly opened medical clinic. Walking up this time was vastly different from opening day a week ago. The line wasn't as long and the clinic's energy had settled into a patient hum from its frenzied pace.

He pinned his posters up in the most obvious spaces he could find. One outside for the people in line to see and two inside. Katrina had made them bold and colorful to attract attention. Looking at them in competition with the other visual noise about handwashing and AIDS and tuberculosis nearby, Ronaldo wasn't so sure they were bold or colorful enough, but they would do for now.

Isadora pushed through a back door into the main room of the clinic as she strode directly to the sink. Deep lines creased her usually smooth brow. She kept her gloved hands lifted above her waist. Dark red stained the blue latex a streaked purple. When she finished scrubbing, she poked her head through the doorway to the back room where she'd just come from and made a few gestures.

Ronaldo watched her movements, unwilling to interrupt her in her zone. It was her childish smile that lit her whole face that he waited on to appear, but deep in his gut he had a feeling he wouldn't see it today. A nurse captured his attention and in an instant Isadora's eyes met his. The sadness welling there pressed deep into his chest. She checked her watch and flashed three fives with her hand with raised eyebrows. He nodded, then stepped outside to wait for her. Good food could cure a lot of problems, but it likely would not solve whatever this was, knowing how much it took to get her there in the first place.

He sat outside on the warm concrete wall to people watch. The world was going a little more insane each year as displayed in small part in Rio. The growing gap between the rich and poor. The war on freedoms from the people who swore to protect them. The gross corruption that bulldozed over every honorable cause in its way. The suppression of women in a culture that pretended to elevate them. The constant need of escape from reality that ended in every type of violence imaginable and abuse of humanity. It pained him. Yet wasn't he part of the problem if he stood by with his hands in the air, clueless as what to do?

A hand fell softly on his shoulder. Dread squeezed his chest with one glance at Isadora's tight-lipped smile. Nothing good could come of that look. He stood and greeted her with a kiss on her cheek and a full embrace. Her small frame felt like a dream in his arms. She pressed into him tightly, her forehead lay against his neck. The hug didn't last long enough. She sighed as she pulled away and took his hand in hers.

"Do you have any dinner plans?" Ronaldo asked as they strolled to her car.

Isadora tightened her grip on his hand. Her hand felt so delicate in his own. "I may not be the best company tonight."

I'll be your soft place to land on a hard day, every day. "I'm okay with a quiet dinner, if you don't mind my presence."

Fishing her keys from her bag, she handed them to Ronaldo. "Sounds perfect."

Ronaldo drove them to a casual seafood restaurant just outside the *favelas*. From where they sat on the patio, they could feel the ocean breeze without being blown away. They ordered before either of them started the conversation.

"My cousin in the United States called today to check in. She wants to provide a couple of scholarships for the new girls' *futbol* league I want to start." Ronaldo sipped his sparkling water and glanced around at the crowd surrounding them. Everyone dined at a different decibel.

In the Shadows

Her worry lines relaxed, but she still hadn't smiled. "What a catch! If they sponsor girls, who knows what other philanthropists will join in?"

Ronaldo nodded. "I put up posters today for the training tryouts and the boys seemed to think we'd be cultivating a nursery while the mamas played."

Isadora grunted, her expression darkened. "I'll be sure my staff talks to every eligible girl we see to let them know. Don't want the girls disqualifying themselves before they get a chance to find out they are exactly who you are looking for."

Ronaldo shifted in his seat, debating the wisdom of continuing the conversation or letting the silence rule like he had promised when he invited her out. Isadora decided for him.

"I delivered a child with microcephaly today. Third this week at that clinic." Isadora tapped on her phone and showed him a picture of a baby. The child had a tiny, misshapen skull covered in patches of dark hair. Isadora scrolled and showed him a comparison shot between the microcephalic child and a baby with an average head. The difference in size was astounding. "The baby's brain didn't develop properly in the womb, thus the skull is not a typical size."

He raised his eyebrows. "How does this happen to three babies in the same week at the clinic? Is it a coincidence? Or is it dictated by DNA?"

"I don't have definite evidence yet, but I believe it's a virus that infects the mother and passes on to the baby. Microcephaly is so rare. According to my research, there is an outbreak of a virus called Zika which started over in Africa, but recently has spread around the world to mosquito-infested areas of the world. The virus isn't that damaging to adults, but there have been a few cases where ambitious doctors linked a microcephaly case to a Zika case. Most of the medical world has dismissed it, but I think that's what we're seeing here. And if that's the case—"

Ronaldo whistled. "All babies in the womb are at risk."

"The results are cataclysmic. We're talking about a significant decline in tourism to the area. And if mothers knew ahead of time that their children were going to have a severe health issues, we could be looking at an unprecedented number of illegal abortions happening. Not to mention, the medical care these babies will need for the rest of their lives—care their parents won't be able to afford. So now we're talking about infantile death, orphans in the system, and an unpredictable national crisis all from a virus that often doesn't display symptoms in the mother."

His arms ached to pull her against him, to soothe the fear discoloring the heavy weight of the world she carried so boldly.

Isadora exhaled hard and sat back in her chair. "I'm planning to run this up the chain, but I'm not sure who will actually listen." Their food arrived, interrupting her thoughts. When the waiter left, she started in again. "And on top of that mountain of stress, at the general hospital this week I did a Cesarean section on a woman who had a phantom pregnancy. She had all the symptoms of going into labor, including a very distended abdomen. No one ran an ultrasound on her before taking her back. So, I cut into her abdomen, only to find there was literally nothing in her uterus. Never in my life have I heard of that. It's very disillusioning."

"You know how much I disdain the press in general, but they ran the story I sent them about the payoffs. Getting attention like that worked in my favor, although it was a gamble. If the authorities don't listen about the virus, take it to the general public. They have a right to know what is happening."

"Even in the face of widespread panic?"

Ronaldo shrugged. "I don't know. Maybe the government would listen to the citizens if they demanded answers. A medical problem only gets acknowledged when it affects the lives of the well-off. Otherwise, it's the poor people's problem."

She smoothed her hair away from her troubled face, a sigh escaping her lips.

In the Shadows

He couldn't stand the distance any longer. His hand slid over hers, relishing her smooth skin. "Forgive my talking out of turn. I hate to see your distress, Isadora. You fight for these mothers and babies every day. You're in the trenches with them. No one cares for them like you do. Be their voice or be their silence—you know what's best."

His plate sat partially touched, but his appetite was quickly vanishing. Isadora wiped the corners of her mouth, feminine to her very essence.

She met his eye and offered him a small smile. "It's never about doing the right thing. That choice is easy. The distress comes from not being heard."

Chapter 7

Gabi welcomed Daniela into the shop as the morning's light stole into the sky. The sales of their goods from two days ago allowed Davi and Cambridge to pay the fee one time yesterday to get inside the facility and search for the materials they needed for projects. Daniela stood outside the fence to catch bag after bag that they heaved over. As a favor to Cambridge, the guards manning the entrance looked the other way when Davi or Cambridge approached the fence.

The materials they launched at her garnered no interest of the other pickers who strictly sought out the recyclables. In fact, the others laughed at them when Cambridge made up a story of why he collected the burlap. Let them laugh. Selling products in Gabi's storefront could change their lives.

When Gabi opened the door for Daniela, she gasped. "My goodness, what is all this?"

Daniela had brought a sampling of various colors of bottles, four woven door mats made from plastic bags, a three-tiered hanging planter woven from old clothes that she had carefully washed and dried, and two small planks of wood with bits of metal and wire bent into hooks for jewelry or bags. It looked like polished pieces of trash to her, but she sent up a prayer that Gabi wouldn't see it that way.

In the Shadows

Daniela scrunched her nose. "Trash" was on the tip of her tongue, but they'd worked very hard over the past day to get this ready. "Cambridge thought you might be interested in a few additional items to offer tourists who love work from the locals."

Gabi sorted through the items without a word, her expression neutral.

"It's too much. I can tell. I'll take it home with me." The humiliation stomped at her heart. Being poor never bothered her before. Everyone around here rowed the same kind of boat she did. Anyone who bragged thought their dirty was less dirty than everyone else's.

"Don't you dare." Gabi's high-pitched scolding stopped the words tumbling from her careless tongue. "We'll put these up for sale and see who's interested. When they sell, I'll order more."

When.

Any fear of refusal from Gabi dissipated. Gabi thought these items might sell. No, would sell. It was madness and hope in one solid plea for survival. They were *catadores,* which was unlikely to be forgotten. But Cambridge seemed to think they could bid for more, and, if they were denied, the status quo wouldn't change. If their attempts were accepted...

Gabi floated around the sales floor snagging items on her way to the front window display. "We'll display them in the 'locally sourced' window. I'll make sure to mention them to anyone coming in." She stuck a yellow sticker on the back of each item and winked at Daniela. "So I remember which items are yours. Now come on back and let's get to work making more magic to sell."

As soon as she stepped into the back room, Gabi hung an apron around Daniela's neck and settled some glasses over her eyes before donning her own. She tugged on a pair of thick gloves. A solid thump accompanied the sound of smashing glass. Daniela sidestepped to peer over Gabi's shoulder.

"I'm breaking the glass to get it ready for laying out the design. Each glass piece will be a little different and catch the light in its own way. Part of the beauty—"

Thump.

The hammer and resulting rattle of the table buried the rest of her words under its quivering. She talked softly as she arranged the glass pieces on another small plate of glass surrounded by a picture frame, dropping bits of sound wisdom offhandedly.

"The tourists like small things they can take back in their suitcases. The smaller the art, the better chance they think they can get it home without it breaking."

Those were things she would have never thought of. She hadn't traveled outside of her city. Daniela needed to remember these tips. She found a pen and paper nearby, scribbling as fiercely as she could.

Big is bad. Breakable is very bad. Use a strong bonding agent that is clear. Creating art on small canvasses takes more creativity.

Gabi went on, but Daniela couldn't write that fast. If Cambridge had his way, learning the art of what Gabi was doing would become second nature to her.

A buzzer chimed in the distance. Gabi finished the piece she had her finger on, then pulled away. A smile lit her face. "Breakfast is ready. Care to join me?"

Oh, she definitely did.

Every day for the next two weeks except on Sundays, Daniela sat quietly beside Gabi—watching, anticipating, discussing, analyzing, experimenting. The breakfast breaks were the sweetest times. They talked about sports, family, religion, fears, art. Never once did Gabi complain about Daniela eating her food with no payment or reciprocation. In fact, she thanked her every day for her company and the thoughtful conversation.

Like Gabi valued her.

Like she mattered in the world.

In the Shadows

It pained her to admit it, but Davi and Cambridge couldn't have insisted she get to know a better person. Not because Gabi was rich and famous, but because she was the kindest, most patient person Daniela had ever met. Even on her bad days when her nose was running and her eyes swollen from a night of tears, she hugged Daniela and told her she was talented, quick, and funny. It wasn't an "I love you", but her words chipped away at Daniela's distant facade.

When Gabi handed her the money from their first few sales, she asked what Daniela would buy.

"Fresh food at the market," Daniela said without thinking.

Her answer didn't faze Gabi. Instead, she celebrated and insisted Daniela tell her all about their meal the next day. If Daniela was honest, she walked away from the store dreading the moment when reality hit and she returned to the dumps to pick trash. This change had been so refreshing.

The next day as Daniela finished the gluing on a project she'd started that morning, Gabi called into the back room. "Davi's here."

His low tones mixed with Gabi's soft laugh in the front room. When she came around the corner, her stomach sank when Davi shifted on his feet and gave her a quick one-sided quirk—the kind he offered in front of people to put on a solid front.

She smoothed her curls into a thick ponytail, off her neck as they left Gabi's. The usual Rio heat couldn't touch the anxiety scorching her inside.

She scrunched her nose at him when he checked his surroundings for the third time in thirty seconds. "You're as skittish as a wild dog. What's wrong?"

He shoved his hands into his short pockets and smiled. "I have a surprise for you."

"Is it something illegal?" Daniela's loud whisper was meant to be a joke, but she did have serious questions.

He glanced at the sky, a longsuffering sigh bleeding from his lips. "No, it's better than that."

They climbed the steep hill and down the other side. They'd explored most every part of the *favelas* as kids, running through mazes of streets adding children to their numbers as they played. But they hadn't had a reason to be in this part for a very long time.

Up ahead, the skeleton of a rusted, deserted factory outside the *favela* lay desolate and ripe for exploration. Although it'd likely already been picked through, her hope simmered.

"Do we get to scavenge through the factory for wire and metal?" She meant to keep her tone neutral, but Davi shook his head at her excitement.

"No, better than that."

What could be better than that? They crossed the street beside it and picked their way through the trees until a flat partially grassed field lay in front of them. People milled around the far end of the space behind the fence.

"What's going on?"

A dark figure strode across the dirt path toward them.

Cambridge.

When he neared, his eyes sparkled as he handed the bag to Daniela. Davi wasn't talking and Cambridge had said nothing.

She opened the bag, preparing to beg for an explanation. The contents stole her breath away.

Tall socks.

Shin guards.

Futbol cleats.

"Whose are these? And what are they for?" She'd never worn any before. Only in her dreams did she see herself running the length of a crisp green field sporting Brazil's green and yellow uniform. And maybe orange cleats so Davi could see her from the stands.

In the Shadows

"Yours now. Try them on. It's the best I could do." Davi swallowed. The flash of disappointment on his face lasting less than a heartbeat said he would have done way better if he could have.

That was her brother. Always wanting to exceed her expectations.

She plopped to the ground to pull on the shin guards and socks. Her fingers skated gently over the surfaces. They weren't new by any stretch of the word, but they were hers.

"And to answer your question, you are going to join the group across the field. It's tryouts for a new girls' *futbol* camp that starts in fifteen minutes."

Her hands froze halfway through putting on her first cleat. A thousand questions raced toward the tip of her tongue at the same time, but the first word that escaped was "girls?"

In bewilderment, she twisted to check out the other side of the field. Cambridge and Davi laughed. She'd not found any other girls in their area willing to play, much less to elbow their way into a crowd of ego-nursing boys with raging hormones, roaming hands, and unpredictable temperaments.

Her heart sank. This league was doomed to failure before the tryouts started.

"Girls of every size and skill level," Cambridge said, crossing his arms. "Some are good, but none of them are as good as you, Daniela. You need to play the best you can. This could be your chance." He stepped in closer, his voice low. "Not to intimidate you, but I heard the man running this tryout is the new president of the FCC."

Daniela rose slowly. Shock reverberated through her. The president. Here? She lifted her eyes to Davi's. The intensity there reaffirmed what she'd already expected.

He knew.

Of course, he did.

He wouldn't waste time on her trying out for a hobby league. For years, he'd promised that he would help her achieve her *futbol* goals whatever the cost.

Cambridge bent over her shoes, pressing his finger into the toe area. They were too big, but certainly better than playing barefoot if everyone else had cleats. He tapped her ankle for her to lift her foot and untied her shoes.

When he had them off, he slipped a couple of thin cloths into the toe. "Try this."

She stuffed her feet back in, wrapping the laces around the shoe before knotting them at the top. She jogged in place. No movement.

A grin stole across her face. "How long have you guys known about this?"

Davi shrugged and walked toward the group. "We've passed a poster about it every day for the past two weeks now that we're doing pickup rounds each morning. If the only good that comes of this extortion from the trash facility is that you make it to *futbol* camp, then I think it's been worth it."

A lot of hassle and heartache just for a chance. If she never tried, she'd never know if her dream was silly or possible, right?

They accompanied her to the coned off area and both kissed her cheek.

"Show them what you've got, Dani-girl."

Her legs balked as reality hit her. Here she was a *catadore*, pretending to blend in with the rest of society. Surely, the other girls would know as soon as they saw her. She wanted to hide, but playing *futbol* was her dream.

A man wearing a ball cap stood to the side of the field with a clipboard in his hands. The line of girls in front of him seemed to indicate that he would have answers for her. When she reached the front of the line, the creases next to his eyes and the gray hair poking from beneath his cap gave her a better guess at his age.

In the Shadows

And when his light brown eyes appraised her, she attempted to wet her lips with an equally as dry tongue.

"Daniela Gomes, Senhor," she said. Many more words and her voice would have shaken.

He smiled and she liked him instantly. "Thank you for coming to tryouts, Daniela. You can call me Coach for today." He winked. "What's your age?"

"Fifteen."

He scribbled on the paper. "Do you live nearby?"

She nodded. "Just on the hill above the high rises."

"Good, good. Go ahead and grab a ball and take a few shots on goal. We'll get started in a few minutes."

The next two hours disappeared in a blur of ball handling, technique discussion, and penalty kick practice. Nothing very challenging, but brand-new information. When she played with the boys, they didn't play by the official rules that Coach was teaching them today. They had their own set and they defended them with as much passion as they played with.

Only eight girls ranging from thirteen to seventeen ran around the field with her. Most seemed like they were only passably interested in playing the game.

As Coach separated them out, five on four, for scrimmage, Daniela tripped over her shoes for the twentieth time. With a grunt, she tossed the shoes to the side of the field. She'd play better barefoot. Boys hung on a chain-link fence and heckled them as the younger kids kicked their own version of *futbols* around. Davi and Cambridge watched silently, arms crossed.

Coach put Daniela as a forward on the team with four players. As soon as the whistle blew, she was on the ball, taking it from her opponent with very little effort. She dribbled past two girls and looked for a teammate to pass to, but no one was next to her. It was her and the goalkeeper, so she shot to the left and scored.

A cheer went up from the fences. Her teammates gave her high-fives.

As they lined up to kickoff again, she sneaked a glance at Coach, his face unreadable. The boys she played with hated when she hogged the ball. He was a coach. He probably hated it even more. She'd dial it back.

This time she snagged the ball that her opponent kicked way in front of her. Daniela shouted for her team to rush the goal. She passed the ball out of the danger area, but her teammate lost it in a head-to-head. Daniela hustled back and recovered the ball. This time sprinting up the right-hand side. Even from far out, she saw the opening and took it, planting the ball firmly in the back of the net.

The whistle blew and Coach called them over.

"Good playing today, girls. Be here the same time tomorrow. Spread the word tonight. Let's fill this field for the rest of the week." They nodded and headed in separate directions. Daniela made a beeline for Davi.

He hugged her despite her sweat. Thank God Coach hadn't chosen the hottest part of the day for tryouts. They walked back to Cambridge's place to finish out the day making items for Daniela to take to Gabi in the morning.

That evening, they sauntered home each with a can of Guarana in hand. She wasn't quite ready for the day to be over.

"This morning when you came to get me, was the tryout the only reason you were acting so jumpy?" The question had burned in the back of her mind all day, but she hadn't had a good chance to ask him without Cambridge around.

His delayed response set her on edge again. "I have a lot on my mind recently, Dani."

"More than work?"

"I don't want to worry you with the thoughts in my head when you have a shot at catching the eye of an important man."

"Davi, if you don't tell me, I'll assume the worst and that will really distract me from my chance at succeeding."

In the Shadows

He grunted. "Chacal approached me two days ago." His words were soft and aimed at her ear.

She stopped. "Why? What does he want with you?" They'd avoided the undesired attention of the resident gang leader by being *catadores,* but that didn't mean they didn't know who he was. Everyone knew him. He was the current head of their *favela* and the unofficial mayor of their housing sector. All the rent money went to him, until someone got money hungry and went after his position.

And someone always did, but they hadn't survived it.

Davi's jaw flexed. "Came to me with a job proposal. Said he heard what happened at the facility and that he could use a man like me on his business ventures." He snorted as if to laugh off his words.

Her lungs seized. She couldn't breathe. Chacal never left without whoever or whatever he came for. If you were approached, it meant you were as good as his.

Or dead.

Daniela forced her legs to take her up the stairs to their apartment. The excitement of the day drained from her body. Davi opened the door and stepped into the darkness.

"Mamãe?" His deep voice rang through the space.

No answer.

He made it to the string hanging from the light bulb in the middle of the apartment as Daniela felt her way along the wall toward Mamãe's room. When the light clicked on, she glanced around. Everything seemed to be in place. In fact, nothing appeared to have been touched since she left this morning.

Davi raised his eyebrows and joined her in front of Mamãe's room in three long strides. He opened the door without knocking. The sour odor of vomit mixed with diarrhea greeted them. Her stomach churned, preparing its own upheaval. Davi motioned for her to stay back. She retreated to the main space, grateful for the chance to breathe fresh air.

"Mamãe?" He asked again. "Daniela, she's not answering. She's barely breathing."

The numbness crept over her first, followed by a submersive wave of guilt. While she'd been chasing her dream of playing *futbol* today, Mamãe could have died.

Chapter 8

The second day of tryouts went much like the first—more male hecklers than female players. If this was the litmus for the state of equality affairs in the country—which Ronaldo very much believed it was—they were worse off than he originally believed. He needed to draw in the girls as well as keep the boys from ruining their tryouts, so he called in a couple of favors.

Three, to be exact.

Two female national players and one male player.

But they came with a price. Namely, their huge brand sponsors who wanted to scoop up the photo opportunity of Brazil's favorite players slumming with the underprivileged.

It was disgusting and he hated it, but since his league assistants were still gathering their sponsors for the camp that funneled the girls' league all the way up to the women's team, that would be part of their payment.

There would be media and extra security. It wasn't all bad. He'd told the kids to spread the word that the stars would be here. And they would be for the last thirty minutes or so of the practice. If he trusted anything, it was the draw of celebrities to the kids. Practically the embodiment of their hopes and dreams.

Despite the raging heat today, he'd gotten here early to register newcomers and to observe.

In the Shadows

Who came from which direction?

Who had family with them? Or who came alone?

He'd brought old equipment with him—used shin guards, socks, and cleats in whatever size he could find them.

A chuckle seized his chest. Yesterday, the best player on the field, Daniela, had gotten so frustrated with tripping over her too-big cleats that she chucked them to the side of the field and played the rest of the scrimmage barefoot. When they huddled at the end of the tryout, her feet didn't have a scratch on them.

He'd checked, because that girl did not need to put herself at risk on his watch. She was quiet, quick, and haunted. Just the kind of girl Mariana would spot potential in. There was fifteen years of pain behind her shuttered expressions.

She didn't show any emotion at all on the field, except the fire that sparked in her eyes. She played like she was born to do it. He'd already pegged her as the potential recipient of one of the Upcycled Life scholarships for his upcoming camp. Her grace and speed kept her light on her feet. Her kind of talent shouldn't be wasted.

Part of Rosanna and Sam's, the women from the national team, jobs today were to challenge his top players to see how far their skills went. He wasn't afraid to segment the team. The girls who were struggling to keep up knew it, but they'd stuck it out this far and that meant something to him.

Especially in the current conditions.

He set the cones in places and constructed the pop-up goal posts. A short huff of laughter escaped his lips remembering the girls' bewildered questions when they first saw the cones and posts. They'd never seen them, much less used them before.

According to his check-ins, some of the other coaches were having better luck at their tryouts in their designated *favelas*. His hope that this might come together wasn't too distant a dream. The girls of this city deserved better, and if they didn't get it today, would they ever get it?

As he pulled the bag of cleats onto the field opposite the hecklers, Daniela approached from the west end of the field. The boy that accompanied her watched her walk in between the cones before giving her a wave and disappearing into the trees again. Daniela's posture was more slouched today than usual.

"Hey Daniela, come on over here for a minute." He adjusted his ballcap so it sat higher on his forehead.

She picked up her head and jogged over to him. For someone without any formal training, respect and sportsmanship came naturally to her.

"I noticed you had some trouble with your cleats yesterday, so I found some old boots in storage that might work. Take a look." He sorted them by size, taking a minute to send up thanks to whoever thought to tie the laces keeping the pairs together.

She nodded. "Thanks, Coach."

"You remind me a lot of my sister when she was your age. She loved *futbol* and always gave the boys a run for their money when we played." He grunted. Those were the days. She was practically Mariana reincarnated.

Daniela's fingers smoothed over a pair of blue and yellow cleats, worn but clean. Bright but not gaudy. "Why did she stop playing?"

Despite the time passed, the truth seemed too harsh. But it wasn't a secret. Her life meant everything to him. Still did. "She caught a bullet from a dealer who was trying to keep her from taking his girls off the street."

Her head jerked toward him, her assessment unabashed. He appreciated the honesty in the way she carried herself. There was no pretense. "So, you're one of us."

The look on her face captured the last few decades of his life. The acceptance, the realized bond was the reason he'd returned to the *favelas*. "And always will be."

She stood and scuffed the blue and yellow cleats in the dirt as if to test their traction. He'd hoped she'd relate to him, but as he

In the Shadows

processed her reaction, his words struck him as taking away hope that she could ever get away from being in the *favelas*.

When she smiled, he could see the satisfaction there. The cleats must fit.

"Coach, I need to tell you something. My brother didn't think I should say anything so as not to hurt my chances, but you need to know." Daniela straightened her posture and looked him in the eye. "My mother is doing very poorly right now. If there's a chance that I am favored to make it past the tryouts to camp, we don't have the money for me to continue."

His heart ached. "I'm sorry to hear about your mother. Has she been to the new clinic on Villa Miseria?"

Daniela shook her head, motioning to where she'd walked from. "My brother is taking her right now."

"I know the head doctor there personally. You won't find a better doctor anywhere." He crossed his arms across his chest. "As for playing, you can be assured that financial status has no bearing here, Daniela. We're in the *favelas* looking for talent, not for people who can pay their way to the top."

She nodded at him but didn't look that convinced.

He snagged a ball and passed it to her. "What's your dream?"

"To play *futbol* on the national team." Her return pass skipped along the dirt.

"What else?"

The silence lingered between them. "To see my brother get the schooling he wants. To get out of the *favelas* and no longer be *catadores*. To sell the art we are making from the trash and use it for good."

All right, Mariana. I hear you. She'll get one of the scholarships.

To his left, a stream of people breached the field. Their laughter and noise carried on the gentle breeze. His pulse thrummed with anticipation. He needed a crowd today. Partly for his ego, but mostly so that the girls who wanted to could find their purpose off the street, to use their bodies in the way they wanted to. He flipped the ball into the air forcing Daniela to chest trap it and bring it to the ground.

"I need to oversee check-in. Run a passing drill until I'm ready, okay?"

She juggled the ball as he jogged to the check-in point. He marked off a couple of players already registered and spent the next thirty minutes registering new girls. His assistants showed up right on time to help conduct the chaos.

With the line of girls now on the field, he tucked his clipboard under his arm and made his way toward the crowd of kids on the sidelines. His whistle shrieked above their noise.

"I want you to be on your best behavior today. Our special guests will be here soon. If I have trouble with any of you, I'll send you home and you won't get to see the guests. Are we clear?"

The boys and younger girls nodded their consent. Almost as soon as he stepped away, they exploded into giggles. As he stalked out to start tryouts, a teenage girl in shorts and a t-shirt gripped the fence a good distance from where the crowd stood. The dirt on her face didn't hide the longing as her eyes never left the girls running drills on the field with his assistants. She was clearly on the wrong side of the fence. He diverted his course.

As he got closer, the reason for her distance was strapped to the front of her with little tan limbs sticking out a the colorful wrap. He cleared his throat as she backed away from the fence.

"Sister, do you play *futbol?*" He motioned for her to step forward, praying she wouldn't bolt to the safety of the trees before they could talk.

"I did." A sad smile captured her features.

So she was a mama now.

He took a deep breath. "I'll hold the baby. You come play."

The hesitancy frozen on her face made him laugh.

In the Shadows

He motioned again. "I'm the coach. Give me the baby and get out on that field. I can tell you belong there."

Her feet moved slowly at first, giving him a chance to change his mind, but then quickened as she realized he was serious. He reached the crowd first to open the gate and let her in. All eyes turned to watch her.

His glare scoured the crowd, daring any of them to repeat the comment about him holding babies during tryouts. A couple of boys wiped the grins off their faces the second he caught them smiling. She didn't stop moving until she was next to him. She unwrapped the sleeping baby and transferred the wrap to him.

The baby's head drooped against his chest creating a hot pocket against him. How did the mom and baby tolerate it in this heat? The teen cinched the wrap around his waist and shoulders as he picked up his clipboard.

"Name?" he said, quietly.

"Valiana, age seventeen."

Practice waited on them. "We'll get the rest of your information after." He motioned his head toward the group as he made a note on the clipboard.

She ran off with her sandals flapping against her feet and a huge smile on her face. As for her baby, the pink bows in her dark hair tugged hard on his heartstrings. He'd missed his chance to have this. He'd been so focused on avenging his sister's death, not a woman in the world could have yanked those blinders off him.

But Valiana didn't have to miss her chance at changing her future because of this child's presence in the world. He might be the only one in her life telling her that, but he wouldn't be the last. Babies and dreams could coexist—it was hard but not impossible. She had a future, if she wanted one.

As he conducted the tryout, he believed that more and more. She was solid with a firm foot and bulldozing speed. Most girls scrambled to get out of her way as she charged.

Except Daniela.

He pressed his clipboard to his lips to hide his smile. Valiana stuttered when challenged. Daniela swiped the ball from her feet like a dog snagging food off an unmonitored plate and headed the opposite direction. With a loud growl, Valiana took off after her.

They were fire and ice on the field together.

These tryouts got a whole lot more interesting.

With the matchup between Daniela and Valiana, the other girls accelerated their performances. With one minor tweak, the team members settled into their teams and gave the audience something to watch. Nevertheless, the moment the audience's energy level changed, he knew the professionals had arrived.

They showed up early, because they knew the drill. Autographs, pictures, talking to kids, getting coach instructions took time he wasn't willing to give away from the practice he'd scheduled. Daniela took advantage of the distractions and powered down the field to score a goal. By the time the other teams' defenders shook off their star-gazing haze, there was no stopping Daniela's advance.

They protested her easy goal. He blew the whistle which resulted in the losing team running a couple of laps. When they circled back in front of him, he smiled at his varied group of players. Every shape and size had joined in today and it did his heart wonders to see it.

"That's the best performance I've seen from you ladies yet. Good work."

They smiled at his compliments.

"We're going to break into three groups. Each group is going to rotate working with a professional player on certain skills, and then we're going to put the pros to the test."

The girls bounced with excitement despite the heat and exhaustion. He left the dispersion to his assistants as he welcomed and filled the national players in on what he needed. The next hour they put the girls through their paces. By the time they left,

In the Shadows

he had three lists of the top players who should join the *futbol* camp.

The lists were impersonal and based strictly on their professional assessments of skill. Objectivity was always hard to come by. After practice ended, he walked home with the leftover cleats and a bag of cones over his shoulder like a *futbol*-themed *Papai Noel*. He dropped the bags off in his apartment and headed to the clinic.

The pep talks he gave himself warned him not to get used to Isadora being so accessible. His fall would be long and hard when he said goodbye to their daily meetings. The sizzle of pleasure through him at seeing her raven hair and golden eyes had become an addiction he hoped to never give up. The second he stepped foot in her clinic, a nurse pulled him into Isadora's office to wait. He paced the length of the room, preferring to be exploring the clinic over staring at gray cinder block walls.

A faint alarm sounded in his head at the speed in which he'd been rushed into an office. No, Isadora would have alerted him to any problems. He checked his phone. No messages. The desk in the corner held an old computer, but nothing personal.

Another reminder of her temporary presence at this clinic.

The door clicked open. Isadora slipped in, closing the door behind her. She slipped off her doctor's jacket, exposing a white tank top and tanned shoulders. He swallowed hard.

She's so beautiful it hurts.

When her eyes met his, a heat flared between them. He covered the distance in two strides and cupped her head in his hands. Without asking permission, he moved his lips over hers, gently claiming her until she responded with more urgency pushing him further from his carefully guarded control.

His hands moved to her shoulders, down her arms to her waist as he savored the feel of her soft skin against his hands. Her weight moved him back a step or two. His back bumped into the wall, but all he could focus on was her silky lips tasting like passion and sweetness against his. His pulse hammering in his ears grounded his high and had him breaking the kiss with an unsaid apology and labored breathing.

"You smell like heat and..." She stopped to sniff again. "Lavender-scented baby powder?"

The alarm in her expression asked so many questions that he couldn't help but laugh out loud. His hand smoothed her along her back. His arms around her felt nothing short of perfect as if it had always been instead of a new sensation. This was what he'd been missing all these years of stuffing the distraction into an unvisited compartment deep in his soul.

A smirk stole across his face. "I made good on my promise today and found a solid player out of it."

Isadora's lips parted, so red and perfectly formed. He inched toward her to kiss her again. Her hand pressed firmly against his chest, stopping his progress.

"You, the impervious Ronaldo Cevere, held a baby during practice for one of your players?" Her tone pitched into a squeak. The laugh that sprang from her sounded as if it came from the depths of her belly. She whipped her mobile phone from her pocket, her thumbs tapping wildly against the screen. "Please tell me someone captured photo evidence of this."

Within a minute, Isadora gasped. "Oh, Ronaldo. That is the sweetest thing I have ever seen." Her hand fanned her face.

What on earth was she looking at? He sidestepped to peer over her shoulder. There on her screen was a picture of him in his ballcap holding his clipboard giving instructions to one of the girls with the baby nestled against him.

"Who was that? Traitor." His grunt held no sincerity. It wasn't a bad look on him.

Isadora slid the phone back into her pocket. "It pays to be friends with your assistants sometimes." Her hands went around his waist, pulling their torsos together. "I'm not sure anything you do from now on could be more attractive than seeing you carrying

In the Shadows

a baby against you while you coach. It thrills me that you have such a soft side to you."

His lips lifted in a grin. The pleasure of having her arms wrapped around him made him feel that he could do no wrong. "Will you be my..." His mind scrambled for a label that wouldn't make him sound archaic or too hip. There were none. "Will you be my girlfriend?"

A huge smile captured Isadora's full lips. He couldn't stop himself from kissing them. When they pulled apart, Isadora laid her forehead against his cheek. "It would be my privilege, Ronaldo."

A knock on her office door forced a sigh from her.

"Duty calls," Ronaldo murmured.

She tightened her grip on his sides. "I'm off at eight. Want to do dinner?"

"Yes. And if you're game, I could use your help matching girls with sponsors. I have to have a candidate and a backup for each organization. And I'd delegate it to Katrina tomorrow, but I'd rather have a hand in the future of these girls."

Isadora nodded. "I can't wait. After that, you can help me draft my letter to the government officials about Zika."

"Oh, Isadora. One of my player's mother came to you today—Daniela Gomes is the girl's name. Said her brother brought the mother in, very sick."

The sadness that stole over Isadora's features took the air from his lungs. He'd seen it a time or two before. If anyone held on to hope too long, it was Isadora. Perpetual sunshine. So when that look came around, it meant one thing.

"That bad?"

Isadora shrugged into her white doctor's jacket. Her eyes trained on him hid none of the pain she felt. "It's Hep B contracted from a dirty needle which hasn't cleared her system like it usually does in adults, but now she has a bad case of pneumonia to compact her already poor health. It's fatal."

The prognosis turned his stomach. "Did they say where she contracted hepatitis? Was she using needles in the home?"

"They're *catadores*, Ronaldo. It's a very serious hazard of the job."

He kissed her cheek and watched her walk away, already measuring the future impact on Daniela's career and her dreams. He had a say where her future was concerned and he never left potential unpolished.

Chapter 9

Daniela didn't get involved in petty gossip. Not when it helped her, nor when it hurt her. But this was getting out of hand. Today was the last day of tryouts. Coach announced this morning that they'd have the list of who made it to camp and who won which scholarships after the practice was over.

His words of "there's still time to win or lose a spot on the lists, so do your best" had brought the sharks out. The girls threw careless words around as deliberately as limbs. What they lacked in skill, they made up for in dirty schemes.

And someone had it out for Valiana.

Based on the conversations she'd heard so far, Valiana was the niece of the former FFC president, the mistress of the coach's brother, a rich girl trying to snag a scholarship from the poor people, and an unfit mom who splashed alcohol into her baby's mouth to keep her from crying.

None of it had any merit, but Daniela kept her eye on Valiana to watch for signs that she'd heard the rumors. Valiana was a fiery competitor, but Daniela liked her. She had honest talent with a temper and a sweet side to match. Sure, her moods swung back and forth like tree branches in a heavy storm, but when the competition was done, she was friendly and complimentary. So she'd attempted to ignore the negativity.

In the Shadows

Daniela even walked away thoroughly disgusted when she heard one of her teammates saying they should "break the diva's legs." But when that teammate shoved Valiana over the outstretched leg of another teammate when the ball was on the other end of the field, Daniela lost her ability to ignore the drama.

"Are you trying to seriously injure her, you jackals?" Daniela flicked a wrist as if to scatter them to the wind. She squatted next to a curled-up Valiana. "You've had it out for her the whole day. For what? Because you think your meanness will force her to give up a spot at camp?" Her loud words drew an audience, but she didn't care. Coach and his assistants jogged over from their spots on the sidelines. "You think that Coach can't see the difference between honest-to-God talent and spiteful playing. She's done nothing but come play her hardest. Which is more than some of you have done. Wipe the target off her back and her reputation. Stop the poisonous schemes. We are sisters out here—all of us. There's no space for petty games when we have so much to prove. Coach didn't have to set up tryouts here. If you keep up that behavior, he might never do it again and you'd be responsible. Is that what you want?"

They had the sense to look chastised, probably to make her speech stop. Daniela gave Valiana's hands a strong yank, bringing her to her feet. Daniela circled her and dusted the dirt off her sweat-soaked clothes. The girls mumbled their apologies and stalked past the onlookers.

Vultures.

She started after them.

"Stay a moment, Daniela." Coach's abrupt command pumped her heart rate to frantic. She could already quote the scolding she'd get from Davi about keeping her emotions in check on the field. His words of wisdom came after she lost her cool from a particularly bad taunting while playing with the boys.

"Let's get that ball back in play," Coach called after the girls. He turned to Valiana, his assessing gaze taking inventory. "Are you injured?"

Valiana flashed a quick smile at him. "Just my pride."

He patted her on the shoulder, a rare display of affection from him. She jogged off to join her team. His focus turned to Daniela, his expression stoic and unreadable. More than anything, she longed to squirm and apologize for the quickness of her tongue, but it didn't feel like he was waiting for an explanation. At last, he nodded for her to join her team.

"I respect your passion for the game and your respect for your fellow players. Your kindness is very much appreciated. Don't be surprised when you earn friends *and* enemies for sticking up for the defenseless. Choose your battles wisely."

She nodded and attempted to swallow the dryness from her throat. The harsh reprimand for her outburst hadn't come as she expected. It surprised and scared her that he didn't consider her to be one of the defenseless on the *futbol* field. She was used to being written off, so much so that she didn't know how to handle being placed on the opposite end of that spectrum.

They finished out the tryouts with ease. They collapsed in the shade to eat the frozen popsicles and packed lunches that Coach brought them today as a celebration of the end of tryouts. Midweek, the number of girls trying had doubled in size, and now two dozen sweaty but happy girls sat under the tree. Daniela stripped her cleats and shin guards off. Her sandals stuck to the sweat on her feet, but the breeze cooled her from top to bottom.

The fact that this could be her last time to don this loaned *futbol* gear trapped the groan in her throat. A small slice of fear stole her peace. She'd wanted this and loved it so much more than she did when she dreamed about it. And it could be taken from her in a heartbeat.

Coach stood at the front of the group huddled over his clipboard with his assistants deciding that very thing. Just how

In the Shadows

badly had she blown it? She tried to focus on her food which was two warm *pastels* filled with meat, cheese, and vegetables and then a side of more vegetables and some fruit. A bottle of fresh water accompanied each bag. Davi would love the *pastels*, but he wouldn't take anything from her if she saved one. He'd always insisted that she eat everything she'd been given unless they found it at work. Then it was fair game to split.

A whistle pierced the air, silencing the talking and laughter instantly.

"We want to thank you, ladies, for coming out in the heat each day to try out for our upcoming camp. We're honored that you took time to tryout. We plan to hold tryouts each year, so if you don't see your name on the list this year, we'd love to see you next year. Keep practicing, because you'll never know the difference you can make in this world. My staff has each of your contact information and we will be inviting each of you to join us as spectators at a practice and a game for our women's national team." A cheer went up from every girl in the group. Coach grinned at his assistants.

"We've prepared an envelope for each of you with the results from the tryouts this year and a few other important pieces of information. When we're done, come grab the envelope with your name on it. Now that you know other girls who live near you that are interested in *futbol* I hope you will continue to meet to play when you can. Don't let the boys ruin your fun. They don't know who they are messing with."

The girls cheered again.

Daniela couldn't keep the grin from her face. These girls might not be her best friends yet, but they were the closest thing she had to it. There was a chance that she'd lose out on their friendships when they found out she was a *catadore,* but for now they were equals.

Coach ended the practice with a "Thanks again for coming. See you again next year." And the girls swarmed into motion. Daniela hung back as each girl found her envelope.

Valiana reached for a hug as she came up next to Daniela. "I can't thank you enough for your friendship out there. It means the world to me."

Daniela hugged her tightly. Gabi would be proud of her for reaching out to others. "You don't deserve to be treated like that from them or anyone." She stepped away and tapped Valiana's envelope. "I hope you made it to camp. Your little girl should get to see her mama chasing her dream."

Tears spilled onto Valiana's cheeks. She nodded. "If not this year, then next year."

Daniela nodded. "Definitely. Hope to see you before then."

She said her goodbyes to the other girls, wishing she could promise to see them soon like they wanted to hear. But with Mama's health and work being upside down, nothing was predictable at the moment. As she grabbed her envelope, her hand shook with the feel of the paper between her fingertips. She forced her hand to stop as she shook each assistant and finally Coach's hand, thanking them for holding the tryouts but she didn't linger.

She couldn't.

The envelope weighed on her as she carried it under her arm to meet Davi at their spot in the trees.

Instead, he met her halfway across the field, his long strides betraying his eagerness to know. "Did you make it?"

She laughed. The nerves were getting to her. "I wanted to wait until I was with you."

A snort rocked his shoulders. He knew. He always did. "You got in. You had to. You were the best one out there. Open that envelope."

She took a stabilizing breath and slid one finger under the flap. She stopped. "Davi, it doesn't matter if I make it or not. We

In the Shadows

can't afford to be spending any money on *futbol* camp. Not when we have to pay for Mamãe's medicine."

Davi placed his hands on her shoulders, his touch a calming force. "Cambridge and I have it figured out, okay? Now pull out those papers and tell me that God has granted us at least one miracle in the middle of this mess."

"And if He hasn't?"

Davi shrugged. "That's not a reason to give up hope that it will happen someday."

The papers came out of the envelope. There had to be at least a dozen to read. She scanned the first page. The words "Congratulations, Daniela Gomes" stood out.

"I made it." She breathed. "But there's more. 'We're honored to offer you a full scholarship provided by one of our incredible partners, The Upcycled Life. They've asked to meet you and your brother, Davi, in person.'"

Daniela squealed and jumped into Davi's arms, waving the papers. With a laugh, he twirled her in a circle. When he set her down, they danced and laughed some more.

"Let's go tell everyone the good news," Davi said as he started the way he'd come.

She cast a glance over her shoulder to check just how big of a scene they'd made. From the shade of the tree, Coach watched their celebration. They were out of earshot, but she could see his smile from where she stood. He stepped out of the shade with a bag of supplies in each hand. She waved. In return, his full hand lifted to touch the rim of his cap.

The *favelas* owned his past. He knew, at least in part, how much that scholarship would change her life. The tear slipped down her cheek where—minutes ago—sweat had taken the same path. As she jogged to catch up with Davi, the reality knocked into her.

Futbol camp.

"Davi, how am I going to do work and camp at the same time? We can't afford for me to be at camp and not earning money for food. It isn't enough that I'm just not costing us money."

His pace slowed to allow her to match his stride. "We're going to be fine. I have it planned out. I knew you'd get in." His happy smile thrilled her. Life hadn't given him much to smile about.

"I'll need to tell Gabi that I can't come in and you'll have to stop by to drop off the goods and collect the money, not to mention collecting supplies, and caring for Mamãe. Are you sure me going to camp isn't too much?"

"Of course, I'm sure." He grunted. "Listen, I was going to wait to tell you this until after we celebrated, but you should probably know everything now otherwise I'll never talk you into going to camp." Her nerves went on high alert, bracing for the impact she could feel coming. He steered them off to a low cement wall on a side street. His hand sought hers, bringing it between his. That was never good. He sighed. "Mamãe's not going to recover. The doctor said Mamãe's organs shutting down."

Not going to recover. The original diagnosing nurse said people could live with Hep B for decades, but she'd also said adult bodies typically cleared the virus within six months. That hadn't happened for Mamãe either. "But the medicine—"

"Is to keep her from feeling the horrible pain that comes with…death. The doctor at the clinic gave us the medicine for free. Said our best option was to keep her comfortable for the remainder of her time on earth. If we were richer, a liver transplant would keep her alive longer, but that's an impossibility for us."

His words bore a hole straight through her heart. Why did the devastating crevice between life and death always seem to be bridged with money—the commodity they had none of? Why

In the Shadows

couldn't it be heat? Or sun? Or sweat? Or ocean water? They had those in bucketfuls.

Resignation came in place of the sorrow. "Were you waiting until she died to tell me?"

He'd walked her to and from tryouts this week without a word of Mamãe's real condition.

"Just until after tryouts finished, if she made it that long. I didn't want that hurting your focus."

There it was. Protecting her from the bad was his number one priority. And for some strange reason, she felt loved instead of hurt. "What else have you not told me?"

"We're not going to be able to stay in our apartment. The rent collector stopped me on my way out with Mamãe. He said that Gerson hasn't sent one *centavo* for rent. He had been good for paying our rent each month, but that stopped after his fight with Mamãe."

Everything he left unsaid filled in the gaps of what he really thought of Gerson. He never spoke a negative word about either of their fathers despite their obvious failings. His actions played out in exact opposition to what they'd come to associate with their paternal figures which spoke volumes as to the value he found in them.

"So where do we go?"

"Cambridge has offered for us to stay at his place. The money we make will help pay for our food and other needs. We're there most of the time now anyway, since he has the supplies and tools."

Why not erase the final traces of everything she'd ever known as normal? Their lives hadn't been that great anyway. Her agreement came from the same harbor of numbness where the rest of her emotions stayed anchored most days.

Except for when she was on the field with a ball at her feet.

Futbol had made her feel again and that was dangerous. Feeling meant disappointment, sorrow, and pain. Long ago, she'd learned the virtues of protecting herself against emotion and losing her ability to feel was her first weapon of choice.

In one week, she'd be back on that field. "Wait, tomorrow is the last day of the month. Are we moving our things to Cambridge's today then?"

Davi gave her a half-smirk. "Our stuff is already there, as is Mamãe. I needed someone to watch her while you and I were occupied this week so Cambridge has been working, feeding her when she'll eat, and supplying her pain medication every few hours. He's been through hell with her this week, but he's never complained."

Daniela filtered through her week on high speed. She hadn't seen or heard Mamãe recently. She'd attributed it to her leaving early in the morning and getting home late, but it's because Davi hadn't told her he moved Mamãe.

Her free hand wiped the sweat from her face and jumped from the top of the wall onto the road, tugging Davi down after her. They needed to get on the other side of the street where they could feel the ocean breeze.

"You've been carrying this on your own. That's not how I want our lives to be lived, with you shouldering every burden and insisting I go after my dreams. You get to chase yours, too."

Davi pulled her into a side hug. "I am. You should see the size of Cambridge's library. People are throwing away knowledge in this country like it's yesterday's newspaper which means that I learn for free what others have paid thousands of *reals* to learn. You should see the prices on the back of some of his books. It's obscene."

She smiled as she debated whether or not to let him divert her from the topic. "When I get the money, you go to school and be one of the ones to spend obscene amounts of money on knowledge, understand?"

Davi laughed. "Agreed."

In the Shadows

They passed through the doorway into Cambridge's apartment. An old radio, his pride and joy, fizzed in the corner between playing pop hits from the eighties— "when life was more whole and love more certain."

As Davi strolled to the food cabinets on the far side of the room, Daniela went to peek in on Mamãe. Her conscience wouldn't let her rest if Mamãe died and her yelling and crying fit was the final memory she had.

A low murmur came from the corner room. Daniela peeked in. Mamãe lay on a plastic-covered mattress, her torso propped up with books cushioned by a piece of foam. Cambridge held a spoon with broth to Mamãe's lips, his quiet words encouraging her to eat something. Perhaps Mamãe knew it was futile too, because her cracked lips didn't part at his request.

Cambridge glanced up at Daniela. "Did you make it to camp?"

"With a full scholarship and a request from my sponsor to meet Davi and me in person." The words came out in a squeak.

He grinned. "That's the best news I've heard in weeks."

Daniela ventured further into the room. "How is she?"

His smile dropped as his eyes cut to Mamãe's face. "Not much longer, I'm afraid."

Chapter 10

"The story is exploding across media and social media outlets today." Katrina perched on the edge of her chair, her excitement level increasing with each word. "The athletes gained unbelievable traction on their social media accounts. Their sponsors are eating this attention up, asking if they can get some of the young players in their gear. I've already pegged those who asked to provide different options for next year. Those old cleats I pulled from storage would be better off at a shoe recycling center." She scrunched her nose. "I cashed in on the sponsors' eagerness while I had it."

Interesting how they didn't care about a few "dirt-poor scamps" when they were asked if they wanted to provide gear prior to the tryouts. But when they got pictures and saw the tidal wave of praise given, suddenly they wanted in. "Perfect. That's just what we need."

"Also, we've had six sports networks call requesting the exclusive interview with you and our sponsorship team can't keep up with the requests to sponsor and donations coming in. The logo page on our website will be five kilometers long."

"Sponsorship *team*?" Ronaldo took off his reading glasses and pinned Katrina with a stare.

In the Shadows

But she only smiled in response to his confusion. "Yes, President Cevere. I hired two extra interns to help us coordinate the massive effort this startup of this league has required. They've been invaluable to our planning."

Ronaldo blinked. "Good work, Katrina. See that they aren't weak links in our armor, if you would." No need for Lenz to go after them to acquire easy access to documents he'd like to change.

Katrina tapped on her tablet with an air of nonchalance. "They don't have permissions to view anything confidential and they've signed their lives and firstborn children away with the privacy policy we have in place."

This was why he kept Katrina when he'd moved into the position. She was worth triple her weight in gold.

"Let's present our interview suitors with an invitation to support a good cause, for once. Send them each a missive with the chance to bid on a donation to our choice of charities—the Villa Miseria clinic with Saving Grace, the Education Fund for a specific number of potential students, or providing free lunch and water for every tryout location we have next year."

With enough money in the program, they'd expand their tryouts to *favelas* in two other cities besides Rio. Other girls out there deserved as much of a chance as the girls in his home city.

Katrina scribbled notes on her legal pad, nodding as she listened. "Anything else?"

"Tell the networks their generous bids will also grant them the rights to cover the camp story when it starts in a week. That way they'll make it worth it. Let's also have consolation prizes in place for the networks that don't win the bid—alternate interviews with players, or whatever would entice them to throw their money our way if we don't choose them for the main prize."

Katrina made it to the door when he stopped her. "Oh, Katrina. It probably goes without saying, but please make sure that everything we put into place is well documented and absolutely legal. This controversy with Lenz is threatening to drown me."

His desk was probably suffering the worst of it. Launching a new initiative in the midst of scandal pushed every one of his staff members to the brink of their tolerance. How genius of Katrina to have thought ahead and had interns on the scene to relieve some of the pressure. He made a note on his to-do list to see she was given a good year-end bonus, even if it meant he paid it from his own pocket.

Since he'd conjured the nerve to ask Isadora to commit to him three days ago, he'd seen her every evening for dinner. They talked and laughed and shared their food. His imagination had filled in the gaps of what a relationship with her would be like, but he had been wrong. It was so much better.

Tonight wasn't any different. Isadora had a medical awards banquet to attend where Who's Who of Brazilian medicine gathered each year. Normally, she went solo and slipped out early, but tonight she'd asked him to accompany her. And—God help him—he would never turn down the chance to see her stunning figure in a perfectly tailored gown. Scrubs suited her temperament, but a fancy gown electrified her radiant glow.

He changed into his dinner suit, the only other option he owned aside from his tuxedo, and left his tie notched slightly below his collar. Cinching it this early would start the evening off too restricted for his liking. His town car picked him up and drove him through the stop-and-go traffic to the Belmond Copacabana Palace.

A man with his position could dine on others' tabs for an entire month straight if he wished. It was a perk and an obligation that accompanied his position, a duty he'd never envied Lenz. The invitations came in with the tide, it seemed. Lenz rarely turned one down, wishing to constantly be in the public eye.

Ronaldo had no such inclinations. Insisting on being so visible made Lenz believe that he was beyond questioning, too far

In the Shadows

past scrutiny. His penchant for the finer things added to Ronaldo's suspicion about unauthorized transactions. Of course, when he looked into it, the answers weren't plain as day. Mara had been smart. She dusted the tracks off the trail but didn't manage to erase the scent completely.

Nevertheless, when it came to being by Isadora's side, her needing him, he would go out every night without question. The medical types weren't his usual crowd. All the grandstanding and gory topics tossed around with little thought for the weak-stomached stretched his social graces to their very limit. He fortified himself with some liquid tolerance at the hotel bar, his eye on the door.

The hum of appreciation that filled his throat when she walked through the door earned him a glance from his neighbors. But they didn't matter. He weaved through the tables and met her with a brief kiss in the lobby.

Her warm gaze melted his pent-up anxieties as her hand slipped the drink from his and lifted it to her lips. She didn't blink at the fire of the scotch, but pushed it into his hand again.

"I'm going to tell them tonight." The normal mask of confidence Isadora kept in place faltered for a split second. They were almost the top of the food chain at their age, but they still battled nerves on the big occasions. One of life's little surprises—aging didn't cure every issue.

He tucked her hand into the crook of his elbow and covered it with his own. "I'll be here for every conversation."

She mumbled something under her breath as she straightened her already perfect posture. The doorman took their names and opened the door to the ballroom. Classical music and polite laughter mingled with the aroma of dinner. He guided Isadora to the appetizer table with hopes of distracting her. She placed a couple of items on her plate but didn't eat them.

Instead, she examined the room with a hawk-like gaze. The lights hadn't dimmed to set the mood so everyone was clearly visible. She knew her hunting ground. He was glad she trusted him enough to be along for the ride.

"There's Dr. Schmitz, the president of the Brazilian Society for Pharmaceutical Physicians. I'll start with him." She set her plate on a table and made her way to Dr. Schmitz's circle of men, crowding out intruders like an elephant herd. Yet Isadora complimented and charmed her way into the ring, introducing herself and shaking hands. The dynamic of the group shifted from the boys' club to the delight at her presence.

He sipped his drink from outside the group, mirroring her movement around the circle so he'd be at her side or near it when she finally snagged Dr. Schmitz's full attention. After fifteen minutes when she still hadn't managed to sequester the man, Ronaldo stepped to her side. At first she blinked at his intrusion, but when he cocked his head and winked, she grinned quickly interrupting the conversation to introduce him.

His gamble paid off. In seconds, the herd reformed the circle around him to talk about *futbol* and the scandal while Isadora pulled Schmitz away. He hated talking about Lenz but it seemed necessary to discreetly field a few questions to aid Isadora's cause. Relief came when a hand clapped him on his shoulder.

The founder of Saving Grace apologized for taking him away, but insisted they get a photo together since he'd heard the FFC had set their sights on making Saving Grace a charity of choice. Ronaldo angled himself so that he could keep his eye on Isadora.

Her expression was unreadable as she talked to Schmitz and another man safely tucked into a corner, their heads together in confidentiality. He pasted a smile on his face for the photo. Then began the steady stream of introductions, that was finally and mercifully interrupted with the beginning of the awards program.

Isadora wasn't up for an award this year, but she'd collected her fair share of awards in previous years. Their place cards sat on a table in the middle of the room, a respectable distance from the

In the Shadows

front but not embarrassing. He sat in his chair and greeted the others at the table. The chair to his left was still vacant.

At last, a scented breeze propelled him to his feet to assist Isadora with her chair. When he tucked her into the table, he took the liberty of moving her a fraction closer to his seat.

"Any traction?" he said into her ear.

"They were understandably alarmed, but they are reactionists. They are too concerned with their perceived standings. They'll wait to see what Guilherme Almaida says before they sound the call to arms within their organization."

As dinner was served, they joined the conversation at their table, exchanging the occasional brush of the hand in quiet reassurance. After the presentation of the awards and the resulting tyranny of droning speeches, Isadora slipped out the door to snag the Minister of Health. It took the stealth of a ninja to avoid a woman on a mission.

He'd just received his requested mug of coffee when a waiter bent over his shoulder. "*Senhor* Cevere, Doctor Rey has asked you to meet her at the front entrance."

Coffee untouched, he strode toward the door saying his goodbyes and shaking hands so as not to look too concerned.

But he was.

Outside of the clinic and hospital, Isadora didn't send staff to do her bidding. When he reached the front door, another man told him she asked if he would wait in her car out front. His eyebrows lifted as he exited the hotel. A red Audi A5 with the top down sat running in front of the hotel. The valets passionately discussed its finer points until he placed his hand on the passenger door.

Was this really Isadora's car? How did she get her hands on a convertible A5?

He might not own a vehicle, but as a man he wasn't immune to their magnetic pull. Tucking his hands into his pockets, he strolled a few meters for a better view of the beach. The wind carried the fragrances of beach food vendors, salt, and whispers of change.

Where was she?

Turning on his heel, he strode toward the car as Isadora clad in white shorts, a peach tank top, sandals, and a hat exited the hotel, looking every bit a tourist. Her toned tan legs looked five meters long in those shorts. A bellboy followed close behind with her dress cradled in his arms. She slid into her driver's seat and leaned over to open Ronaldo's door in a silent invitation.

He slid his jacket off his shoulders, sighing in relief as the sweet breeze whisked the heat from his body. His right hand tugged at his tie while his left hand eased the buttons beneath it open. He laid the suit and tie in the trunk alongside her dress and closed it before hopping into the passenger's side. A strange current of energy vibrated through him, as if he were about to do something dangerous or illicit.

Instead, Isadora pressed the gas pedal and they flew from the parking lot like a sprinter off the block. A local rock radio station filled the silence at the stoplights, as they headed south then west along Avenida Lucio Costa away from the suffocating crowd.

A foreign peace settled over him. She was taking the lead tonight and seemed happy to do so. The wind whipped her hair from her perfect updo and plastered it to her serene face. This Isadora—so comfortable with herself, no appearance pretenses or pressing need to speak when she had nothing to say—she was without question the woman who made his blood run a little redder and a lot hotter.

Despite their proximity, he couldn't get a read on her emotions, except to think her encounter with the Minister hadn't gone as she desired. The ache that her fears came true formed deep in his chest. She pulled off into a wooded area, weaved through a quiet town over a bridge, and finally stopped the car off to the side of the road on Restinga da Marambaia. She hopped out

In the Shadows

of the car, dropped her hat on her seat, and trotted down a sandy bank until she reached the beach.

He watched for signs of distress from his vantage point at the top of the bank. When she waded into the water, he shucked off his socks and shoes and followed her down. She didn't bring him here so she could be left alone. If she'd wanted that, she'd have left him at the hotel. No, this was an invitation into her hidden life. The one she'd agreed to let him be a part of when he asked to date her.

The white sand cradled his feet with a residual warmth from the day's heat. Isadora stood in the waves up to her knees. He waded in behind her and wrapped his arms around her waist, his cheek pressed against her ear. Her back melted against his chest. The tension drained from her body.

The water tugged on his suit trousers, protesting the drag they created. He tightened his grip as peace anchored his heart. There was nowhere else in the world he'd rather be. He didn't dare tell her after such a stressful evening.

With a sigh, she twisted in his arms and looped her hands behind his neck. Fresh air mingled with her perfume in the most enticing aroma he'd ever smelled. Her body, flush against his, swayed in slow rhythm. The sand disappeared beneath one foot as they shifted to the other.

"You're my dream come true, do you know that?" Isadora murmured against his ear.

In his younger years, he might have made a funny remark to deflect the intensity of the moment or brushed past her compliment with the firmly rooted false bravado. Instead he absorbed her words, letting them linger in the vulnerable parts of his inner man.

"I need you to be strong for me, Ronaldo." His name was a purr off her lips.

"All the strength I have is yours."

"I'm questioning my sanity on this, but I think I'm the person to take this fight to the world. These families and babies deserve better and all Almaida could do was try to hide his fear behind his mountain of an ego as he threatened my license if I pursue a 'path sure to swallow those you wish to defend with Brazilian chaos and worldwide panic'."

"The only thing I can counsel you to do is what I did myself. Gather the evidence until it's so substantial that, when presented to the world, it does the damning for you. Names, faces, test results, blood samples—they can't be manufactured. And when that's done, you find the most sympathetic audience and start there. It's not foolproof, but if you're going to take a fall for something, it might as well be for the truth." He swung her into a dip, her hair hovering right above the waves. His breath caught in his throat. "And I'd be vastly remiss if I didn't take this chance to tell you how stunning you are, inside and out. Irresistible. I'm the luckiest man."

A real smile stole across her lips as he brought her back to standing. "I should bring you to the middle of nowhere more often."

His fingers caressed her chin. "Middle of nowhere sounds perfect to me as long as I'm with you." They kissed as the darkness stole a bit more of the sky. "I'll see you home and call a town car to come get me."

She looked like she was going to argue, but there wasn't a chance in a million that he was going to let Isadora drive him home to edge of the *favelas* at night. Not that she knew where he lived.

Yet.

For some reason, he wanted to keep that information for another time when there wasn't so much turmoil and anxiety at the forefront of their minds. Although with the way things were headed, a break didn't appear to be coming any time soon.

Chapter 11

Daniela spent her week off working at Gabi's during store hours, collecting recyclables from their partnered businesses in the evenings, and tending to Mamãe while the guys gathered supplies and produced more items to sell. Davi and Cambridge took turns hawking their goods on the main tourist stretch, calling out in as many languages as they knew "handmade, locally sourced goods." They'd found remarkable success so long as they avoided the police who patrolled, looking for proof of the extortionately priced vendor permits.

Since moving into Cambridge's place, the distribution of money had become easy. With Davi's full agreement, Cambridge took the brunt of creating the goods that Davi sourced from his days in the recycling facility. It was on principle that Cambridge, the perceived leader of the *catadores*, stayed away from paying the facility fees, since the idea of a strike came from his mouth in the first place.

In the dark on the brink of sleep, Daniela's mind buzzed with the week. Yesterday, Mamãe begged her to give her all the pain pills and let her end it. Daniela shivered in her bed. That seemed a kinder way to let her go. What would Davi say?

Instead of asking him, she listened to Davi whispering that Cambridge's knees and back limited his quickness on the mounds

In the Shadows

these days. When Davi saw he could collect almost triple what Cambridge could bring in a day, he stepped in to volunteer for the job permanently.

Any thought of being a burden to Cambridge fled her mind. Her role in the house came naturally to her. She'd taken on cooking the meals of rice and beans in the evening, cleaning up after Mamãe, trying to quiet her choked screams and cool her frequent sweats.

"The day's coming when we won't need to collect to stay alive. I can feel it," Davi said in a whisper.

She let his prediction go unanswered. His steady breathing of sleep picked up a few seconds later. What a coward she was. For days, she'd been meaning to ask Davi about Chacal's unwanted "business proposal", but she couldn't find the words. Davi instructed her not to tell anyone where they'd moved, so she assumed he operated under the same rules.

With camp due to start in two days, the worries hit her full force, but especially at night. Mamãe's swollen limbs and yellowed eyes haunted Daniela every time she closed her eyes. Mamãe had never been an overly affectionate mother but that didn't stop Daniela from recounting the few good memories they had together each time she walked in to feed Mamãe her ration of broth and pain pills. Only thirty-eight years old, Mamãe said she couldn't remember those times. Some days she didn't recognize Daniela at all.

Dying was stealing her memory.

It wasn't in Daniela's nature not to fight, to sit back and let sickness suppress vibrancy, so watching Mamãe fade away was taking pieces of Daniela's heart with her.

The next morning, Daniela didn't wait for Gabi to prod her about Mamãe's condition. She spilled the pain and heartache as soon as Gabi set breakfast on the table. Gabi listened intently, interrupting only to pray over the food and for Mamãe. And when she'd exhausted Mamãe, she moved on to everything else.

"You're going to fit in nicely at camp, Daniela. Don't doubt yourself. I know being away from your normal isn't ideal right now, but the timing of this gift is no accident." She held out her palm and brought Daniela's beside hers. "Look at my hand. And look at yours. They are so different—the lines, the texture, the colors, the length of my fingers and the width of my palm. I can see yours and wish I had them, but I can only ever have mine. So I must make the most of what I've been given whether I find them to my perfect ideal or not. You understand?"

Daniela nodded. Gabi's words felt like a prism catching sunbeams, deflecting light into the dark corners of her constant worry. She didn't scold or talk down. She taught with sensitivity and grace. If anyone deserved to serve God in the way they longed to most, it was Gabi.

"Cambridge is bringing new goods to sell this afternoon when he comes to pick me up." A twinge of disappointment trickled through Daniela when Gabi didn't react to her mention of Cambridge.

Gabi's hands wrapped around her mug of tea. "Is he treating you respectfully at home?"

She swallowed at the implication of Gabi's words. Her defense of Cambridge was on the tip of her tongue—that he would never touch her in an unacceptable way, but Davi taught her over the years that it was the people she least expected that were the most dangerous predators. "He does treat me with respect. Our living with him has been an easy adjustment. Davi and I shared a room in our other apartment, too. And Cambridge sleeps in the main living area with all the supplies and tools. He says it's to protect our livelihood, but it's really because he gave Mamãe his room." She paused, but then decided to meddle. "He's a really good man."

Gabi smiled. "God knows our world needs as many of those as we can get."

In the Shadows

The timer buzzed in their work area. Leisure time was over. As Gabi readied the registers, Daniela straightened items on shelves, arranging and rearranging. After Gabi unlocked the doors, they made quick work of opening boxes of new shipments. Gabi left a final small box for Daniela to open as she organized clothing according to size.

The box opened to a smaller box and that box to a smaller box.

"What is going on?"

Gabi laughed as she watched from beside the clothes rack. "I got you a congratulations gift."

Daniela stopped her progress through the boxes and stared at Gabi. "You bought something new? For me?"

"Open it." Gabi crossed over to her nesting all the boxes inside each other again as Daniela opened the small rectangular box in her hands.

When she slid it open, a shiny gold necklace lay perfectly across the box. In the middle were three small flat pendants of a cross, a *futbol* ball, and a heart. Her jaw tingled as her eyes watered.

"I know you can't wear it during games, but I thought it could remind you of your first loves as you find yourself on a new adv—"

Daniela didn't wait for her to finish before throwing her arms around Gabi's small waist. The surprise had settled into a humbled awe.

"No one has ever given me anything this expensive or beautiful before. How can I repay you?"

Gabi giggled. "By wearing it as often as you'd like. It's a gift—an object to represent what really matters. So don't hide it away because you're afraid of breaking it or losing it."

Funny how she was thinking of doing just that. Never had she owned something so precious or valuable. Gabi unhooked the necklace from its fasteners and draped it around Daniela's neck, securing it in the back.

Daniela faced the mirror, her fingers grazing the gold against her bronzed skin. It looked so foreign and out of place on her. But her unease spurred a kind of hope, a joy, that perhaps one day she'd be the type of girl to look at home in a simple necklace without it screaming how much of an impostor she was for wearing it.

She floated through the rest of the day. When the doorbell jingled over Cambridge's head, she checked the clock. Hours had passed in what felt like minutes. She hurried around the desk to unload the goods from Cambridge's arms.

"*Garota,* where did you get that necklace?" His whisper was as harsh as his gaze which was glued to her neckline. "You must put it back."

She laid her hand over it as she'd been doing most of the day. "It's a gift from Gabi. She bought it for me to celebrate my making it into camp."

"It's a small token of love for Daniela to take with her wherever she goes." Gabi winked at Daniela and took the final items from Cambridge's arms.

His frown eased into an easy smile. "That was very kind of you, *senhora.* I am very sorry, Daniela, for coming to a negative conclusion so quickly."

She shrugged. "I've never had a necklace before. You had every right to question it."

"Daniela, why don't you set up the window display? You're so good at it. I'll get the payments for today for Cambridge," Gabi said.

Cambridge hesitated, then followed Gabi to the counter. They spoke in hushed tones with Gabi emitting an occasional full body laugh. It was Daniela's favorite laugh of Gabi's. It meant she was genuinely humored and at ease with the company she was in. Daniela sneaked glances at the two. Cambridge leaned over the

In the Shadows

counter, a huge smile on his face. Gabi sat perched on the stool within arms' reach, also smiling.

Perhaps her casual comments about Cambridge's good character found their mark when she wasn't looking.

After letting them talk for a few minutes, Daniela finished fussing with the window display and edged closer, but they talked of their experiences with formal learning, nothing secretive.

Gabi left her stool and wrapped Daniela in a big hug. "You're going to be so wonderful at camp tomorrow. I can't wait to hear all about it when you finish."

Daniela grinned. Strange how Gabi had quickly become such an important part of her life. Cambridge scooped the money off the counter and shoved it in his pocket.

Gabi waved them off from inside her shop. As usual, they made four stops by businesses to pick up the recycling and then sell to their buyers what they couldn't take home and use as supplies. On the way out of the buyer's shop, a shout of her name halted her steps.

"Child, you respond to me when I call your name."

Daniela turned to see Gerson stumbling toward them, a bottle in his hand. She'd never seen him in this part of town before.

"I thought that was you, but seeing the trash man confirmed it." Gerson snorted.

Cambridge eyed Gerson with a cool stare. "What do you want, Gerson?"

Gerson stepped forward, and grabbed for Daniela but missed. Cambridge moved between them. "I want to see my daughter is all. I have that right, don't I? I want to know if she's alive after her mother ran me off with hateful words."

Daniela longed to tell him of her success on the *futbol* field, the very thing he'd curled his lip at when he found out she loved to play.

Cambridge answered for her. "She's doing fine, but we need to get going."

Gerson swayed. "What ? Are you doing her like you did her mother?"

Cambridge's hands balled into fists and he rose to his full height, towering far about Gerson's short frame. "I have never inappropriately touched either of them. You will never speak of Patricia or Daniela like that again. You know nothing of their good character."

Daniela inched away from the men, watching for a telltale sign from Gerson that he was about to swing a fist. Cambridge backed up.

"I'm surprised Patricia hasn't come running back to me after I cut off her drug supply. Turns out she loves to hate more than she needed those hits she always begged me for," Gerson said, his face scrunched in a sneer.

Daniela bit her lip, suppressing the gasp that threatened to come. Mamãe had been doing drugs? Cambridge glanced at her and then shoved Gerson, saying words so low she couldn't hear. Gerson landed on his backside with a loud thump.

When Cambridge returned to her side, he led her home without a word. Was that why she'd been so sick? Her faint murmurs for drugs Daniela had written off as pleas for another pain pill to stifle the agony of dying. Her compassion had been misplaced.

At home, Daniela marched to the stove and immediately set to making dinner. She should have checked on Mamãe, but she couldn't face her yet. The anger welling inside her slowed her pace, although she could have made the meal blindfolded. She heard Davi's footsteps approaching before he settled against the wall not far from where she stood. He stood there with his hands in his shorts' pockets, watching her.

"Did you know Mamãe was doing drugs? Is that why you moved her here? Is she even sick? You promised no more secrets." She huffed, frustrated that she was mad about this in the first place. Davi should have told her a week ago.

In the Shadows

"I suspected she was doing drugs a few times, but she always seemed sober when we got home and I never found evidence. That night we found her sick, I found a few used needles in her room when I went in to check on her. I thought maybe she'd overdosed, so I moved her here to detox. Cambridge has experience with people coming off drugs. Chacal approached me, because he wanted to know why she wasn't buying anymore. We needed to get out of there so he didn't become a problem in case she had debt."

Chacal was already a problem and Davi knew it.

"I know that when he approaches someone he doesn't let them go until they join or they are unable to join." The thought made her want to grab Davi's hand and not stop running until they were too far away to be reached by Chacal.

He moved closer so that his mouth was close to her ear. "We won't be here forever, Daniela. When things clear up with the facility and we have money from selling goods, we're going to move closer to wherever you need to be to play *futbol*." He laid a hand across his chest. "Businesses and learning happen everywhere. We just need enough money to get out."

"We should do it after Mamãe passes away. I won't have you being found by Chacal. You are my only brother and he can't have you." She shook the stirring spoon at him, causing him to smirk.

"Here is the truth, Daniela. Mamãe is dying. The drugs she took to cope with her sickness has weakened her immune system so much that she can't fight the pneumonia."

Daniela flinched when Davi touched her shoulder. It stung that she'd been so blind. "Are you doing drugs, too? I might be young and a girl, but I deserve to know the truth."

Davi sighed. "No, Daniela. Of course not. And I didn't keep the truth about drugs from you because of either of those things. It's because I was trying to protect your memory of Mamãe so that at least one of us could still remember the good."

His face was so sincere that it made her ache inside. "I accept your apology."

"No more secrets, I promise." He hugged her shoulders, pressing her to his side. "Now tell me what Gerson said to you."

Daniela grinned. "You should've seen his face when Cambridge pushed him. It was like he never expected Cambridge to stand up to him."

Davi laughed.

"And I think Cambridge likes Gabi and she likes him from the looks of their talk today."

Davi's eyebrows lifted. "Trying to play matchmaker? Cambridge will fall—" He paused, his eyes on her necklace. "Beautiful necklace. Where'd you get it?"

She unclipped it from around her neck and handed it to him. "A gift from Gabi."

He smoothed a thumb over the pendants. "She's been a godsend. Maybe I'll push Cambridge to find out if he plans to keep visiting Gabi while you're away. We'll need someone to drop off the goods and pick up the money from the sales."

Matchmaking was contagious.

The next morning, Daniela woke early. She checked on Mamãe, kissed her cheek, and squeezed her hand. How much longer would Mamãe have to suffer with her labored breathing? She grabbed her secondhand cleats and shin guards and met the guys outside, where they planned out their day each morning.

"To survive you must be strategic, Daniela," Cambridge said.

Davi stood when she exited, his smile making his eyes sparkle. "You ready for your first day?"

"I think so. I have my paperwork and my gear." She shrugged. "Anything I'm forgetting?"

He reached down and pulled a brown paper bag from beside his stool. "Breakfast. To give you a good start to the camp day."

For the second time in as many days, her heart swelled at the truly generous people she had in her life.

In the Shadows

"A bun and a couple pieces of fruit," he said as she peeked inside the bag.

She bounced on her tiptoes and planted a kiss on his cheek. "You are too good to me. Thank you. You two be careful while I'm gone today. Don't let trouble find you."

Cambridge offered her a salute and Davi just smirked. He walked her to the bus station at the meeting point at the bottom of the *favelas*.

"I'll be here to get you when the bus comes back this evening, okay?"

Daniela nodded. She knew her way back, but Davi would never agree to it. She ate her breakfast and they made small talk as a handful of other girls arrived looking bleary-eyed at the hour. She could see Davi assessing them and for the first time, she hoped she would meet someone that she could introduce him to. He'd never shown interest in dating or going out with girls, because he spent so much time surviving and keeping her alive.

But that had to change someday.

A white passenger van pulled up to the station right on time. The driver was a young woman with an FCC logo on her polo.

She exited and walked right up to their group with a clipboard in hand. Her straight black hair was pulled into a long ponytail. Her build was athletic. "Hi ladies, are you here for *futbol* camp?"

They nodded.

"I'm Kiania. Let me check each of you in and we'll head out. It's going to be a great week for you. I hope you're excited."

Davi stood beside Daniela as Kiania looked over her paperwork. "The girls will return around six tonight, Kiania?" Always worried.

Kiania smiled. "We will be as prompt as possible. You're all set, Daniela. You're officially a part of the *Guerreiras* now. Welcome to the camp."

Warriors—a chill ran down Daniela's spine. She felt anything but that. Her mind urged her body to get into the van, but the moment felt too monumental to breeze by. She hugged Davi's neck hard and murmured goodbye—a goodbye that seemed to encompass the reality she knew now. She swallowed hard, propelling herself into the van.

There was no going back now. Only looking forward.

Chapter 12

Ronaldo sat pressed against his office window, unable to take his eyes off the field far below him. Forty girls from around Rio were given an exclusive invite for this camp. This was a tryout of sorts for an under twenty (U20) team that fed into the women's national team that played in the Olympics or the women's World Cup. The girls didn't know they were on trial, but the coaches watched and assessed.

Fifteen of those girls came on scholarships from the *favelas*. He'd given the staff strict instructions to listen for discrimination from any player and punish it. This league wasn't a game he was toying with, or a fun girls' party. It was business and a chance to change how Brazil treated its women, starting with sports. That meant everyone on the field was to be treated as equals.

He checked his watch. The press should be arriving in two hours. Katrina worked her magic and charmed every penny and promise she could out of the networks. So much so, that he really only knew of a couple of items, but he didn't care much so long as it was taken care of.

One of the networks paid for all fifteen girls from the *favelas* to receive paid tutoring in school basics for the year in exchange for interviews with the girls about life inside. The girls had every

In the Shadows

right to turn down the tutoring and the interview, Katrina had made sure of that.

The winning sports network had decided to run a special on the new girls' *futbol* program. Ronaldo had done part of his exclusive interview last week, but he'd agreed to give them additional audio for their program while they videoed the girls playing. The program would air in three months which gave the network enough time to edit and track any girls they tagged for special interest and follow their stories.

With a sigh, he turned back to his computer. The email at the top of his inbox was from an anonymous sender that threatened his work, saying he'd find himself losing everything he cheated and lied for. A hunch told him the email was from Lenz or Mara or someone close to them. If that was the case, he needed to send it on to authorities. A threatening email while he was angry didn't mean he'd act on it.

But what if he did?

Ronaldo hit the forward button and sent the email on to his contact on the investigation team. It was probably nothing. Lenz had nothing with which to take aim at Ronaldo. The investigation team was scouring his documents and reports like they were Lenz's. If there was more corruption tied to Lenz, they were going to find it and get rid of it all at once.

An hour and a half later, Katrina trotted by his door and called, "The press is here."

He pushed back from his desk and took the stairs to the field. Katrina would brief them on the expected decorum and angles. And he'd be there to shut it down if they stepped out of line.

The girls had another hour left before they broke for lunch. After that, they'd train in the fitness center and the girls from the *favelas* would move into an afternoon of tutoring, starting with anatomy and health and then the tutor would talk to each girl and recommend a topic of interest and what level to entertain that interest at to study with them. It was a specialized education. The girls from outside the *favelas* didn't get that privilege, but they had school. And he didn't want anyone to feel they had an unfair advantage or disadvantage.

The coach, Ian, strode over to where he leaned against the rail watching the drill being run. "Presidente Cevere, this field holds lots of talent."

Ronaldo nodded. Ian Frade was one of the up-and-coming coaches from the collegiate level and had sat right seat to the men's national team coach Alves on many games at a national level. But, unlike Alves, Frade loved the game regardless of who he coached. Alves sneered at the women's teams, calling them sub-par and a shadow of what the men were. That was a worldwide sentiment, unfortunately.

"I have a good feeling about these girls. When the Coach Leal comes to visit at the end of the week, he's going to have a lot to take into account," Ronaldo said. Coach Leal led their women's national teams to medal in the last three world tournaments—two Olympics and one World Cup.

"A few obviously have no formal training, but they are quick learners. Thankfully, they are young enough that we can break bad habits easier now."

Valiana jogged past them and waved. "Hey, Coach!"

Ian glanced over at Ronaldo with raised eyebrows. "She one of yours?"

Ronaldo nodded. Not only had her scholarship paid for her camp, but it also paid for safe, reliable childcare for her baby while she was at camp. Her sponsor had been overjoyed to know they were giving two girls hope for a future, especially since teen moms were at risk of getting lost in the crowd.

On Wednesday, two days later, Ronaldo checked in again as he had every day. He watched for an hour. Daniela was off of her usual form, reacting a second too late or missing easy shots. He flagged down one of the field assistants and asked to be called when camp broke for lunch.

In the Shadows

Ronaldo finished his initial task list and got rid of a stack of papers from his desk in the time it took the assistant to buzz him about lunch break. He took the stairs once again to the field level but then scanned his badge to allow him access to a side hall that led to the inside of the stadium where the players ate, worked out, and let off steam.

The girls already sat with their lunches in front of them. As he suspected, Daniela didn't engage the others much, so it was no difficulty to catch her eye and motion her toward a table out of earshot of the other girls. She gathered her lunch and met him there as he sat with his own bagged lunch.

A bonus of being the one in charge.

"How are things going for you, Daniela?" He sunk his teeth into a sandwich, satisfied that the girls were getting decent food after working so hard on the field each day.

"I'm really happy to be here at camp, Coach. This is better than my best dream."

"Mine too, most days. How is your mother doing?"

Daniela's smile wavered. "Failing fast. We have to crush her pain pills into her water now to get them in her."

"Is that the main thing on your mind today? You seemed distracted on the field." When her shoulders sagged, he scrambled. "We all have those days, Daniela. Don't be upset about it. I just wanted to make sure everything was all right with you."

"I have been off today, Coach. I know I have." She sighed, picking at her food wrappers. He held his breath, afraid to breathe and scare away the thoughts on the tip of her tongue. "I've told you before that my brother and I are *catadores*. We're fighting against really powerful people who want to charge us to do a job no one else wants to do. We get paid for the recyclables we pull out, but only from buyers who may or may not want what we have. Then to hear my own father assume I was a whore and the fact that Mamãe wouldn't be dying right now if she hadn't killed her organs with drugs. My father wasted money on alcohol but she wasn't any better, using drugs like she did. Yet she still blamed him...I blamed him for our severe poverty and Mamãe's illness. And Davi's done everything in his power to make sure I get the chance to pursue this." She scrubbed her face with her hands. "The guilt about everything going on and the fear that I'm going to really mess up this dream has been weighing heavy on my mind. My future and Davi's counts on me succeeding here."

Ronaldo dusted the crumbs from his hands. He'd doubted she had spoken that many words at one time in her time at being at camp this week and, judging by the slight embarrassment on her face, he suspected maybe ever.

"Daniela, did you know I first joined on Brazil's national team when I was nineteen?"

She shook her head.

"It was so many years ago now. I was a nobody kid from the wrong part of town who dared to show up to open tryouts for the national team one day with the other guys who had shiny, new cleats and a history of playing in leagues. The coach that day saw some talent buried deep inside me." He lowered his voice. "And I mean, deep."

Daniela smiled. That felt like a sizable victory.

"I sat on the bench for two years before I ever set foot on the field for a game. But the coach worked with me, pushed me to the edge of making me want to quit, and then helped me fall in love with the game all over again. Meanwhile, my family was struggling to stay alive. The guilt I felt that I wasn't contributing to the family funds like I had been since I was ten riddled my soul, but I never felt more alive than I did when I was playing *futbol*. I couldn't imagine a life without it."

At that, Daniela nodded. "I feel the same."

"My dad used to ask me when I was going to quit messing around and see that survival meant working hard." Ronaldo grunted. "He didn't see what I was doing as preparing for my

In the Shadows

future. He saw me playing a silly sport and shirking responsibility. It especially annoyed him that I did all that and still sat on the bench. But the next year, Coach started me almost every game. I made money my parents only dreamed of and I sent them what I could to try to get them out."

"Then he didn't care so much whether you played *futbol* all day or not," Daniela said.

Ronaldo chuckled. "No, he suddenly became very supportive. They decided to move from the *favelas* and get a house in a respectable neighborhood. One night while I was out celebrating a tough win with my team, my sister Mariana was gunned down by a gang leader in the *favelas* they were about to move from."

Daniela sat frozen with wide eyes, not moving.

"The 'what if's' and the 'I should have's' plagued me for years. And eventually, I had to face the fact that Mariana supported my dream like it was her own. She wouldn't have wanted me to be or do anything different than I was doing. And I shouldn't have wanted her to do anything else than what she was doing that night—which was trying to save some girls from the gang they were involved in." Daniela still hadn't moved, but her scrunched brow told him she was still tracking. "What I'm trying to say, Daniela, is that there is plenty of space for guilt and fear in your life if you let it, because you'll make mistakes in front of everyone you love and maybe even while the whole world is watching, or at least your whole world. And those times you did the wrong thing or said something foolish or tried to be someone you weren't, they will come back to haunt you in your moments of peace, but you can't let them win. If you do, that's when you will actually risk losing your dream. But that knowledge has to go from here." He tapped his forehead, then his chest. "To here in your own time."

Daniela shook her head. "Don't let them sign me off yet, Coach. I'll do better tomorrow."

"I know you will. In the meantime, I'm going to get in touch with a special friend of mine named Tiago. He specializes in art that gets attention and I think he could be a huge benefit to your *catadore* cause." Ronaldo paused. "The introduction is strictly private, though, understood?"

"Understood, Senhor. So Tiago would make some art where the facility leaders could see it and they'll start listening to us?" She looked skeptical.

Ronaldo grinned. "Something like that."

This relationship was going to be fun to watch. Quirky and nimble Tiago was the most brilliant social change artist in Brazil, but he did most of his work anonymously in case there was any grounds for legal repercussions. "Some art" didn't come close to describing Tiago's mural masterpieces that he left on unsuspecting surfaces. And the man loved a good cause like most men loved a chilled beer.

As Daniela moved from lunch to afternoon tutoring, Ronaldo made his way upstairs, his chest lighter than it had been in too long. The tryouts and the camp felt right, like his interaction with Daniela was just a small ripple of the seismic activity taking place beneath his feet.

Inside his office, he closed the door and picked up his phone. Tiago was very picky about who he let have his phone number. He suspected everyone of malicious deceit and treated them as potential whistleblowers on his art operations. His day job kept him well compensated and out of the public art world, so no one would suspect him.

The phone line rang twice and then stopped. "Senhor Cevere, to what do I owe this honor?"

"Old friend, I have a project you may be interested in. The work would be for *catadores* in the *favelas* off Euclides da Rocha."

Tiago clucked. "Poor area. Lots of crime. Who is the target?"

In the Shadows

"A recycling facility is taking advantage of the poorest of the poor and I think you could get their attention in a way they haven't been able to yet."

"Of course, I can." Tiago excelled at humble arrogance. "Have the leaders of the movement—I'm assuming there is a movement, Ronaldo or else you wouldn't have called me—meet me at the bakery behind the Santa Clara taxi stand tomorrow night at eight-thirty. And you might as well be there for the introductions so they don't go asking every fool in the place if they are me. The fewer who know my name, the better."

"We will be there, friend. Your dedication to the art is inspiring," Ronaldo said.

"Yes? How inspiring?" Tiago's tone pitched upward in an air of hope.

Ronaldo chuckled. "You'll find out tomorrow night."

Mariana was the reason he felt so involved in Daniela's situation. For over twenty years he'd been positioning himself to be the voice of the poor, to do something to end the senseless violence. Now he was in place and calling in favors to get involved in a fight he had no business being in, except that was how fights were won, weren't they? When stronger forces involved themselves in the plight of the underdog, defeat didn't seem so inevitable anymore.

The rich perhaps remembered too well what it was like to have nothing, hoarding and distancing themselves from the constant drain of resources that it took to help the poor. Why help one if you can't help them all?

But Mariana saw it differently. They'd been sitting by a bonfire on a section of beach that was marked as too dangerous for pedestrians since it was tucked away, hidden by a particularly cruel outcropping of loose, slippery rocks. They scrambled over those rocks in the dark with the ease of risk-immune teenagers. Friends were supposed to accompany them that night, but they'd been stood up. That's when she laid out the logic of her vision.

Multiplication.

"If you truly help someone and instill a vision while you do it, they will understand the necessity to give back and help another person. Then by helping one, you help tens and hundreds and thousands." Mariana's voice rose above the rhythmic waves into the sky.

Ronaldo smiled at the memory. They were so young and passionate about everything in those days. No mundane routine intruded on their exciting future of hope. With a sigh, he dug into his work until a knock interrupted his flow.

"Come in." He sat back, his head aching at the tiny print on the pages of papers he was supposed to read.

Katrina entered and stood rigid on the opposite side of his desk, her expression pinched. "I just received word that there will be an emergency board meeting tomorrow morning to discuss the success of the girls' league. Apparently, an anonymous tip led them to believe that unauthorized committee funds are being used to make this look better than it is."

A colorful curse ran through his head. Just the idea of shutting down the girls' league made him sick to his stomach. "We have nothing to hide. Everything is documented and above board, right?"

Katrina nodded, looking slightly relieved.

"Then let's make sure they have every reason to keep our girls' league running." Or they'd be right behind Lenz on the way out the door.

Chapter 13

The next day, Daniela hopped out of the van and was greeted by a pacing Davi. Coach caught her after she left tutoring yesterday and told her to bring the *catadore* leaders to the meeting tonight. And when she'd told Davi and Cambridge, they stared at each other without speaking for long enough that she suspected they had a silent man language they'd developed. Finally, they broke into smiles at the same time and set to work so they could take the evening off.

Now, Davi looked ill.

"What is it? Is it Mamãe? Did she—?" Daniela choked on her words. After her talk with Coach, she'd been mentally attempting to push the guilt from her mind, especially on the field. But talking about death brought those buried feelings to the surface again.

Davi swung his arm around her shoulders. "It's not Mamãe. I'm nervous about our meeting tonight. It sounds like we have a chance at making a huge statement and we don't want to mess this up."

Which was exactly the thought that ran through Daniela's mind two hours later as they sat across from a twitchy Tiago. Ronaldo had purchased a plate of baked goods and drinks which Cambridge and Davi devoured quietly. Tiago didn't acknowledge

In the Shadows

the now empty plate, instead his eyes shifted from left to right at alarming speeds as if waiting for someone to jump him. Daniela checked around her for the danger several times before trying to imitate Coach's relaxed manner.

She'd expected a man with a commanding manner, elegant sentences, and paint stains on his fingers, not a short, balding bundle of nerves with beady eyes that appeared to have never been taught to sit still.

Coach motioned at Cambridge and Davi. "Why don't you guys start with what's happening?"

"Don't leave any details out," Tiago said as he slid his chair closer to the table and leaned in over his pad of paper with a pen.

Cambridge started the story with describing their former normal, adding details of the working conditions in a succinct, factual way that made it clear he wasn't looking for pity as much as clarity. Davi jumped in to offer some details that Cambridge overlooked as they moved into the changes that happened recently. Finally, Davi ended the story with the current conditions and Cambridge added that the resolve of other *catadores* was waning. They were going to give in to the demands to pay soon and end up working to pay to work and only have a tiny bit extra for surviving each day unless they could intervene somehow.

Tiago doodled and made occasional notes on the side of the page as they talked. He didn't answer for a long time after they stopped talking, just focused completely on his paper. Coach took up the questioning about long-term plans. Daniela couldn't take her gaze off of Tiago hunched so close to his notepad. His focus kept him from constantly assessing the room.

What was he doing over there?

At last, he slapped the notepad on the table with great flourish and slid it to Cambridge. "This."

Daniela craned her neck to see what was on the paper. Gnarled and baby hands poked through a gate holding *reals* to a stoic guard in front of a trash heap.

"The colors, of course, will be bold and symbolic and the art could be up to three stories tall on the side of a building," Tiago said.

Cambridge sat back against his chair with a huff. "You want to put this on the side of the recycling facility?"

Tiago laughed, a snort-high-pitched combination that sounded like a dying bird. "No, no, no. That would be too secluded and far too easy for them to remove since they own the building. No, I'd put it on one of those eyesore apartment walls that are ugly and huge and that everyone on the highway and on the beach at Copacabana can see. I know the owner of the one I am thinking of and could easily get permission, since he owes me a favor."

Tiago's eyes were on Coach who nodded and said, "The more visibility the better. And if we can tip the right media off about the story behind it, the recycling facility leadership won't be able to ignore the public protest."

"How long will this take to produce, Tiago?" Davi asked.

A scowl formed on his lips at Davi's use of his name, but he didn't address it. "Many hours of my free time, but I will give the art the time it deserves. Brilliance and accuracy take up most of my time, and when it is done, you will know. The whole city will know."

Daniela raised her eyebrows when Davi looked her way. He gave her a slight nod and a smile. His reaction scared her, because for the first time in many years, she felt the lightness of hope invading her heart. Their situation wouldn't be ignored forever and she almost wanted to allow herself to dream that one day, the people she loved climbing those mounds each day would be treated like humans.

As they walked out of the bakery, Coach grabbed two bags from the man at the counter. One he handed to Daniela and the other he kept in his grip.

In the Shadows

"For your culinary pleasure. Since I know Cambridge and Davi wouldn't accept them from me, perhaps you will take these home and persuade them to enjoy it as a gift from me."

Daniela nodded, taking the warm bag in her hand. Coach didn't treat his generosity like charity, but couched it with respect in a way that made it feel necessary. When they exited, Tiago went straight to his car. Coach turned to the left, as Cambridge and Davi turned right to go home. As Coach walked, he pulled a cap onto his head. Already it was dark and there wasn't a great need for a hat, but it fit with his outfit of nondescript clothes, not the wardrobe of a president of anything.

He was one of them.

She jogged to catch up with the guys who were a few paces ahead deep in conversation. As she approached, Davi stepped away from Cambridge creating a space for her to fill between them. Her chest tightened. He was always thinking of her safety.

"Without a doubt, this will be our biggest chance to make a statement to the world about who we are and how we want to be treated. A show of that degree shouldn't be planned for a small-time effect. No, we should visualize a world impact so we are prepared." Cambridge's fist connected with his other hand.

The streets were fairly quiet tonight. A few groups of older teens and young adults stood illuminated by the occasional orange street lamp. They passed around joints and laughed at each other. Were they truly happy with their life? Was this what Coach's sister had been doing when the bullets caught her?

Cambridge ducked into his home first as was the habit and clicked on a light. They'd been gone less than an hour, but the air seemed still. Davi felt it too, because he motioned for her to stay near the door. Cambridge reappeared from the rooms with slumped shoulders.

"She's dead."

Daniela swallowed against the tightening in her throat. Davi strode to Mamãe's room, then walked back out slowly, dragging a hand over his face.

"Mamãe asked me that morning I took her to the clinic not to spend any money on a funeral for her, but we still need to take her back so they can give her a death certificate. I think we should donate her body to science and education. Should we carry her on the mattress to the clinic tonight so we're not parading through the streets in the morning with her?" Davi asked.

"If we want to avoid suspicion as to why we aren't following tradition with this death, then yes, it'd be better for us to go under the cover of night," Cambridge said.

The community would find out. They always knew everything. If someone saw you, it was guaranteed that others would hear about it soon. The bonus was that they didn't know Cambridge's neighbors like they knew theirs. A tingle started behind Daniela's eyes and crept down to her nose. She swallowed hard and tried to distract herself with clearing a path for the guys to walk across. Cambridge's feet came into view just as she finished.

"Daniela, don't watch." Davi's voice was soft despite his command.

"I'm not a child anymore, Davi. I want to say goodbye the real way." Daniela approached the mattress. The odors emitted made her eyes water, but she hugged Mamãe's bony shoulders and kissed her cold, lifeless cheek. "Farewell, Mamãe. I will always remember you. How fierce you were."

Her whisper felt unnecessary, yet vital at the same time. The numbness sweeping over her would be an emotional free-for-all that needed reining in on the field tomorrow.

The next day was more painful than she expected. With meticulous care, she left every emotion that dared bubble up on the field—in warm-ups, in drills, in sprints, and in scrimmages.

In the Shadows

Each word of praise she received or any guilt or frustration, she redirected towards her grief.

Halfway through the day as she squirted water into her mouth from a community water bottle, she pinpointed the ache deep in her chest. Mamãe's secrets stung with the acid of betrayal which overshadowed the relief and sadness of the final goodbye. Why had she killed herself with drugs while ranting so violently against Gerson for his use of alcohol?

The facts didn't settle into an easily solved puzzle. They grated and pushed against each other. How had she hidden that addiction for so many years? Even asking the questions in her head seemed wrong in a way now that Mamãe had passed.

To add to the guilt, there was no burial place as a memorial. More proof that they were desperately in need of a livelihood that could grant them dignity in death and life.

Coach Frade separated the girls into teams, specifying each position. On this final day, they were going to play with eleven on eleven, full field. The rest of the girls stood on the sidelines on their respective teams. Behind them in the stands sat three or four rows of spectators. For a split second, she allowed herself to imagine Davi and Cambridge and Gabi in the front row supporting her, wearing her jersey number and name, screaming in excitement. She smiled briefly and took off at a jog the second she heard the kickoff whistle shrill.

The whole week, she'd watched the other girls who were older or faster or had team experience. Her mind picked out her main competition, cataloging each strength and weakness. Quietness often worked in her favor. She read their tells and listened to their complaints, then watched for them in practice. After a week, she read people like one of Cambridge's books.

By the second half, each girl had moved positions or substituted off the field altogether. When Daniela came off, Coach Frade switched her to the other team. Her legs caught their second wind, and kept her moving, light on her feet until the final whistle blew. Sweat dripped down her face as she slapped hands with the others, smiling and laughing.

Not until Coach Frade stood in the front of the room calling for silence did the nerves hit her. Off to the side, a line of four people waited against the wall. Coach Cevere was one of them. First up was Coach Cardoso, the women's Under Twenty national coach. Next was Coach Leal, the former women's national team coach who Frade said was helping scout. Then he introduced Coach Rocha, the new women's national team coach, who had the final say of who they scouted.

Finally, Coach Cevere looked over the group. Daniela relaxed slightly, his presence familiar and comfortable now.

"You ladies are the best the city has to offer in *futbol* this year. I hope you take great pride in what you've done this week. You were invited to this camp to train with some of the best coaches in the business, but this week wasn't just for fun. And the presence of these coaches is testimony of that." Coach Cevere motioned to the other coaches still standing nearby. "Today, they came to watch you, to choose from this amazing pool of talented women who they'd like to invite to train with their teams for the next season."

The room erupted in a buzz. Daniela gulped her water aggressively. She'd been so busy thinking about everything else going on in life that she hadn't stopped to really think through the implications of camp.

Camp wasn't the final prize. Camp was a doorway to a bigger prize.

"Each one of you has a thank-you gift waiting for you in the hallway. It contains various items supplied by incredible sponsors and vendors, maybe some girly stuff we guys know nothing about—"

Daniela laughed along with the other girls, although she might not know some of the items either. She'd never gotten gifts.

In the Shadows

"Most importantly, your gift contains an envelope. Coach Cardoso and Coach Rocha and all their assistants watched you play today. If they liked what they saw, they invited you to an interview this afternoon. So some of you will have invitations. If you don't have an invitation, don't think your *futbol* journey ends there. The FFC is excited to share that we will be starting a girls' league and a good number of you may represent Rio on that team as you play against other cities and even countries. We're committed to building a better environment for girls' *futbol* and we're grateful you joined our first attempt."

He started clapping and the adults joined in. The girls clapped for each other, too.

A new beginning.

The excitement stirred inside her. She was a nobody and she had been chosen to be a part of this.

As with the tryouts, she let the rush to the bags subside and the tension build. Her emotions had driven her playing today, not in an overt display but internally. She found her name without any trouble and carried the bag to a secluded corner.

If she could have, she would have waited to open the bag when she got home, but waiting wasn't an option. She dug around the hair ties, water bottles, t-shirts, sports drawstring bag, and extracted a thin paper packet.

Her teeth snagged her lower lip between them. The last one had been thick and full of information. A thin packet could only mean one thing.

The deep breath didn't calm her nerves. The first paper was the FFC letterhead thanking her for coming to the camp. The second paper was an invitation to join the *Guerreiras* girls' team.

She'd made it. She was on the team!

The third paper was an invitation to meet with Coach Rocha who headed up the women's national team.

The wave of nerves crashed until it became a ripple of nausea. Coach Rocha would dismiss her in a blink. She wasn't national team material yet. And maybe she'd never be. Maybe her dream was just a kid's wish to escape the poverty and squalor and rise to the top doing something people assumed she couldn't.

But that was just it.

Anything she did successfully, she'd be doing something people assumed she couldn't. That could be art with Gabi or creating items with Cambridge and Davi, but none of things spoke to her whole self like *futbol* did. Nerves or not, she needed to follow through with where her future was going.

She asked an assistant where to be for the interview and followed the hallway to a door past the locker room. When the door opened, Coach Rocha thanked another girl for coming and spotted Daniela immediately.

"Daniela, come on in."

She fought to keep the shock from her expression. He knew her name? Summoning every ounce of shaky confidence, she strode into the office-like room and sat in the seat Rocha motioned to. Coach Leal sat in a seat off to the side.

"Ignore him. He's not really here," Coach Rocha said with a wink.

Ignore a man whose international fame had every little girl learning his name hoping to catch his eye someday for her skills.

"Daniela, I need to be up front with you. We're not looking to add anyone to the national team right now based on the roster we have. According to your file, you're fifteen which is still young for a professional career on a national level."

Daniela's heart sank. There was always some reason to disqualify her. She was a girl. She was too young. She lived in a *favela*. She was a *catadore*.

"But I wanted to have an interview with you to let you know we're going to be keeping our eye on you for the next few years. We're opening our training sessions at the Olympic Training Center to a select few and we'd like you to be there if you can afford it. The cost is considerably higher than this camp, but that

In the Shadows

top tier training is what's going to move you to the next level." Coach Rocha's warm brown eyes assessed her. She met his gaze without blinking. This moment felt unreal. "You're a talented player. Your instincts are natural and you have a stunning grace about you on that field. I think you have potential for professional *futbol* and a long, healthy relationship with sponsors and ad agencies. We aren't looking to rush you into anything. You have time, but I want you to keep your sights set on the future. Hope is the most potent weapon I can give you right now. And trust me when I say, what's ahead is well worth preparing for. So give your team the best you've got and we'll be watching you and thrilled to have you with us for training events when you can be there."

Daniela nodded. The chaotic nerves came surging back. So she hadn't made history as being the youngest female to make the squad right now, but he'd invited her to the Olympic Training Center.

She stifled her laugh of disbelief, then shook his hand. "Thank you, Coach Rocha. This is a dream come true for me." Turning to Coach Leal, she offered him her hand as well. "I've wanted to meet you since I was a little girl. I've admired your coaching so much."

When he grinned, the wrinkles on his face deepened, but charmingly so. Davi was going to be so jealous that she'd met Coach Leal.

She kept her head down the rest of the afternoon and occasionally joined in the van banter of the other girls on the way back to the *favela*. She'd enjoyed their company this week, but shame reared its head every time she thought of Mamãe dying alone and not receiving a proper funeral or burial. She longed to acquit Mamãe of the role she'd played in her own death, but she couldn't.

One of the girls gasped. "Look at that. I wonder what that will be."

Daniela leaned forward to see what the girls looked at. There in the waning sunlight, solitary figure swung himself back and forth by a rope and harness, marking the brick in front of him with great arcs of color. Chills raced across her skin.

Tiago had started their final battle with the recycling facility. And it'd be no small comment, either.

Cougar Dating

The Secrets to Success for Older Women Dating Younger Men

by Jackson Sparks

Table of Contents

Introduction 1

Chapter 1: Why It Doesn't Matter That Age Matters 5

Chapter 2: Playing It Light Is Playing It Right 9

Chapter 3: Where to Prowl and How to Growl 13

Chapter 4: Dressing the Part 21

Chapter 5: Romancing the Younger Man 25

Chapter 6: Shooting for Long Term 29

Chapter 7: Side-Stepping the Pitfalls of Cougar Dating 33

Conclusion 37

Introduction

Just because he's younger than you by a good ten years, or even twenty years, does not mean he can't feel intense attraction for you. Every day and every hour, a young man pines intensely for the affections of a woman many years his senior. When an older woman knows what she's doing, she can powerfully captivate the imagination and desire of younger men just as effectively (or even more so) than much younger women.

Attracting and successfully dating younger men boils down to learning how to flaunt one's assets, develop a sense of mystery, and minimize one's vulnerabilities and insecurities. If you're interested in having fun, you definitely want to read this book. And if you're interested in developing a long term relationship with a younger man, you absolutely *need* to read it.

This book will provide a concise yet thorough step-by-step guide to help you become the fiercest and most fabulous of cougars. Get ready to prowl.

© Copyright 2014 by Miafn LLC - All rights reserved.

This document is geared towards providing reliable information in regards to the topic and issue covered. The publication is sold with the idea that the publisher is not required to render accounting, officially permitted, or otherwise, qualified services. If advice is necessary, legal or professional, a practiced individual in the profession should be ordered.

- From a Declaration of Principles which was accepted and approved equally by a Committee of the American Bar Association and a Committee of Publishers and Associations.

In no way is it legal to reproduce, duplicate, or transmit any part of this document in either electronic means or in printed format. Recording of this publication is strictly prohibited and any storage of this document is not allowed unless with written permission from the publisher. All rights reserved.

The information provided herein is stated to be truthful and consistent, in that any liability, in terms of inattention or otherwise, by any usage or abuse of any policies, processes, or directions contained within is solely and completely the responsibility of the recipient reader. Under no circumstances will any legal responsibility or blame be held against the publisher for any reparation, damages, or monetary loss due to the information herein, either directly or indirectly.

Respective authors own all copyrights not held by the publisher.

The information herein is offered for informational purposes solely, and is universal as so. The presentation of the information is without contract or any type of guarantee assurance.

The trademarks that are used are without any consent, and the publication of the trademark is without permission or backing by the trademark owner. All trademarks and brands within this book are for clarifying purposes only and are the owned by the owners themselves, not affiliated with this document.

Chapter 1: Why It Doesn't Matter That Age Matters

Let's not be unrealistic. If you're serious about being successful with dating younger men, then you need to face facts. And the facts are that being an older woman in the dating game has *some* disadvantages. Mainly two:

1) Younger women, in general, are perceived as being more physically attractive. This is the result of generations of evolutionary programming, though as with many other facets of nature, exceptions to the norm are widespread.

2) Men interested in longer term relationships tend to be more comfortable with a large age spread if the woman is younger and the man older.

Now, keeping our grip on cold reality, let's assess each of these potential obstacles. Regarding physical attractiveness, there are multiple factors that go into a woman's overall level of physical attractiveness: fitness, style, attitude, femininity—just to name a few. And, unlike the age factor, most all other measures of attractiveness are measures which can be controlled and improved upon. If you're able to really dial in these other aspects of physical attractiveness, then the age factor will quickly shrink into the background. At any age, a woman who takes good care of herself is going to be more attractive than a woman who does not.

For older women who are just looking to have fun on the dating scene, the likelihood of finding a successful long-term relationship may not be of the utmost concern. But for older women in search of a longer term Mr. Right, it's important to realize that a twenty-year age gap may seem a bit daunting to the man twenty years your junior. A ten-year spread is a lot more palatable, and it's not uncommon to find couples who are married or in serious long-term relationships where the woman is roughly ten years older than the man. The advantage of being a cougar is that you have the power to enamor, and men who are enamored aren't really all that concerned with what their relationship might look like several years down the road. In romance, men are creatures of the moment. For the rest of this book, we'll focus more so on the here and now of attracting younger men rather than worry too much about what the future may hold. After all, being a cougar is about being free, wild, and passionate in the present moment. Life's too short to worry.

Chapter 2: Playing It Light Is Playing It Right

From this point forward, the world is your playground. You are dating to have fun. If you were dating to find security, then you'd be shacked up on a ranch somewhere helping some codger burn off his IRA. You wouldn't be going after younger men. As an older woman, it's important for you to realize that dating younger men means dating immature men. Women are more mature then men from the get-go, so it follows that older women are veritably light years ahead of younger men when it comes to maturity. Do not expect anything different or you will be setting yourself up for frustration, failure, and possibly heartbreak.

The number one rule of dating younger men is Light is Right, not in the dietary sense (though that helps too), but in terms of one's attitude. The easiest way to make the fact of your age stick out like a sore thumb and detract from your sex appeal is to present yourself as a gravely-serious dater with very serious, well-defined, and perhaps urgent reasons for involving yourself in the dating scene. A cougar is powerful, mysterious, and playful, not desperate, transparent, and glum.

The way of the cougar is playful by way of mystery, not playful by way of ditsy. This is how you turn your age into an asset. Be flirtatious without being aimlessly talkative. Men like to be kept on their toes and younger men will respond more to an older woman who doesn't give away too much about herself as opposed to blabbing on and on about her ex-husband(s), her kid(s), job, etc. An air of confident reserve will spark the imagination of the men you're pursuing. You'll come across as a woman whose broad life experience has added to, not detracted from, her vitality, and that's sexy. Just keep things light and mysterious in the early stages of dating and you'll be surprised by the amount of attraction you can generate.

Chapter 3: Where to Prowl and How to Growl

Meeting younger men isn't as difficult as you might think. For starters, any time you go out, it's important that you look and feel sexy. Remember, fitness and style are two factors of attraction that, when properly leveraged, can take the age issue right off the table. Look good, feel good, and have a light and mysterious attitude. Here are some venues where you can find success on your next prowl:

The Supermarket: The mecca of cougar dating, the supermarket is full of hot young stock boys and wandering bachelors who would like nothing more than to spark up some flirtations with a sexy older woman. A simple smile, or perhaps a question, can start a conversation: "Where's the bread aisle?"

Clubs and Meet-ups: What are you interested in? Scuba-diving? Tennis? Politics? Whatever it is, there's probably a meet-up group for it you can join online (www.meetup.com). Would-be cougars can do quite well at physical club activities such as softball and ultimate Frisbee.

College Campus: No, you shouldn't stake out the student center and troll around for younger guys, unless you're exceptionally ambitious. But if you're interested in improving yourself, take a college class or two. You'll get to learn a little and you'll also increase your proximity to a limitless supply of young studs.

Night Clubs: There's really no reason a hot older woman can't live it up until late hours at the club. You may have to dodge a few drunken idiots, but you may also be approached by a young hottie or two who finds your mature debonair sensibilities to be irresistible.

The Shopping Mall: Malls are full of young guys on the hunt. Try sitting on a bench in clear view of the heavy foot traffic. If you've got nice legs, show them off. You're bound to be approached.

The Park: What better way to spend a sunny Sunday afternoon than with a nice prowl through the park. If you're lucky maybe you'll bring back some fresh meat.

Swanky Bars: There's something a bit incongruent about a suave, confident, older woman guzzling cheap beer at a dive bar. But not all bars are created equal. Micro-breweries can often be very classy venues and wholly appropriate haunts for hip and sexy older women. Take a stroll downtown and look for other venues where you'd be comfortable throwing back a few. And go out on a Wednesday or Tuesday night, so you don't get lost in the commotion. There's something positively scintillating about meeting a hot older woman at a quiet classy bar. It's what the best fantasies are made of.

Concerts: What better than music to break down intergenerational barriers? Meeting a guy at concert will automatically give you something in common to talk about.

Online: The most obvious place to meet younger men is on the world wide web. There are a handful of specialty dating websites that cater to cougars and the men interested in dating them. Remember to play up your profile with lots of fun and attractive pictures of the awesomeness that is you.

Regardless of which venue you choose, the most important thing to remember is to keep your hunting spirit alive and healthy. Some people like to say that you tend to meet people when you're not looking. This is rubbish. The truth is that you do often meet people in unexpected ways, but if you're not trying then you're probably not going to have much success. Cultivate the mentality of the hunter. Go out and prowl about and have a good time in the process. Your moment may come at an unexpected time or location, perhaps somewhere not mentioned in the list above, but it will be much more likely to come (and you'll be more prepared for it) if you're taking all possible actions to maximize your chances.

Most men will take the lead if you send them the proper buying signals. Start with a smile. If you need to be a little more aggressive then escalate up to a random question. Young, old, or otherwise: if a guy likes you, he'll take the lead if he thinks you might be interested.

One of the allures of dating or even flirting with an older woman is that they are usually not afraid to be a little more direct. They know what they want and don't play games. As an older woman, it's ok to take the lead at times during the courtship process if need be. For example, inviting a guy out for lunch, for a drink, or to a club activity is fair game for a cougar so long as it doesn't come off as needy. A cougar should have thick skin and should act and speak with confidence. If you're interested in a guy, you're going to let him know, and you will escalate where appropriate. There's nothing wrong with that. If it turns out he's attached or not interested, so be it. It's his loss.

When flirting, you can be bold without being too direct. If you're flirting with a guy who is strikingly attractive on a physical level, you can bring it up subtly and always with an air of sultriness: "You look like you take really good care of yourself." Now, the normal woman would stop here, but in order to assert that you are a bold and beautiful sexual being, hot on the prowl, the cougar might add "If you want, I could take good care of you too." At this point, if he's interested you'll know it. He'll be a little nervous, his pupils might dilate a little bit and if he's got game, he may fire back his own line to advance the banter. If he's not interested, the remark you make can easily be laughed off without anyone having to suffer a bruised ego.

Remember to always keep things light and fun, even if you're nervous. In fact a little nervousness when talking to younger men is a good thing so long as you also evoke an inner confidence. A touch of nervousness can give you just the right amount of vulnerability and damsel-in-distress femininity to balance out your powerful and independent attributes brought out by graceful aging. The best advice, really, is to not think about it too much, try and have fun, and don't act surprised if you get asked out on a date.

During your dates, you need to be yourself. Don't try to dress or act younger than you really are. Also don't feel that you need to pick up the check, even if you make double his salary. Don't anticipate being smarter or wiser than him. Instead, you should be open to learning things from him that you didn't know. This will help to add some healthy balance to the dynamic. Avoid saying things like, "When I was your age," or anything else that sets you apart generationally. Your goal for the date is to connect, not delineate yourselves from one another. It's also very important to maintain your air of independence. Don't try and get him to commit to another date right there on the spot. If he likes you, he will pursue you. Avoid the subject of commitment or exclusivity for at least the first several months of dating. If he brings up the subject and it's something that *you're* interested in, fine, but for your part, strive to keep things as light as possible.

Chapter 4: Dressing the Part

As is true with so many other aspects of dating younger men, the most important key to dressing attractively is learning to play to your strengths. An older woman is going to look her best when she dresses in a way that's classy and elegant. If you're not twenty-one, then don't try to dress like a twenty-one year old would dress. No need for skin tight miniskirts and six-inch heels. Instead try a sexy leather skirt and dark boots. Dark colors tend to work nicely on older women overall.

For makeup, think elegant. A lot of older women try to use make up to cover up their age when they should be using it to accentuate their best features. If your makeup is caked on by the pound you risk turning guys off by looking like you're desperate and trying too hard. Your goal should be to look like an attractive and confident older woman and your makeup should be employed to this end. Focus on smooth and light application and use eye shadow, mascara, and lipstick for subtle and elegant highlights. Smell is the great equalizer when it comes to female cosmetics. If you smell sexy, men will have no choice but to be attracted to you.

When it comes to dressing, your years of experience should put you at an advantage over younger women. You should be very comfortable and knowledgeable about your own body. You should know what looks good on you and what you can't pull off. An older woman should wear her clothes with comfort and confidence. She should not be fidgety or self-conscious. Exploit the experience advantage for all it's worth. Be the sexiest, classiest woman on the scene, and the young guys will be turning their heads.

Chapter 5: Romancing the Younger Man

One of the most satisfying aspects of dating younger men is being pleasantly surprised by how fulfilling of a romance a younger man can offer. And this extends well beyond just the bedroom. Younger men are from a different generation and the way they view women is going to be different from the way men from your own generation view women. Many younger men come from homes where their mothers were the sole or equal breadwinners for the family. They will be more inclined to be supportive of your dreams and ambitions and less inclined to be dismissive of them. Rather than viewing women as eternal helpers, they will be more likely to appreciate your sense of power and self-determination. A younger man can provide a very satisfying romance or relationship for a woman who has lofty aspirations for herself professionally or personally. If you want to open your own business or hike the Appalachian Trail, a younger man is more likely to encourage you to take real action on these ambitions rather than steer you towards a stable, work-a-day lifestyle.

There may be some palpable generational gaps. For example, the two of you will likely have differing tastes in music and in other artistic media. But these factors really shouldn't put a damper on the relationship.

The most challenging hardship for dating a younger man will be issues that stem from disparate maturity. If you're dating a man in his twenties, then don't expect him to want to settle down any time soon. Men at this age are often trying to maximize their experience by dating a lot of different women and a so-called "cougar" may very well be their next fleeting fancy. It's important to be realistic in this regard and manage your expectations appropriately.

In his late twenties, a man will have more knowledge about what he wants in a relationship. He will also likely have had some success in his career and will thus be a little more stable. By his early to mid-thirties, a man will probably have even had his heart broken a time or two and will begin to understand his values in a relationship and what he needs and wants long-term. Don't count your chickens though, a lot of men remain serial daters well into their forties— another byproduct of generational differences.

Though the role of the sexually-experienced cougar may be prevalent in pop culture, it is not necessarily factual. The younger generations, thanks in large part to the internet, have grown up in an environment where sex is much less taboo.

Young men especially tend to be exposed to pornography very early in life and are often sexually active in their early teens. The attitude towards sex among the younger generation is much more casual.

Don't be surprised if your younger man has more bedroom experience than you.

The best approach to relating to a younger man is similar to the approach you will use when attracting him—play up the positives. Dating a younger man is an opportunity to be adventurous and spontaneous, to expose yourself to new views of the world and possibly yourself. Pack up and go to India for a few months. Go skydiving. Open a bakery or audition for a role in a movie. Remember you're not in this for security; you're in this to feel alive.

Chapter 6: Shooting for Long Term

If the young guy you're dating makes you feel appreciated, excited, and happy overall, then maybe he's a keeper. If, by contrast, he makes you feel your age, if he's difficult to relate to, or if you're otherwise incompatible, then it's certainly ok to move on, regardless of how old you are. Don't ever settle for something that doesn't work just so you don't have to be alone.

If you're thinking you might have a long-term relationship on your hands, then start having some conversations about longer term issues. You should be aware of and forthcoming about your ability and desire to have children. If you are too old to have children, then you should talk about the possibility of adopting.

When it comes to families, regardless of the age difference, if the two of you truly make one another happy, then your respective families should acknowledge this and support the progress and development of your relationship. It's important that you don't treat your partner like a show-dog—don't try and show off to your family or anyone for that matter that you're dating a younger man. And if projecting an image for yourself of youth and vitality is a primary reason for your continued dating of a younger man, then definitely don't proceed with creating a longer term commitment. Instead, ask yourself honestly if you're ready to spend the rest of your life with this man.

If you decide that you do indeed want to pursue a longer term relationship, or even the prospect of marriage, then you'll need to think about the different spheres of responsibility in the relationship. Since you're older, you may be making quite a bit more money than him, so you may find yourself to be the primary breadwinner of your pending committed relationship or marriage. Therefore, it's important to recognize and encourage some other important area where your younger husband-to-be can contribute. Otherwise you risk an inappropriately lopsided dynamic that will end with you feeling drained and used and him feeling unfulfilled and helpless.

If you do plan to have a child or to adopt, then there's nothing wrong with having the man oversee daily childcare and other domestic duties. It's also perfectly acceptable for both of you to continue to focus on your careers and not have children. Even if he's making less money than you, if he has a fulfilling job and has you to lean on for encouragement and support, then the two of you have the framework for a very healthy and prosperous partnership. It may also be a good idea at this point to think about retirement realities. Are you putting enough away into retirement to continue to support the families quality of life after you retire? Is your husband-to-be okay with the possibility of having to take care of you in your old age, when he's perhaps only 50 or 60 years old?

The realities of highly age-disparate couples may present some challenging situations to consider, but in the end if the two of you are happy being together as a couple and wish to continue as such, you shouldn't let age get in the way.

Chapter 7: Side-Stepping the Pitfalls of Cougar Dating

For a woman to have success dating a younger man, she must exert expert control over her ego. Too many women quickly fall too far into the role of sole decision maker, know-it-all, or worse, mother. Dating and relationships are a two- way street, regardless of age differences. It's important that you strive to make your partner feel important and secure.

There will inevitably be times when he shows his age in a way that's not very flattering. Whether it's a naïve opinion or a shortfall of maturity, there will be times when you're tempted to criticize him under the warrant of being older and knowing more. Don't give in to this temptation. Find other ways to introduce him to your wisdom by showing him by example that your ideas are about sophistication, manners, class, and respect. If he appreciates and admires you as he should, then he'll take your example to heart.

Learn to appreciate him for all the unique and insightful things he brings to the relationship. Even if his only strong suit is high competencies in the use of Twitter and Instagram, look for things that you can learn from his unique generational experience and don't discount them.

Unfortunately, a lot of younger men with low self-esteem will regress into very dependent roles when dating an older woman and this can lead to disaster. You date someone so you can be their girlfriend, not their mother. Here are a few things you can do to prevent this type of regression:

Don't Be Anyone's Sugar Momma

There's nothing wrong with a woman picking up the check from time to time. If you are an accomplished female of independent means, then you should be proud and feel free to flaunt your purchasing power. Just don't do it too much. If you're dating a younger man, the age spread makes it easier for you to slide into the role of constant financier. The key word of concern in "Sugar Momma" is "Momma." In a romantic partnership, it's important to let your man play the part of the "man" by letting him be a provider and procurer, even if his income is a piddling fraction of your own. As a good rule of thumb—try and avoid the unemployed types.

Avoid Younger Men with Drug or Alcohol Dependency Issues

Men who struggle with issues of addiction should never be at the top of your "to-date" list, and especially so if you are dating younger men. If you're older, wealthier, and more experienced with life, a younger man with a drinking or drug problem will find countless avenues to suck you dry. From classic addict behaviors, such as borrowing money that he never intends to return, to frequent emotional outbursts, your role will quickly transform from girlfriend to both mother and therapist. And no matter how nice he is to look at, after dealing with an addict for a few months you'll get to a point where even looking at him fills you with dread and disgust.

Avoid Low Self-Esteem Cases

Even if he's not jonesing for his next fix of heroin, dating a younger guy with terrible self-esteem is going to make for a terrible relationship. He will constantly depend on you to validate him since he can't do it on his own. He will prove helpless in the face of any new challenge and become accustomed to you taking charge in all trying situations. Your roll will be that of a mother mixed with a cheerleader, which does not make for a happy hybrid.

The best cougar matches are with young men who have a good sense of discipline, pride, and self-worth. Go after guys who are self-starters, young entrepreneurs, or artists who are passionate about life. Look for young men who are involved in hobbies and communities, who take their grandmothers to church, and volunteer to serve the poor. Make sure he's worthy of you.

Conclusion

The overarching principle of dating younger men is playing up your strengths and accepting — not hiding — your weaknesses. Men are biologically programmed to want younger women because the instinct-driven part of their brains tells them that a younger woman has the best chance of producing healthy offspring. There's nothing anyone can do to change the biological basis of attraction, but you can and should play up the exoticism of being an older woman. You do this by being confident and mysterious, bold yet feminine, and by always being on the hunt.

Finally, I'd like to thank you for purchasing this book! If you enjoyed it or found it helpful, I'd greatly appreciate it if you'd take a moment to leave a review on Amazon. Thank you!

Made in the USA
Columbia, SC
16 November 2022

Chapter 14

Since they'd started dating, Ronaldo found that Isadora rarely had a free Saturday. And after a long, stressful week, he couldn't have been more delighted that today was the exception. He'd planned the whole day himself. His only instructions to Isadora were to bring swim clothing and dress as casually as she liked.

He picked her up at her place in his town car and took a short ferry ride. They'd spent the day touring *Ilha Grande* hand-in-hand, snorkeling at their leisure off the beaches, and relaxing with each other as their sole company. He didn't shy away from touching her, nor did he avoid her touch. The day was theirs to explore as they wished.

They had a laidback dinner for two on the water, enjoying the fresh seafood. After a romantic ferry ride back to the mainland, they slid into his town car. Ronaldo's request for the driver to "take us home" likely meant something very different to Isadora than it did to him. He'd promised her dessert and drinks at his place this evening, but also knew such an invitation brought a hard conversation when she saw what home meant to him.

Her place was very comfortable and secure with cameras, covered parking, and an incredible view. He also had an incredible view, but that was only if you were willing to climb to the rooftop on a precariously secured ladder. Isadora didn't seem

In the Shadows

to be impressed by finery and he'd be tremendously disappointed if he were to be wrong about her, especially after the amazing day they had.

The car pulled to a stop outside the *favela* where the bus stop sat on the main road. Ronaldo helped Isadora from the car and then leaned in to ask the driver to stay nearby for when Isadora wanted to go home.

She didn't say a word as he took her hand and walked into the apartment building that bordered the *favela*. They greeted everyone with a nod and a smile who acknowledged them. Isadora's beauty earned her attention everywhere she went. He certainly didn't mind being the one whose arm she held.

He led her up the concrete steps and stopped at his door. She chuckled when he pushed a key into the lock. Inside, he flicked on the lights illuminating his small space and, suddenly, he felt bare to her as his inner life lay open to her scrutiny.

"It's charming, Ronaldo." A smile tinged her words as she made her way to the kitchen area to pour herself a glass of wine.

The inside of his lodging sported considerable upgrades compared to the units beneath his. He owned the apartment building, and once had considered making the two units on the top floor into one. But logic overruled his frivolous thinking, and he'd instead chosen to loan it to families in need. Families not unlike the Gomes family whom Isadora had signed the mother's death certificate for just yesterday.

With her wine glass in hand, she returned to his side to give him one as well. "I like your secrets, Ronaldo. You've been so honest and forthcoming with me. It's something I love about you. There are no pretenses or false fronts. And this is just another example of how beautiful your heart is. You live next to those you want to serve." She shook her head. "So incredibly beautiful."

Her shoulder brushed his as she moved to pass him. He caught her hand in his and brought it to his lips. An explanation for his choice hovered on the tip of his tongue, but he held on to it hoping she wouldn't ask.

She didn't. She moved in and brought her lips to his, their bodies pressing against each other. Her mouth tasted of bright fruit flavors and her skin like fresh air.

A heady combination.

When they broke apart, she leaned her forehead against his.

He spoke first in a whisper. "Isadora, I'm afraid my feelings for you are too deep to continue with our relationship if you don't feel the same way." His hand cupped her neck. "If there's any hesitation, you should tell me now, because once I'm committed, I won't back down until I have what I want."

Her eyes blazed, reflecting a heat that coiled inside of him. "Your loyalty is one of your best features, Senhor Cevere. I depend on it heavily." She lingered with her breath fanning his lips. Just as he decided to close the distance, she stepped back. "Do I get the grand tour?"

A grunt of dissatisfaction escaped his lips which earned him an infuriatingly coy smile from Isadora. "Yes, but then I must take you home."

She curtsied with a laugh. "Ever the gentleman."

He stood in the doorway as she circled his plain bedrooms. The pride he held that the room was free of mold and stains of unnamable types dimmed in the enjoyment he received from her unveiled interest in his space. In the common space, she tested his extremely comfortable couch, ran a finger along the books in his bookcases, and opened every cabinet door in his kitchen area.

A smirk had settled on to his face and wouldn't be moved. He could just imagine how she was improving the space in her mind, giving it the woman's touch it so badly needed.

"It's poetic and simple. Despite my knowledge of the danger out those doors, I'm so taken with the uncluttered life you lead. It's therapeutic." She collapsed on the couch next to him, her head resting in the crook of his shoulder. "Thank you for today. It has

In the Shadows

been magical and restful to step away from my normal chaos and burdens and see the outer reaches of our city the way others see it in an unfettered way."

Her words ran like cool water over his parched heart. He drew his fingers through the silk of her dark locks and sunk a little further into his couch. "You fit here. Maybe the scene is tainted from my perspective of how much I enjoy your company, but I've admired for so long the way you suit a ball gown like you do your everyday scrubs. I've never seen a woman so comfortable with being present where she is."

"Perhaps the secret to my comfort lies in who is present when you see me in each of those situations."

Dared he hope that he was a source of confidence for someone so wildly independent and attractive as Dr. Rey?

Yes, he dared.

They sat in silence for a while as they listened to the *favela* settle into its nighttime rhythm. He glanced at his watch in hopes that time wasn't so silent a thief tonight on a night he didn't want to end.

"I'll see you home."

Isadora mumbled and buried her face into his neck. It felt too good to stay like that. One day he'd not have to let her go and it'd be soon if he had his way.

The next Monday, Ronaldo sank into his well-cushioned office chair. The task ahead of him was clear cut but daunting. He had to secure permission from every donor and sponsor to release their information to the board and the shareholders. That was no easy task for those who'd asked to stay anonymous. Anyone could leak that sensitive information to the press and the feast would be laid out for the predators with little effort.

Someone had managed to make important members of the committee's board believe that Ronaldo was given drug money to hold tryouts in the *favelas*. The logic was baffling. He'd done it to prevent the girls from being forced into a life they wanted no part in, yet somehow it was twisted so that the drug dealers were paying him money to take their easy income from them?

That afternoon when he stood in front of the conference room full of grim-faced board members, he started by thanking them for their dedication to the job, for taking the board's ethics seriously. He reminded them of confidentiality and then proceeded to go over every single donation and the donor's job and address to prove the money had nothing to do with drug dealers.

It was a necessary waste of time to prove to others as well as himself that he'd been above board in his dealings. Katrina wasn't slacking either. If anything, his team deserved his most devoted thanks for their dedication and backing. Could a good leader be perceived as so if his whole team was corrupt?

Hours later when they finally left the room, everyone's questions had been satisfied. Jackets were off, sleeves rolled up. They looked as if they'd gone to war on the paper, but the board members left with smiles on their faces. And Ronaldo did as well as he marched the excess copies to the shredder.

Katrina waited for him at her desk. "How did it go, senhor?"

"Smoothly, thanks to your detailed records." He scrubbed a hand down his face. "The hounds are held at bay for now until someone gives them another reason to doubt us and the good we are trying to do. There will always be naysayers to object to progress."

She cleared her throat and flashed him a hint of a smile. "That's part of why I'm here still. I didn't want you to be surprised when you left."

His eyebrow rose. "At?"

"The protesters who are marching in front of our office entrance. They're upset that you're taking the girls away from their duties at home and filling their heads with unrealistic dreams and ideas that they should fill the male roles."

Ronaldo snorted. "We did away with all that nonsense in the eighties. Are they old-timers?"

In the Shadows

"No, senhor. There's a variety."

"You're telling me I'm older than some of them and I'm still more knowledgeable about womens' rights than they are? That's surprising. Go on home, Katrina. Have security walk you to your car out the side exit, if you need them to."

She nodded and said good night. She excelled at everything she did. Not to say that she didn't make mistakes, but she learned from them and he gave her space to do that. Kids didn't get that much these days. The pressure to be perfect while learning was crushing their ability to pick themselves up and start again.

He finished his work and locked up. The protesters had left before he did. Nevertheless, he took a roundabout way home and found himself wishing for the day when the promise of coming home to Isadora made him close up the office early. Tonight, she taught classes at the hospital. Brazilian medicine wasn't what it needed to be, but with teachers like her, it wouldn't be long before they were returned to their places.

Ronaldo paused just as he passed under the highway above him. From here, Tiago's art of bold colors and heart-twisting graphics took shape in awe-inspiring form. Tiago had been right. His building was the perfect place for the display as it was possibly the final structure Mariana saw before she closed her eyes for eternity. For years he'd avoided allowing Tiago the privilege of repainting his building exterior for what seemed like temporary causes, but now he wanted to ask him to create a mural on his ceiling, too. It seemed like something Mariana would ask for and Isadora would love.

This happened because he held tryouts right outside the *favelas*. The nearly finished mural struck a nerve deep inside him. But what would have happened if he hadn't? Just how would they have won this battle?

They would've fought but lost.

How easily he fooled himself into believing he was a force of change.

When was the last time he sat and talked with others who lived in his building? He'd grown so regimented in his comings and goings that he never made time for socialization to become acquainted with many of the people around him. Sure, he was living near the people he wanted to serve, but was he serving them if he was gone early, out all day, and tucked inside for the evening after dinner? When did he have time to learn their names? Or find out their struggles and help them fight their battles?

The thought scared him. For years, he'd blamed Mariana being at the wrong place at the wrong time for her death, so he'd kept to his known places and predictable times so that wouldn't happen to him. All while trying to help from his nest of relative safety.

But what if she had been at the right place at the right time to protect others? He swallowed hard. Not once in the past years had it occurred to him that she had been there willingly and selflessly present with the girls who wanted a way out.

Wouldn't that have been the most selfless serving—to sacrifice her safety and possibly her life intentionally so those girls would have a way forward?

Anger rose uninvited.

Perhaps she'd been careless in her youthful heroism, but starker was the prudishness of his carefully guarded life with every sacrifice and service rendered from the protection of his whole being.

Was that who he wanted to be? How did a man go about tearing down the correct strongholds without leaving the castle recklessly unguarded?

Or was the purpose of service to leave the castle vulnerable?

He stopped by a local eatery across from his building. The place was otherwise empty, so he sat at the bar one seat away from a couple of locals who chatted to the bartender. They had no food or drink in front of them. A replay of an old *futbol* game ran

In the Shadows

on the television behind the bar. Before he ordered a drink, he stood and walked out the door he came in.

The restlessness in his heart wouldn't settle. He turned toward Isadora's clinic. With her, he was the man he longed to be. On the sidewalk ahead, a little boy and a younger boy sat quietly, holding their hands out to strangers who walked by. Ronaldo stopped.

"Are you hungry?" he asked the older boy.

They both nodded, their eyes downcast.

Although he suspected the answer, he asked anyway. "Where are your parents?"

"Working to pay for rent for our family." The boy's answer was prompt and too articulate for Ronaldo to believe it was the truth.

"Bring your brother. I will take you to dinner and send you home with food."

The little boy's eyes widened. "No, Senhor. We can't leave our place. If we don't return home with money, our mother will be very upset."

Ronaldo sighed. "I will bring you something to eat and food to take home. Is that agreeable to you?"

The little boy nodded with a smile that revealed crooked and missing teeth. He'd never regretted not having children. They were a distraction from his purpose, but he did wonder just what kind of father he would have been.

Ronaldo walked across the road and down the street toward a food shop to fulfill his promise. He should have asked more questions about the boy's family. Beggars were shameless and rampant, as common as bugs in the dirt. So why did he stop for these boys?

Next to the food shop, a window display caught his eye. It wasn't the bars in front of the bulletproof glass. Rather the sizable ruby ring surrounded by a circle of diamonds that made him stop without warning.

Nothing had seemed more like Isadora to him.

C.D. Gill

He hurried inside the store to get groceries for the boys, delighted for the sign. If she helped him be the man he wanted to be, then he needed to do something about that. And he knew just what he'd give her when the time came.

Chapter 15

Daniela's first work of art was finished and strategically placed for sale in Gabi's store near the front where each customer could see it clearly when they entered. The artistic process had been tedious to learn. Art had always seemed to be the one thing that people didn't have to work at, as it was an expression of the soul. Now that she understood that expression came with a great amount of labor and exacting, she didn't take on a second piece so willingly.

Life with making and selling had fallen into a new rhythm in the time Daniela had been at *futbol* camp. They sold enough to scrape by most days. Gabi had agreed to sell so much of Cambridge's work that Cambridge went to her store almost every day now for product drop-offs. They hadn't made many sales at the store.

Today was her first day back with Gabi and she had her suspicions that Cambridge didn't always come for business like he made it seem. As Daniela unloaded a couple of new shipments, the yearning for *futbol* came in loud and clear. This—storekeeping and managing a business front—wasn't what she wanted to do with her life any more than sorting through waste.

To be fair, it hadn't been Gabi's dream either, but the convents still wouldn't take her.

In the Shadows

Until recently, Daniela's enjoyment came from playing *futbol* in the evenings, eating fresh food, or making Davi happy by finding lots of recyclables to sell. None of that pleasure stemmed from what made her feel most alive. Now that she could recognize the feeling, she craved the rush, the anticipation, every moment of the day.

Gabi's influence illuminated a piece of her she didn't know existed. Making something beautiful and decorative had been something she learned to better herself. Playing *futbol* on a field with a real team was what she did to feel alive. That life blossoming inside her made colors brighter and the air fresher. She'd never known life could be like this.

Playing *futbol* was her art.

The store's door burst open with a harsh jingle. On instinct, Daniela dropped to a squat behind the box she was emptying. She peered over the edge to see Davi's looming form and bright smile appear above her.

"We—we—" His breathing was heavy as he pulled a rolled newspaper from his back pocket. The unscrolling took too long. Whatever he needed her to see, he'd ran here to show her and Davi rarely ran anywhere.

"We made the news today. Front page. I mean, Tiago did. His colossal painting made the city sit up and take notice." Davi laughed his laugh of genuine, unfettered happiness. She jumped to her feet and skimmed the article, grateful Cambridge insisted she learn to read all those years ago.

There in black and white, the newspaper outlined the *catadores'* biggest struggle, their fight with wealthy recycling center owners, and called for the rich businesses to be held accountable when dealing with the poor workers. A smaller picture of Cambridge standing on the mounds of trash graced the second page with a long quote from him, telling the world in no uncertain terms how life was for them.

Cambridge didn't exacerbate the problem despite the unique way in which he described the gross misconduct of authorities. Gabi pressed against Daniela's shoulder, reading from behind and making the occasional comment.

"Think it's enough?" Daniela asked, afraid to hope just yet.

Davi grinned. "It's why I came. Shop owners who turned us down last week stopped me in the street to tell me we could come pick up their recyclables every day. Now no matter what the authorities do, we might not have to pay any more fees to get the supplies we need."

"But why? Why do the shop owners suddenly care about us now when they hated us so strongly only a day ago?"

He shrugged. "I guess they hate bullies even more. They don't want to be on the wrong side of history."

Gabi shooed her out the door to capitalize on their good fortune. Not a moment too soon, either. By the time they sold what they didn't need and dragged the rest of their resources home, night had begun to take command of the sky.

People dancing and cheering filled the street outside Cambridge's apartment. Someone passed out cans of cheap beer and handfuls of sweets. Daniela and Davi stashed their things inside, then joined the party. Daniela grinned at Davi, and he raised his eyebrows as he surveyed the crowd with a smile.

A man strode up to him, his arms open for an embrace. They wasted no time on frivolities since, overnight, they had become scholars and knowledgeable businessmen discussing the finer points of business and strikes.

Daniela wandered into the crowd, careful to stay within eyeshot of Davi. She held onto the unopened can of Guarana that was shoved in her hand. As she wiped the lip with her shirt, someone bumped into her back.

"*Foi mal!*" a male voice said.

She glanced up to wave it off but stopped to stare at the smooth-skinned guy grinning down at her. His height felt like a

In the Shadows

rich boy's size—someone who was well-fed every day, able to grow at will. A shock of dark hair fell across his forehead, giving him a boyish look.

"This party is a crush."

He nodded and snagged the can from her hand. The party-goers' drunken cheer for the merits of art drowned her protests. Those same people would have sneered at the frivolity of art yesterday. But today—specifically this evening—a more noble pursuit they'd never seen. After all, how bad could something be if it made them money and gave them free drinks on occasion?

Holding the can away from his body, he popped the tab in a small explosion, letting the liquid drench his hand and arm on its way to the dirt. Her lips parted in surprise as he winked.

When he leaned in to give it back, she caught a whiff of cologne. He wasn't from around here to afford that kind of luxury. His words in her ear distracted her focus. "Don't be impressed yet. The kid that was handing these out shook every single one like it was a cheap maraca while he danced to the music. It's to his good fortune that most people are too drunk to care and everyone else is treating it like it's a poor man's champagne."

Laughing, she raised her can in thanks and took a sip. The cherry flavor burst on her tongue right behind the bubbles. Her good-looking rescuer appeared in no hurry to leave her side.

"Whom do I have to thank for rescuing me from a cherry bath?"

"My mother calls me Macalister, but my friends call me Maco." A spark of humor lit his mud-colored eyes underneath long eyelashes, and a dimple appeared in his left cheek.

"What should I call you?"

He didn't hesitate for a second. "How about Mac?"

"Okay, Mac it is. I'm Daniela."

He tipped his chin and winked. His shoulders had a tension to them as he stood with his back against the wall so that he could see in every direction.

"You're not from this neighborhood."

By the way his gaze took in the scene, she didn't need to tell him how foolish and dangerous it was to sneak into a *favela* at night.

"What makes you say that?" His muscled arms folded across his chest. No visible tattoos. Decently straight white teeth. Healthy looking. Smelled good. She could continue.

She shrugged. "I haven't seen you around before."

"Are you the party bouncer?"

"You're pretty and the *favela* is a tight-knit group. Newcomers aren't always welcomed around here."

Mac brushed his arm against her shoulder, a roguish grin on his face. "You think I'm handsome?"

Her long ponytail swished against her neck as she smiled. "I think it's a good thing it's dark and people are drunk, otherwise you'd be drawing unwanted attention." A thought wiped her smile away. "You're not here to start trouble, are you?"

Mac grabbed her free hand and spun her around, jiving and bopping like the others around him. "I'm here to enjoy the party, Daniela. You should, too." He pulled her in close, so her body pressed against his. She glanced at his pink lips, then back to the crowd. "And I'm the one that brought the drinks."

So, he was rich enough to hand away drinks to poor people. "And yet you're not drinking. Suspicious."

He waved her comment away. "No suspicion necessary. I'm here on business to talk to Cambridge, but would I be Brazilian if I didn't enjoy a party when I find one?"

"In this case, you'd be a smart Brazilian to avoid a party in the *favelas*. I'll help you find Cambridge." It didn't escape her that Mac had yet to let go of her hand. His warm fingers grasped hers and it felt like the most natural thing in the world even though she'd just met the man and knew virtually nothing about him. Her neighbors would be talking when they saw, but her

In the Shadows

holding his hand labeled him a friend. She could only hope the *favela* owner or his enforcers didn't stop them for questioning.

She gave him a small tour as she checked all the places Cambridge might be on an unusual night of partying like this— anywhere that was considered hiding to the normal party goer. At last, she found him tucked away in a neighboring apartment bent over a book with two small children, a mom, and three teenage boys looking over his shoulder. He sounded out syllables and spelled words.

On a night of celebrating, he was teaching his neighbors to read. No scene depicted a more accurate version of Cambridge in her mind.

Mac watched for a bit from the doorway, content to observe. She made no move to end their physical contact yet.

Only when he quietly turned to leave did Cambridge glance up once, then twice, his gaze landing on their interlocked hands. Daniela attempted to pull away, but Mac held her firm. Cambridge mumbled something to the group and stood to approach them.

"Macalister, didn't expect to see you tonight. Are you covering the aftermath of your article?" Cambridge gripped Mac's free hand in a familiar way.

Mac was the journalist covering their story. Inside, Daniela cringed. Cambridge knew how inexperienced she was with male attention. And the way he angled himself so it was them against Mac made her want to pull away and run. He'd caught her holding hands with a guy he knew better than she did.

Which was to say, not at all.

So when Davi called her name from down the stairs, she seized the opportunity to wrench her hand loose and fast walk to where he stood at the bottom of the cement stairs. A relaxed smile lit his face and he had a girl with six layers of makeup on her face tucked under his arm.

A girl who was known to make her money on the streets. At night. Wearing enough to freeze to death in the dead heat of the summer.

What was he thinking? Daniela set her jaw. This night kept getting worse.

Davi held out an arm to her. "Heloisa said she loved me. Isn't that sweet?"

Davi never had trouble pushing away unwanted females. Nor did he fall prey to the streetwalkers who were out for extra cash. He must have had one drink too many. She grabbed his arm and excused them, leaving the lovely Heloisa to glower at their backs and plan a thousand ways to poison their water supply and steal their money.

As he walked quietly beside her without so much as a generous sway, her heart sank. He wasn't drunk and she hadn't saved him. He'd seen her with Mac.

"I don't want to talk about it," she said.

"Okay." His tone was light and easy. Maybe he'd forgive her stupidity that quickly, but she wouldn't. He picked up two more full cans of Guarana, popped the tabs outside, and followed her into their apartment.

They slid two upside-down buckets beside a makeshift table and Davi dealt out the deck of cards for her favorite game. She always beat him in *Truco* (Trick). He joked that it was a sure sign of her character, but tonight it fit her mood just fine. She needed to beat someone in something. After not playing *futbol* for three days that had felt like three years, she had a taste of that exquisite flavor of passion and she needed it like a hit.

That particular revelation made her agitation grow exponentially. Needing something or someone set her up to be crushed later when that was taken away. It was her reality.

The good things always ended.

Two days until the *Guerreiras's* season began and it couldn't come soon enough.

In the Shadows

Her hands slapped the card onto the table a little harder than necessary. To Davi's credit, he didn't flinch or respond. If she'd wanted to go toss trash at the government building, he'd probably take her to do it.

Her interaction with Mac had been nothing but talking and hand holding, regardless of how charming and good-looking the reporter was. After beating Davi in three rounds straight, she sighed.

"You didn't have to save me. I knew he didn't belong here."

Davi played his card. "I know."

Cambridge stepped inside and closed the door behind him. Daniela felt his assessing gaze on her, weighing her mood. She wanted to ask what they'd said after she left. Surely, he didn't let their handholding go unaddressed despite its innocence.

She slapped her cards on the table, eliciting a groan from Davi. Four wins in a row. She was beginning to think he wasn't trying. If that was the case, she appreciated his attempt at making her feel better.

Cambridge overturned a bucket and joined their game. "Today was good, but the coming days are the ones that matter most."

Davi grunted his agreement. "With the influx of materials we can gather each day from our section, I'd like to teach others to make things and we'll sell their products and take a few *reals* off each sale for our resources."

"A solid plan." Cambridge studied his cards. "Practice starts in a few days for you, Daniela. Gabi said she already misses you."

Daniela let her eyebrow raise as she shuffled the cards around in her hand. "I'll miss her, too. But I think she'll be fine without me since you're there to keep her company." When he didn't respond, she continued. "She likes you a lot, Cambridge."

He let the silence linger long enough that she figured he would drop the topic altogether. "The feeling is mutual."

C.D. Gill

She sneaked a glance at Davi. His grin mirrored her own. Their Cambridge was falling in love. He deserved someone as angelic as Gabi. While Daniela hoped for love someday for herself, a part of her doubted she would ever draw the attention of the kind of man she longed to have—not with her life the way it was. Not to mention, the judgment from the men already in her life would probably scare any sane man away.

Her initial draw to Mac was that he didn't shy away from her because she lived in a *favela*. That wasn't a normal reaction from outsiders. Nor did he avoid her because she was a *catadore*.

She was kidding herself. Maybe their conversation made fodder for another article.

But that was just it, wasn't it?

She slapped her hand on the table with a triumphant *ha*. The guys grunted and tossed their cards in to be reshuffled.

What would it take for her to finally feel like she was good enough? Whose approval did she need? Davi's? Mac's? The world's?

Like an overly ambitious bee, she stopped at every available sweet spot to make sure she kept herself full on self-satisfaction. Her need of approval had become a life crutch, but she couldn't command herself to stop caring. That hadn't worked before.

No, the only way was to know for herself that she'd given everything she had plus a little more to whatever she did. If it wasn't enough, then she'd have to live with that. But if it was, she'd have to live with that, too.

Because needing a relationship or *futbol* to complete her was too dangerous a game to play. And one that would never end well for her.

Chapter 16

Katrina and her team of miracle workers hauled their chairs from Ronaldo's office as a knock came at his door. Isadora's dark hair framed the smooth, tan face that poked from behind the door jamb. She grinned and strolled in. As she closed his door, Ronaldo waved his thanks at the security guard watching them from a distance.

"You had me on your approved list of visitors despite the fact that I have never once visited you here." Isadora leaned against the wall nearest his giant windows facing the stadium field, her arms crossed over her chest. She wasn't in scrubs today which had him scrambling to remember if she'd told him today was her day off.

He shrugged. "I had high hopes that you'd break your visiting fast someday. And here you are looking fresh and gorgeous as ever." He stood and placed his hands on her hips, bringing his lips to hers. Her fresh-aired scent and the softness of her skin beneath his fingertips was blissfully familiar, a treat on a mentally taxing day like today.

A big meeting! That's what she had.

"How did your meeting go with board members?" He pulled her onto his lap as he settled into his comfortable chair.

In the Shadows

She sighed and dropped her head against his. "Jury's still out. The statistics I've put together aren't convincing them. I don't know how they can ignore the data. They live and die by 'the numbers.' How is it meaningless to them at such a critical time?"

"What's our next step in exposing this?" Involving Katrina and her brainstorming team might very well be the answer they needed. Frontline doctors weren't given the resources that *futbol* organization presidents were.

Her warm brown eyes held his. "I love that you're in this with me. You're trying to fix it and I love you for it. Never has a man treated my problems as his, and I wonder now if it's because the men I chose were never emotionally mature."

They laughed together. Her thoughts amused and flattered him. Serious relationships weren't something he'd done in the past. On many levels, he questioned whether his actions and reactions were normal for relationships such as theirs. But then he decided he didn't care as long as she didn't care that theirs might be an unconventional love.

"If one part of you is suffering, it affects all of you, which in turn affects how quickly I need to don my superhero cape." He ran his fingers down her arms. "Your pleasure and pain are my weaknesses."

She leaned in and showed him just how much of a weakness he had for her.

As he kissed the spot behind her jaw, he murmured, "Come with me to dinner tonight."

"I'd be honored." She planted another kiss on his lips and stood, straightening her clothes and smoothing her hair.

She was the most stunning woman he'd ever seen. How had he gotten so lucky?

As a professional *futbol* player, there had been no shortage of beautiful and enamored (yet vapid) females, but none with her grace and character. He glanced at the clock. It was midafternoon and he had plenty of work to do, but he was the boss and tonight's date was going to be one for the books.

Ronaldo grabbed her hand and walked her to her car. After she ducked in, he leaned in for a last kiss. "Dinner will be fancy, but bring a jacket and walking shoes for afterwards."

Isadora's eyes glittered. "Can't wait."

"I'll pick you up at 7:30."

And at 7:29, he stood outside her door peering at his watch, waiting for the second hand to give him permission to knock. When the hand rocked into place, he rapped on the door and stepped back.

Everything was in place for tonight. Tonight, he'd make his intentions for the future clear and hope she felt the same way.

The door opened to reveal Isadora's slim figure giving an incredible shape to a forest green cocktail dress. The rich color highlighted her gorgeous skin and perfectly coiffed hair in one breathtaking sight. His hand rested against his breastbone as a reminder for his heart to continue beating and his lungs to fill with air.

Yes, tonight would be one worth remembering.

She draped her shawl around her shoulders and secured the door's lock behind her. Her warm hand gripped his arm just above his elbow as they stepped down her stairs. She smelled of flowers and mint.

Her presence incited the ferocity of his need to protect her, to see her smile and hear her laugh, to know she was happy. Being with her put his deep inner self at peace, a feeling he'd never felt with anyone else. He closed them into the town car, and the driver took off.

They stopped a few blocks from their dinner location.

"Are your shoes appropriate for a short leisurely walk?" he asked, eyeing her heels.

Isadora smirked. "Leisurely, I am always game for."

In the Shadows

He nodded to the driver and received a subtle thumbs-up in return. They first ducked into a small bakery to enjoy a shared *brigadeiro*— those exquisite chocolate truffles—and a passion fruit mousse. Dessert needed to precede the meal, because if the evening took a sharp turn, they would otherwise have to cut out the sweet part of their culinary experience.

His goal was to delight her at every turn this evening. Keeping her off balance allowed him the upper hand. which was just what he needed if he was going to pull off what he had planned.

"My *vovó* adored *brigadeiros*. She'd make two or three dozen at one time so she could hide a batch, freeze a portion, and still have plenty to eat. And when her sweet tooth took over her whole mouth before she died, there was no telling how many she ate every day." Isadora's warm laugh washed over him like the sea breeze. "I miss her fiercely."

An overpowering sensation burgeoned in his chest. Isadora would without a doubt become feistier as she aged. He could feel it in his bones. The question, though, was would he be the one sneaking chocolates with her when they banished the buttons and zippers in favor of elastic waistbands and overstuffed recliners?

Her thumb rubbed across the back of his hand as she peered into his eyes, her mouth turned down in a concerned frown. "Did that conjure up some bad memories?"

Ronaldo laughed. "I only wish I could have known more of your family."

She waved him off as she leaned back in her chair. "You'd see the same patterns of insanity on repeat throughout each of my brothers. And then you'd get to my mama and understand the origin."

"My sister would have said the same thing to you, if she were here." His words sounded rueful even to his own ears, but Isadora gave him no look of pity. "But seeing your mama would have given me insight into your future."

Isadora leaned in close, her eyes flashing with heat. "Then, there'd be nothing for you to discover on your own."

Her words made his breath catch in his chest. "I have a long way to go before I have discovered everything I want to know about you, *meu amor*." When he sneaked a peek at her reaction, her look of contented happiness gave him reassurance that she wasn't objecting to his pursuit of knowing her fully. He tucked her hand under his arm and stood.

Their next reservation awaited.

They sauntered down the path and across a few busy roads to end up at the front door where his favorite highly acclaimed chef ruled the kitchen.

Isadora raised her eyebrows, stepping aside as an attendant opened the front door for them. "Of course, Ronaldo Cevere has a way to get reservations at O Figo Gordo."

His wink was her only answer. The aroma inside short-circuited his brain for a minute as he inhaled deeply. The host bowed with a murmured welcome and stepped to their side. "Welcome. Please follow me, Senhor Cevere."

The host led them toward the back and slowed briefly when the space opened enough to allow Ronaldo to offer Isadora his arm again. He'd worked this out with the host beforehand as he wanted to be able to see her face for the next part.

They continued past the tables towards the back hall. Isadora's eyes widened when they pushed through the door into the kitchen. The staff buzzed around, executing their tasks with the precision of their five-star establishment. Still the host led them on and stopped at two chairs in the corner near where the head chef worked.

"Is this legal?" Isadora murmured into his ear.

He shrugged. "We have to wash the dishes after this, but it'll be worth it."

To his relief, she laughed with delight. Immediately, place settings appeared. And the meal began. The head chef talked them

In the Shadows

through each course, its paired drink, and quizzed them on the subtle flavors. Each perfectly plated dish was a few bites or less, but by the time they were finished they were full.

They walked into the late evening laughing at the kitchen antics. Ronaldo's driver waited for them in front of the restaurant to whisk them away to the final destination of the evening. He nodded at the driver who nodded back. Everything was in place.

They drove forty minutes outside the city to the base of Corcovado Mountain to Parque Lage.

"Here's the part where we slip on our jackets and you wear your flats." He flicked on the interior light as the driver came to a stop. She shrugged on her jacket as he opened her door. He patted his pockets to check one final time. Still there.

The ground lighting illuminated the paths in the dark surrounding them. A representative from Lage's mansion met them at the entrance.

"*Senhor* Cevere and *Senhorita* Rey, welcome to Parque Lage. The grounds are yours to explore tonight. We have refreshments waiting for you by the pool for when you are ready to relax."

Ronaldo heard the hitch in Isadora's breath as they rounded the bend in the path to get the full view of the mansion at night. Above it, Christ the Redeemer stood way in the distance with powerful lights spotlighting His open arms.

"Ronaldo, tonight has been so perfect. How many favors did you have to call in to do all this?" She giggled and snuggled in closer to him.

He kissed her forehead as they stopped by the fountain. "One or two. You are an experienced lady. You have seen many things and been so many places. Every day you care for others in the most extraordinary way. It is time for you to be taken care of."

They wandered around the outside of the mansion taking in the sweet smells of the flowers mixed with the intoxicating scent of cool night air. Tree-lined paths disappeared into the dark.

"This reminds me of the peace I felt the night before Mariana died. Everything felt in place. The world was right," Ronaldo said.

Isadora squeezed his hand. "It's terrifying, you know? Feeling the peace and knowing the storms, whatever they may be, are coming. Will they take your breath away? Or will they puncture a lung and leave you to suffocate?"

Ronaldo nodded. He had fallen to the earth gasping for air, but taking in none until the despair smothered him. A fish out of water flopping along, hoping to squirm back into the water. He could breathe again, now. But he'd never forget the crushing weight of grief.

"I felt it when my very first patient died in my care. The inability to save him was incomprehensible. I'd gone to school to get answers so they could live. And here he was unable to be saved." She stopped at a huge rose bush. Her fingers cupped a bloom. "They couldn't show off more perfectly."

He led them, at last, up the stairs lined with palms. "I suppose it's not romantic, but you have the strength of these palm trees. When the hurricane comes, they only bend. Never break. That is you." They paused under the first arch and looked out over the grounds. He kissed her tenderly. Yes, this was right.

The final flight of stairs led them into the pool area. Carved pillars supported arched walkways surrounding the pool. Small white lights dangled over the pool, their reflection glittering in the night. A cushion sat on the edge with a tray of chocolates and drinks set up, once more.

"Oh, Ronaldo. It's gorgeous." They settled onto the cushion, sipping their drinks.

"Isadora, I've hardly been able to see anything else tonight besides your joy and fervor for life. You are the reason I look forward to every day." He pulled her hand to his lips and kissed her knuckles. "I want you to be my tomorrow. Isadora, will you marry me?"

In the Shadows

Isadora's face transformed before his eyes. Her smile glowed brighter than the stadium lights at night. "Ronaldo, my charming *amado*. I would love to be your tomorrow. Yes."

He kissed her soundly before pulling the ring from his pocket. Her shock at the sight of the ring. "I walked past this piece and knew immediately that yours was the only hand it belonged on."

She slid it onto her finger with a huge smile. "Ronaldo, this is stunning. Truly, but I can't wear this to the clinic. It'd vanish before mid-morning."

Ronaldo chuckled. "We can find you a something that you like to wear to work, if you'd like. Just so long as everyone knows you're mine."

Her eyes narrowed as she moved into kiss him once more. "Oh, they'll know."

The weight and depth of her kiss carried him through to the next morning, as he accomplished his morning routine out of sheer habit. His thoughts floated hopelessly over last night's date. She'd said yes. She wanted to marry him.

Isadora Rey wanted to marry a man like Ronaldo Cevere. He laughed out loud. She was so far out of his league that it surprised him, yet it fit like a comfortable shoe. His lonely nights were numbered. It was all he'd ever known, but they didn't have any appeal compared to coming home to Isadora every night. For her, he'd happily change his set ways.

On his way to the office, he picked up his usual paper and tucked it under his arm. He was too distracted to read while he walked today. Instead, he dropped a few *reals* into the homeless man's cup, proud of himself for having changed his routine so successfully already.

Just to prove that he was a man of adjustment, he decided to take the elevator instead of walking the stairs to his office. While he waited for the car to finally descend, he snapped his paper up to browse the headlines.

There on the front page was Ronaldo's face, a picture of his apartment building complete with its new art, and his address for all of Rio de Janeiro to read. The floating feeling dropped with the two-ton rock into his stomach. His days of relative incognito were over.

When the elevator opened, Katrina met him at the door. Her usual collected look was already askew.

"We need damage control quickly. I'll call my town car to take me home. I've got to move out immediately."

"The moving company is already on its way your place, Senhor. They'll be at your house in an hour. I hoped that wasn't too presumptuous." She wrung her hands as she walked beside him.

"I'll meet them there. Thank you, Katrina. You're a life-saver. I'll be giving you a bonus when I get back to the office."

Chapter 17

As Daniela laced up her cleats and pulled on her shin guards, she shoved the embarrassment with Mac out of her mind. Again. As she had every day for the past week. Her skin wouldn't recall how soft the skin on his strong hand felt in hers. She wouldn't suck in air hoping to scent traces of his intoxicating cologne. This turf, this field in front of her was all that existed right now.

Being a warrior, a *Guerreira,* felt surreal. Davi's promise of a new life all that time ago had been a seed floating on air, rainwashed into a crack in the concrete to make its home.

Unexpected.

Out of place.

Sprouting recklessly.

Even though they had a couple of years before Coach Rocha would consider her for the national team, Davi doubled down, determined to come up with money for her to go to the Olympic Training Center. They'd never made even close to a third of what was being asked. Truth be told, her chest ached when she thought of missing the chance, but the cost was impossible.

She'd never tell Davi that. Water pooled in his eyes—Davi who never cried—when she'd told him they'd selected her to be on the short list for the training center. Over and over again, he whispered to her how proud he was and how much she deserved

In the Shadows

to find a future doing what she loved. Cambridge, too, gave her a firm hug, his expression pleased.

But did she love it because it wasn't survival? Because it wasn't endless work?

The fear of her dream being a mirage never strayed far from her mind. Perhaps Coach Rocha didn't know her background. Most people despised them for their poverty. For once, her ability on the field gave her equal standing with the girls around her. It was an intoxicating feeling, a high she didn't want to lose.

The whistle blew, yanking her from her brooding. She couldn't afford to be distracted today or any day. She had to prove to everyone that she deserved to be here before they realized she didn't belong.

Coach Cevere and his assistants ran them hard. They had to be in shape. Some of the other cities' teams they would be playing soon had been together for years. This mix of girls from every walk of life had a lot of catching up to do.

When practice was over, they were dripping with sweat. Coach Cevere was in an unrelenting mood today and didn't mind making them work. She'd take sweating from *futbol* over sweating from the heat on the trash mounds any day though.

For the first time in her life, she enjoyed and anticipated time with other girls her age. Her friendship with her teammates began to blossom as Coach insisted on them rotating drill partners each day. There would be no cattiness in their rivalry, but a joint pursuit of excellence as was fitting for professionals, he reminded them daily.

She'd already been paired with Valiana the mom, Andressa the strong, Pedrina the trapper, Noemia the boot, Lecia the cheerleader, and Gilma the wall (who was also the goalkeeper). Today she partnered with Aline, the fastest girl on the team. Aline was so fluid and exact in her movements Daniela forgot herself for wanting to watch.

Aline, too, came from the *favelas,* and was working hard to learn how to keep the balls she so easily chased down. The ball often went too far in front of her to give herself room to run which was okay for a drill, but meant a turnover in a game with opponents. In the Teach Me Something New time, Daniela showed her a quick tap with the outside of her cleat which kept the ball close without hurting her foot since they now wore shoes to play. Aline gave her a tip on running smaller so her form didn't meet so much resistance.

They put their new skills to practice in the scrimmage and saw a huge change. Everyone noticed Aline's handling skills improving immediately. They laughed together as they walked over to the sidelines to grab their things and head to the showers before starting school.

An assistant coach jogged over to her. "Daniela, Coach Cevere wants to meet you in the manager's office. I'm supposed to take you now."

"Did he say what the meeting was about?" Prickles spread across her skin.

"No, but he didn't look happy when he gave the orders."

Daniela toweled off and reworked her ponytail. There wasn't much she could do to look better without a shower. She trailed the coach through the tunnel to an alcove with three doors in it. Was he going to kick her out because she wasn't following the team's nutrition guidelines? She didn't have the money to have six servings of green vegetables a day and she honestly didn't know what a lean meat was. Maybe he'd found out about her mother doing drugs and thought Daniela might have done them, too. Or had he been told about the party and someone told him she'd been drinking when she hadn't been?

Her chest felt too tight for a breath. Nausea knocked into her. She was about to lose everything. She could feel it.

The assistant coach knocked on the manager's door and cracked it open. "Daniela, Senhor."

In the Shadows

"Yes, come on in, Daniela. Have a seat." Coach Cevere stood, motioning her in to the office. A man and a woman sat in the other chairs, leaving two open chairs next to the woman.

She perched on the edge of a metal chair closest to the woman, so as not to be rude. The man had white skin, dark hair, and straight teeth like a toothpaste billboard. He spoke quickly in what sounded like English and Coach Cevere answered. When they laughed, panic snaked through her. Once again, she was the odd one out.

"Thank you for coming, Daniela. Coach Cevere has told us so much about you," the woman said gently in Portuguese. She had a slight accent, but her warm tone immediately set Daniela at ease.

"Daniela, this is Gia Carter and Xander Reinerman. I told them all about your situation and they wanted to meet you and your brother in person. Xander doesn't speak Portuguese, so Gia and I are going to be translating for him so he can keep up with our conversation."

She nodded. "I don't know much about what Cambridge and Davi are doing with the other *catadores*, Coach. I won't be much help."

Gia smiled. "We wanted to hear your story and talk to you about *futbol*, if that's okay. Can you tell us about how you grew up and how you came to the tryouts for the camp?"

This she did know about, but if they found out how poor she really was they'd want her gone immediately. "It's not a very interesting story. I grew up not far from here. I've been working with my brother for a few years now. He saw the posters for the tryouts and wanted me to go. So I did. I'm very lucky to be here."

Coach Cevere translated quietly to Xander and then paused. "Daniela, you are safe here. These are friends. They want to see you succeed, and to help you do that they need to know where you came from. Will you share from your heart?"

Everything inside her screamed no. It wasn't safe. Davi would definitely tell her not to. Explaining her life to outsiders was not normal. It didn't feel right. Her eyes scanned Coach's face, full of sincerity. Gia smiled and even Xander looked kind as they watched her.

How badly would this hurt?

Against her discomfort, Daniela started her story, pausing on occasion to let Coach Cevere finish translating as she gathered her thoughts. Stories about her parents, Davi, her work, Gabi's kindness, the new laws and their thoughts on how to survive flowed more easily than she imagined. When she mentioned Davi and Cambridge's ideas for selling things, Xander inhaled sharply. Not once did Gia look away, her attention rapt.

She let the silence swirl around them as she examined their reactions. Coach Cevere nodded for her to continue. "After the week of soccer camp, Coach Rocha kindly invited me to the Olympic Training Center to train since I am too young to be considered for the national team."

"And will you go?" Gia asked.

Daniela stared at her hands. "I've told you my past. Our kind doesn't make that much money in two lifetimes. Even with our new efforts, we could work for years and never see half that. I can't take that survival money and waste it on a wish. It isn't fair or right. This team, for as long as it lasts, will be where my *futbol* dream ends."

Her throat tightened.

Xander spoke and Coach Cevere agreed.

"Xander wants to tell you his story as I translate," Coach Cevere said.

Xander began to weave his tale of being a *futbol* coach, being wrongfully accused of giving his players steroids, and then spending five years in prison. He met Gia who helped him build a life that he loved, one where they paid it forward.

"We watched you play, Daniela. You are extremely talented. Not having the means to afford training is a roadblock for your future that we can help you overcome. Gia's parents and other

In the Shadows

generous Brazilian companies have donated to our nonprofit that is structured to help people have a chance at their dreams. We want to pay your way to the Olympic Training Center."

A knock interrupted his words. Pay her way? The idea swirled around in Daniela's mind as they answered the door. At what price? They'd just give it to her? She could go to the training center and actually try to become a professional?

Davi walked into the room. His eyes widened. "What's wrong?" Turning on his heel, he stood inches from Coach Cevere's face, his stance aggressive. "Why is she crying? What happened?"

Daniela hadn't felt the tears slipping down her cheeks. They were the culmination of her relief, joy, grief, and excitement. Somehow Coach Cevere's murmured words had Davi sitting in the chair next to Daniela, holding her hand.

"Tell me." He squeezed her hand.

She swallowed back the lump in her throat. "They want me to go to the Olympic Training Center." The others nodded as she spoke.

"I do, too, Daniela. We're working towards that." Davi inched closer.

"No, Davi. They want to pay my way there so we don't have to."

The understanding dawned in his eyes. His conflicting emotions scrolled across his face and she felt each one of them. He'd been the one to believe when she didn't think there was prayer to be said for it.

"Davi, we brought you here today because we wanted to talk to you, too. We run a business that sells products much like you and Cambridge have just started making." Xander turned on a small screen where pictures of all kinds of items appeared. "We take materials that would normally be dumped in a landfill and give them a second life as you are doing. I want to talk to you about selling your products internationally."

Now it was Davi's turn to be speechless, to stare blankly at the room. Then he laughed so long and hard that he couldn't catch his breath.

"I'm sorry." Davi held a hand to his chest. "I'm having such a hard time believing this is real. You don't know us, but you want to give Daniela free money to play *futbol*. Nothing in return. And you want to sell my products that you've never seen to people around the world who also have never seen them." He turned to Daniela. "This is real?"

Daniela shrugged and nodded.

Gia scooted her chair forward. "Davi, I know it seems unimaginable, but Xander and I are staying with my extended family here in Rio, so we could spend time developing the reach of our international nonprofits. Others have helped us when we had nothing and we want to do that for someone in need. You don't have to agree to any of it, but if you'd like to do business, we want to be the ones you do it with. I spent my summers playing with kids and cousins near here. Brazil is a second home to me. It would mean so much if we could support your entrepreneurial dreams."

Xander grabbed Gia's hand and smiled. "We can work out the details, Davi. We just want to talk over the business opportunities with you if you're interested."

He nodded. "I am interested. I'm stunned, too."

They laughed.

Coach Cevere spoke up. "Xander and Gia, you work out the details with Davi. I'm going to walk Daniela back to the locker room so she can get changed. I'll explain what you have in mind, then we'll all reconvene for dinner."

They pulled out a pad of paper for Davi and began to answer Davi's questions before Daniela left the room.

"What do you think, Daniela?" Coach Cevere said in a quiet tone so the tunnels didn't echo with his voice.

In the Shadows

She glanced at his face, the kindness it wore unobscured. "It'd be like living someone else's life, Coach Cevere. What you have done for me, I will never be able to repay."

"The time will come, Daniela, when you are in a place to do good for someone in need. That is when you can repay me by doing good in that person's life."

"I will. I'll make sure of it."

"You'll find the Training Center is a different world than this place. The standards are very high. You eat, sleep, and breathe *futbol*. Every exercise is tailored to maximize your impact on the field. Every drill focuses on honing your eye and sharpening your reflexes. A lost ball on a bad judgment call could lose you the World Cup or an Olympic medal. The stakes are the highest they will ever be, because the world is watching."

Daniela stopped outside the locker room and looked Coach Cevere in the eyes. "Do you think I'll actually make it that far?"

Coach Cevere's forehead creased as he lifted a finger. "Make no mistake, Daniela. You'll make it. Not only that, you have the potential to be the best Brazil's team has ever seen. Dig to the deepest part of your mind and heart where the game is actually played and don't stop until you are among the best in the world."

He patted her on the shoulder, leaving her standing slack-jawed outside the locker room door.

She went through the motions of cleaning up and preparing for dinner. Her mind kept replaying Coach Cevere's words. His faith in her was stunning. She didn't see much of anything that was special in her. How did he see 'the potential to be the best Brazil's team has ever seen'?

Outside the locker room, Gia waited against the wall. When Daniela walked toward her, she motioned toward the tunnel that led to the field. Gia gave off a faint whiff of something wonderful and flowery. Her beauty and poise were intimidating.

"I wanted to explain what all The Upcycled Life wants to do for you before you make your decision on whether to accept." Gia twirled in a circle on the stadium field. "Playing for a packed stadium must be the biggest rush."

Daniela smiled. She'd thought the same thing.

Gia sucked in a huge breath of air and let out a yell. It echoed through the stadium. Would that echo say her name in the future?

"Anyway, we want to cover rooming, food, as well as supplies and some spending money for a year. In a year's time, you'll be sixteen?"

"A month from seventeen."

"And Ronaldo says teams will be fighting for the chance to get you on their rosters. That's when we'll talk about a sponsorship with Invicta, the athleticwear company." Gia pulled out a list of required items the Training Center wanted. "You and I can go shopping for everything on this list over the next few days and we'll pay for your transportation to and from the center. I'll be your contact person since I'm here in Rio for the foreseeable future. If you need anything, and I mean anything, you call me."

Daniela glanced over the list. A mobile phone, clothes, a host of items she'd never heard of, a computer. She swallowed. "Gia, this is a lot to pay for. I—"

Gia grinned. "And that list isn't everything that you'll take. Xander and I are serious about setting you and Davi up for success. We want to invest in you. More importantly, Brazilian companies are jumping at the chance to sponsor women's *futbol* and young entrepreneurs. They want to be on the right side of history."

Her stomach ached in a mix of anxiety and excitement. This could be it. Gia and Xander really could be their ticket out of barely surviving each day. Just for today, she allowed herself to believe it, to see it, to want it so much she could taste it. Because tomorrow's reality didn't always match today's good fortune, but as Cambridge reminded her—the best time for worry was always tomorrow.

Chapter 18

With the moving company's help, Ronaldo had his place boxed and in a truck in less than two hours. The majority of one of the hours had been dedicated to navigating the seven flights of narrow stairs with heavy boxes and his bed. The rest he left for the next tenant. After loading his things into a storage unit, his town car drove him and his suitcase to a place he hadn't been in far too long.

His knuckles rapped on a door he'd almost forgotten. Locks snapped and the door opened.

"Hi, Mama." Ronaldo leaned in to kiss her weathered cheek. The dress hanging on her thin frame pictured faded flowers that used to be bold and bright. A grin lifted her whole face. The foggy-eyed growling mop under her arm bared its tiny teeth.

"Ronnie, my boy. Welcome home. Leondardo, look who came for a visit." She shuffled back as Papa came around the corner.

They embraced with a laugh. Papa patted him on the shoulder. "I saw your face on the newspaper this morning. Thought my old eyes conjured up your image."

Ronaldo ran his hands through his hair. "That's why I'm here. The media has no moral boundaries anymore. My address was sent out to the world. We had to organize a security detail for the

In the Shadows

building to make sure none of the tenants get harassed on my account. Lenz had an avid following that didn't like his corruption being exposed."

Mama reappeared in the family room with a tray of tea and cookies. They were finally using their fine china. "Stay as long as you need. Your room is ready and we miss the noise of having company these days."

Papa sat with a huff into his overstuffed recliner, the television droning on in the background. Mama liked watching the day drama reruns. They were like old friends, she said.

They sat in companionable silence. Would this be what he and Isadora did at this age? "I'm engaged."

Mama's teacup clattered on to the saucer. "Ronaldo Felipe Rafael Cevere, it's about time you found a girl. For too long grief has spoiled your heart for love. Loving deeply doesn't always leave you in pieces, *amorzinho*."

He was starting to believe that. "I will bring her for dinner one night while I am staying here so she can meet you."

"Does she have a name? Leondardo uses his mobile phone to spy on all sorts of people these days."

Papa grunted from his chair. "It's not spying. It's research." When Mama wasn't looking, he winked at Ronaldo. They'd talk about *that* later over a drink.

"Isadora Rey. She's a gorgeous, kind-hearted, award-winning doctor. Far out of my league."

"You're a good-looking man, Ronaldo." Mama reached over and patted his cheek. "You've taken care of yourself. Women like that in men. Look at my prize. He gets out and walks this stubborn nightmare of a creature each morning to keep his and the dog's limbs functioning."

Ronaldo made the mistake of making eye contact with The Stubborn Nightmare, making it rumble again. He pushed to his feet. "I need to get back to the office to find out what other messes

Lenz has made. I'll set my suitcase in the room and call Papa's phone to let you know I'm on my way back this evening."

Papa waved him off. "Don't call. Send me one of those short messages. I can read just fine."

Back at the office, Ronaldo abandoned his attempt at embracing change in favor of using the exercise to clear his mind on the way up.

Katrina jumped up from her desk and met him in his office. "The security detail you put on your apartment building already stopped thirteen people from entering the building that had no business being there."

"And it's not even noon yet." Ronaldo shot off a text to Isadora explaining that he'd be staying at his parents for a bit while things settled down. "Any collateral?"

Katrina shook her head. "Not that we've picked up yet, but we've had a huge number of extra hits and donations for our girls' leagues."

"That's perfect. Let's see if we can twist this in our favor. I'm sure news outlets will be asking for comments from us."

"They are," Katrina murmured, her head bent as she scribbled on a notepad.

"Also, let's find a family to live rent-free in the apartment I just vacated. We could get an at-risk family to safety. Isadora would be a perfect resource for this." He tapped his pen. "You know, I met a family at the clinic recently. A mother with three children whose names are Taynara, Quim, and Eliana. Can you contact the clinic to see if we can get information on them? The mother says she works and leaves her nine-year-old to babysit. Let's see if they'd be interested in a safer environment. If not, let's compile a list of possibilities."

"Great idea. What would you like your statement about Lenz releasing your address to the world to say? It's free press."

"No such thing as bad publicity, right? Say nothing about Lenz and his scandal. We'll not stoop to his level. Highlight the

In the Shadows

girls' leagues again and mention the free schooling for the poverty-level players thanks to donations. This could bring us more options for players and give organizations a glimpse at what we do with their donations."

"We are five million shy of hitting our twenty million *real* goal. A few more foreign donations would seal that up nicely."

"My cousin's daughter and boyfriend and their team are staying here with family for a bit. I'll see if they can send out information to their contacts."

After *Guerreiras* practice, Ronaldo sat down with Xander and Gia in his office to work out the logistics of The Upcycled Life International being an official sponsor of his new league.

"So you have eight existing teams registered for the league so far with the potential of forming more teams in the coming years if you keep running the camps in the *favelas* each year?" Gia asked, typing notes into her tablet.

Xander cleared his throat. "Do you need coaches for these teams?"

Gia's eyebrows raised, but she didn't look up from her tablet.

Ronaldo hid his smile behind his hand that he rubbed across his chin. She was so much like Sophia. "Yes, but these coaches would be seasonally paid at first, so I doubt it'd really attract talent."

Xander shifted in his chair. "Could you offer university credit for sports majors in nearby universities to coach the teams? Eventually, if you generated enough income, you could hire full-time coaches that were responsible for overseeing the girls' education and connecting their families with community resources to get the jobs and health care and safe housing. You'd be creating jobs and helping break the poverty cycle."

"That's going to require an enormous amount of capital, Xander, and could take years to implement," Gia said.

Ronaldo nodded. "I think it should be in our long-term plans though. *Futbol* is a means to an end. We're setting these girls up to live a life they wouldn't be able to otherwise. They may not continue past our league, but the best ones will feed talent to the national team."

"Maybe once Gia and I get things established here for our nonprofits we can come down here for *futbol* season and take over one of the teams." Xander cast a hopeful glance at Gia. "I'd love to coach again."

Gia nodded. "We'll get back to you on that one, Uncle Ronaldo. So what can Invicta do to get this league on its way?"

Ronaldo checked his list. "For now, game jerseys in the teams' chosen colors. Some of the teams may already have sponsors, but for the ones who don't we'll need jerseys: shirts, shorts, socks. We'll create banners for all our sponsors to be on the sidelines for all our games."

"I'll have an Invicta representative contact Katrina with size order forms and charts."

The list's length overwhelmed Ronaldo. Solidify names, assign colors, ensure all teams are properly equipped, and on the list went. Most of it his team would handle. Anything that didn't happen would of course blow back on him and his enemies would be waiting to strike.

It was six-thirty when his stomach ached enough for him to glance at the clock. He called his town car and packed his briefcase. The oddity hit him that he didn't need to change into his street clothes to walk home tonight. He'd walked to his cozy apartment for the final time last night and didn't know he'd never again follow the routine he loved so much. He'd counted on change, but not like this.

In the main office area, Katrina sat at her desk with her gaze on her computer. Tears ran down her cheeks as she sniffled. He froze.

"Why are you here so late, Katrina?"

In the Shadows

She swiped at her cheeks. "Oh, I had a few things to finish up before heading home. Donations just surpassed twenty million. We're fully funded!" Her hands raised in celebration.

"That's incredible news." Ronaldo grinned. He'd let her think her tears had gone unnoticed for now. "Do you have dinner plans? Let's go celebrate!"

Katrina grabbed her things. "I'll meet you in the lobby. I need to stop in the restroom."

Ronaldo took the stairs and sent a text to Papa's phone about his plans. Surreal. It'd been almost thirty years since he'd felt he needed to keep his parents apprised of his plans. Katrina exited the elevator as the town car pulled up to the curb.

"Any preference?" he asked Katrina. When she shook her head, he mentioned a new casual restaurant he'd been meaning to try for a while.

They managed to snag a table next to the window to people-watch. When they'd placed their orders, Ronaldo waded in.

"I noticed your tears at your desk. Is work overwhelming you? If there's too much for you to handle, we can spread out the work load. I can move forward our plan to hire someone to take over the girls' league administration."

Katrina gave him a weak smile. "It's not work, but I agree that we may need to hire someone soon since we are fully funded and can implement the plans we put into place." She drew a shaky breath, her fingers toying with the silverware. "My boyfriend received his dream fellowship offer for next year. He'll be participating in an anthropological study in the heart of the rainforest. An incredible opportunity for him." She sounded as if she truly believed that. "It means limited contact with me which would be manageable, but he asked me to marry him now instead of us planning for a big wedding next year. I would have full custody of his son while he's gone. And I'm grateful for the chance to be a family but also I'm really overwhelmed at being a new mom and wife without him around to help me adjust."

C.D. Gill

Ronaldo waited to see if there was more. Here was life reminding him once again that he really never knew what someone was going through at any given moment no matter how much he thought he knew about them. When she didn't continue, he jumped in. "First of all, congratulations. That is a huge step. Second of all, how can I support you best?"

Katrina sat back in her chair. "Well, we'd be honored if you and Isadora came to the wedding whenever it is." She laughed. "I guess I need to know if I'm going to lose my job when I become a solo parent and have to do parent things. Please be completely honest with me."

He let out the breath he'd been holding. She didn't quit. Relief flooded him. "That's a very simple answer. No, you will not lose your job. Becoming a parent will not affect your employability whatsoever. It will change your availability to the job so we may need to start looking at restructuring your team so you're able to delegate when you need to be home with a sick child. What's his name?"

Her smile lit up her face. She obviously loved him a lot. "Zico. He's two and a half."

Ronaldo pulled out his phone and made a himself a note. "We'll get you a laptop, phone, and secure remote access to the files you need."

Katrina's hand landed on his arm. He glanced up in surprise. Tears streamed down her cheeks. "I can't thank you enough, Senhor. You're in the middle of a personal upheaval and you're helping me. I'm incredibly grateful."

He patted her hand in an attempt to dislodge her touch which felt far too intimate for his comfort. The harmless touching of anyone made him feel uncomfortable. Perhaps it was time to change that. "Do me a favor and spread the word that people who work with us do not need to be afraid for their job if they happen to experience a big life change. Work is part of life. Work is not

In the Shadows

the entirety of life. If Lenz gave that impression, we're changing that right now."

They finished their dinner and he dropped Katrina off at her home. He sank back into his town car seat as his driver navigated to his parents' house. Was he doing enough? It never felt like it.

How many other women in his office felt they couldn't have a job and a family in the same lifetime?

That fear stopped tomorrow.

He'd worked so hard to position himself for this moment, his hour in power. But now that he was here, he didn't know what other gross oversights sat lurking in the shadows of his blind spots.

His first night sleeping at his parents went surprisingly well considering he much preferred his mattress and sheets to others. He grabbed a simple breakfast and called his town car. Mama smirked as he kissed her cheek and patted Papa's shoulder on his way out the door. The company in the morning was refreshing actually.

His incredibly insightful driver had his favorite morning paper sitting on his seat waiting for him when he got in. "So thoughtful. Thank you, Alfonso."

The drive in to the office took long enough that he had time to read his paper and see new scenery along the way. A familiar face waited for him at the guard's desk in the lobby.

"We need to talk." A gorgeous and apparently furious face. Isadora's voice was low and her words clipped.

Dread flooded his chest in a tidal wave that he had not experience in a very long time. "Of course. Let's go to my office." He nodded at the security guard and placed his hand on Isadora's elbow, moving with her to the elevator. The negative energy rolled off her in waves. "I thought you'd be opening the clinic early this morning."

"I called in for a delayed start, so I could see you."

Uh oh. He barely remembered how they got to his office, but he gently closed his door behind him. "Say whatever you need to, but please don't raise your voice in my office."

Her curt nod was his only answer as she tapped at her phone. She turned it around to show him. "What am I looking at here, Ronaldo?"

There on her screen was a picture of Katrina sitting across from him last night with her hand on his arm and his hand on top of hers as he smiled at her. The title read "Is FCC President Bedding his Barely Legal Assistant?"

Oh no. He swallowed hard. "I wonder how much the paparazzi made on that picture with that title. That looks very bad and I imagine it looks like betrayal to you. It's not."

She raised her eyebrows, but said nothing. Ronaldo stepped toward her, gauging her tolerance. His body had no problems anticipating her touch.

"On my way out of the office, I saw Katrina crying at her desk. She tried to cover it up by telling me we hit our donation goal. So I took her to dinner to cheer her up under the pretense of celebrating. Her boyfriend wants to get married and then take a fellowship for a year while she raises his kid by herself. And she was worried—no, terrified—about the life changes and whether or not I would kick her to the curb for becoming a parent." He shook his head in his lingering disbelief. Isadora's expression was slightly less furious, but hadn't relented its hardness yet. She could be very scary. "I reassured her that she would not be fired because she was getting married and having a family." His hand ruffled his hair to distract her from the next step he took toward her. "And that we would do everything in our power to make sure she had what she needed to succeed in her job as her home life changed. Today, I'm going to make sure all the women in the organization know their jobs are not in jeopardy for wanting—" He inched toward her, craving the feel of her relaxing into his embrace. "the most precious gift life could offer—a family."

In the Shadows

As he reached for her, she spun toward his door. "I want to hear it from Katrina." She walked out the door and reappeared with an alarmed-looking Katrina in tow. "Katrina, please explain to me what happened after you left this office last night."

"Oh," She laughed. "I thought I might be in trouble. Senhor Cevere and I went to dinner to celebrate reaching our donation goal."

Isadora waited a moment. She raised her phone to Katrina's eye level. "What was happening in this moment, specifically?"

Katrina gasped, her eyes widening. "Doctor Rey, I was thanking Senhor for—well, for not firing me when he heard about my upcoming life upheavals. It was nothing more than overwhelming gratitude that I realize now I should not have done. I'm very sorry, Senhor. You are my boss and despite my gratitude, touching was extremely inappropriate." She rubbed her temples. "The last thing this office needs is more scandal. Doctor Rey, please forgive me."

Ronaldo and Isadora insisted they forgave her and sent her on her way. When she closed the door, Isadora whirled around, melding her body to his.

"Marry me," she said into his chest.

The tension in his muscles disappeared as he rubbed her back. "Of course, *paixão*. Your questions didn't threaten my deep love for you. It didn't change our bond."

She stepped back with his hands in hers and stood up straight. "No, today. Come with me to register our intent and file all the paperwork. When everything goes through, I will have my minister on call to marry us."

His brow furrowed as he struggled to read the situation. "I am truly very excited to marry you and I can tell you're serious about this idea." That part was a guess. "Tell me more about why you feel this way."

Isadora dropped his hands. "It's silly to wait, Ronaldo. We're grown adults. I wake up every morning and wonder what you're doing. In the evening, I come home to an empty place wishing instead I was with you. I'm tired of wondering and wishing, Ronaldo." The longing in her deep brown eyes stunned him, yet it matched the feeling in his chest intimately. "I have never known you to rush one thing in your life. Even on the field, you calculated every move and every decision. You must be ready to marry me since you asked me."

All of that was very true. He'd had no doubts about her for a long time. If anything, he should have been rushing her to the altar, so she wouldn't have time to change her mind. He pulled her back into his arms.

"My lunch hour is from noon to one. Can we fit it in then?" He laughed as she smacked his backside in protest. When he looked into her eyes, they reflected the hope and desire in his heart. "Will you have time to find an outrageously priced dress to wear at the ceremony? I want you to have the wedding of your dreams and no regrets."

"Being married to you, my best friend, the most respectable man I've ever met, is my dream."

Ronaldo grunted. "I noticed you left devastatingly handsome off that list."

She kissed his neck. "That's a bonus feature. Attractive bodies fade away. I see deterioration every day. Anyway, we can still have a big party and say our vows in front of our loved ones, but saying them to each other in private and then living them is what matters."

"You're right. Let's register today." What did formality matter after years of wooing her?

The goal was wide open. Time to take the shot.

Chapter 19

"I'm not going, Davi. My stomach hurts so bad." Daniela laid back onto her mattress, scrunching herself into a ball. They'd been arguing for most of the morning as they packed up what they wanted to take from their *favela* home. Davi packing his things right alongside hers made the work easier.

Outside it was still dark. Chacal hadn't delivered on his promise to get what he wanted from Davi, but he'd come for it. They had to get out of here under the cover of darkness to limit the chances anyone saw them. People weren't given free passes out of these places, especially not if they grew up here.

They were giving up the home they'd had with their parents in favor of something small, safe, and closer to the stadium for Daniela's practices. Cambridge hadn't decided yet if he wanted to take Xander up on his offer for a new place in exchange for the apprenticeship. He'd accepted the apprenticeship for now.

Davi crouched in front of her, smiling through his exasperation. "You're going. Your stomachache is from the nerves. They'll calm down once you get going. We can't hold off much longer. Gia is waiting for you at the bus stop with your suitcase and a ticket to your future. Your bright, untainted future as an Olympian away from the recycling center and perpetual hunger."

In the Shadows

"Our life right now is not that bad. At least I have you."

One side of his lips quirked up. "You won't have me forever and then you'll have nothing but regrets."

It was all too much. Her feelings had never felt this big before, but she'd also never been faced with separation either. She pulled her knees to her chest and rested her forehead on them. "I can't leave you. What if Chacal comes after you?"

"You will be a thirty-minute bus ride away for a week of orientation. It's not another country."

"It might as well be," she whispered into her knees.

"And I would definitely be happy with accompanying you to the women's *futbol* training center. Those women are—" Her glare stopped the rest of his sentence. He laughed.

"Those women are not pieces of meat for eyeing up at the butcher. Same as me."

In the kitchen area, he pulled the last two pans off the shelf. "I was going to say they are skilled professionals." He dropped them in a nearby bag and lifted her chin. "Something can happen just as easily with you here. Cambridge and I will get us moved into the new space and when you get back, you can make it homier. This apprenticeship with Xander is exactly what we need. It's a huge life change for Cambridge, too. If you're not going to get on that bus for you, then get on it for me. I can't live happily knowing that you didn't give yourself a chance to become an Olympian, a world-class *futbol* player."

He hoisted a garbage bag over his shoulder, stopping at the door. "Let's go see if you have what it takes to be an Olympian, Daniela."

The admiration in his eyes pulled her from her place. An Olympian. It sounded impossible. A very expensive, shiny dream.

He slung his arm over her shoulders as they used the shadows to escape from their *favela* for the last time. No looking back. No regrets. A hope and prayer that Chacal didn't come after them.

With their possessions in hand, they met Xander and Gia in a parking lot down the road right next to the bus stop. Davi stuffed the garbage bag into Xander's trunk and Gia wheeled Daniela's brand-new suitcase over to her.

"Here's to a new beginning!" Gia grinned. Daniela mustered a return smile. "Oh, I almost forgot. We got these for you both so you could keep in touch with each other. They should have enough minutes and texts for the time away. If it's not enough, Davi can let us know and we can buy more." Gia handed them each a compact mobile phone with its box.

A phone. Daniela blinked. She'd always wanted one. A laugh bubbled inside her. She threw her arms around Gia and squeezed. Her clothes smelled fresh. "Thank you will never be enough, Gia."

Gia squeezed back. "I know this is a lot for you to take in right now, but Xander and I and Coach Cevere have complete confidence in your abilities. Don't let fear blindside you. This is your time to learn and grow and become the best player you can be. If you go to orientation and realize pro *futbol* is not for you, you come home and find a new path for your life."

Right. A test run. The thought hadn't occurred to her that she would turn down this opportunity. People like her didn't turn away a dream like this. There was nothing better in her book.

She said thanks one more time as the bus hissed to a stop at the curb. She circled her arms around Davi's neck and peppered his face with kisses. "Thank you for your support. I love you. See you soon."

Davi laughed but didn't push her away. He wasn't embarrassed of her. He was her protector and now her support from afar. "I'll call and text. Let me know your schedule when you get there, so I'm not interrupting."

"That's something we've never said," she whispered. "We have phones now?"

In the Shadows

A light glimmered in his eyes. "Well, we actually need them now." He gave her another big hug before stepping away. "I told you we'd get out of there."

Her heart ached in a happiest way. He'd seen a way out when she'd not been able to see past the trash hills in front of her. Almost as if he had spoken their future into existence that day her father left and didn't come back.

Daniela stashed her suitcase on a rack, then picked a seat in the front. This was her first bus ride out of town. She didn't want to miss anything. As the bus jerked to a start, she waved like a fool from the window until Davi was out of sight.

Someone sat next to her at one of the stops, but Daniela didn't look away from the window. She had never been this far away from home and she was going to see it all. Her phone had a button on it that opened a camera and grabbed a picture. She took a lot so she could show Davi next week.

Gia said a representative from the training center would meet her at the bus stop in Barra da Tijuca which put Davi's safety-conscious mind at ease. True to her word, a man her father's age with a Brazilian flag and the Olympics rings waited at the stop holding a sign with her name on it. When she descended the stairs with her suitcase, he stepped forward to grab it.

"Welcome to the training center, Daniela!" He checked her paperwork, and then handed her a packet with her name on the front of the envelope.

Behind her, a few older girls crowded around the man, seeming to already know who he was with their choruses of "Hi, Duarte!"

Duarte smiled. "Four. Looks like everyone is here. Let's get going." He turned to walk to a van across the street. "Girls, this is Daniela. She's here for *futbol* orientation this week. I'll let you introduce yourselves as I drive to the dormitories."

Although friendly, the girls didn't seem different than normal girls. They invited her to watch their water polo practices sometime if she was near the aquatics center. Since she was the newest, Duarte insisted she sit in the front so he could give her a tour of the facilities. With a flash of a badge, Duarte drove them through the gates onto the grounds. Gymnasiums, aquatic centers, tracks, indoor snow sports facilities, restaurants, spas, medical centers, shopping, and on and on the list went. The place was a small city within itself.

On her left, the buildings disappeared into fields. The green *futbol* fields had small stands on one side and the other side opened up to stunning blue water with outcroppings in the distance. She captured a picture to show Davi. He would love that and she could definitely get used to that view.

When Duarte parked, the others filed out and disappeared into one of the food centers. Daniela closed the van door behind her and turned in a circle taking in the village bustle. Wouldn't Davi love to see this? She took another picture.

He said it wasn't another country. It was a whole different world.

"It's incredible, isn't it?" Duarte said as he lifted her suitcase from the back. "I never get used to seeing this. Brazil's most elite athletes walk around here like they're out for an evening stroll with a normal life." He shook his head, laughing. "Well, just roll your bag into the lobby of the dorms there and check in. The host will get you situated and connected with your teammates. Good luck this week!"

She lifted her hand in a wave, desperate to call him back. He was the only person she kind of knew in this soup of humanity. But instead, she did as he said and checked in at the lobby. The host gave her a wristband that looked like a watch that he said would act as her key to open her room door, pay for her meals, and get into the training facilities.

Her room was on the fourth floor with the rest of the women's *futbol* team. Squatting, she hugged her suitcase to her chest, then walked up the flights of stairs stopping occasionally to let someone pass her. They must really be serious about the team being in shape if they had to do this many stairs every time they went to their room.

Stairs beat the uneven footing of unpacked trash mounds. One wrong step would sink your foot right into muck. The thought brought a smile to her face as she wheeled her bag down the hall in search of her room.

She followed the numbers to 438. With a tap of her watch against the handle, a light flashed green followed by clicking. Wow. That was serious magic.

Inside, she passed a bathroom on her right to get to two beds with pristine, white covers on them. How did they expect her not to get that dirty when she was going to be playing *futbol* all day?

The chair had a purple cover on it, so she sat on that instead of the bed. The folder in her welcome packet had a schedule in it that gave her one free hour a day. Running, breakfast, workouts, drills, lunch, film study, scrimmage, team bonding, dinner, free hour, evening sauna and spa (muscle recovery). Start date on the schedule was tomorrow at 6:30 AM. She could sleep longer than usual.

Today she was supposed to see the team nutritionist, physical therapist, and get familiar with the layout. A click interrupted her silence. The door pushed open as a girl walked into the room.

Jet black hair hung like curtains next to the girl's face. "Oh good. You're here already! That makes my job of teaching you the ropes easier." She laughed to herself. "I'm Cana Pinto, four-year veteran right defender."

Daniela shook her hand. "Daniela Gomes, first-year right forward or midfield."

Cana punched the air. "Right side, best side." She dropped her bags on the ground. "Have you eaten recently?"

"Is it lunch time already?" Daniela checked the clock.

"No." Cana snorted. "But the food here is amazing so I like to eat brunch on day one. Food is already paid for so we eat as much as we need. Let's go get a snack. We'll be on a strict diet during the season, so now's the time to make the most of all those amazing chefs they hire."

Daniela started to walk out behind Cana.

"Oh, you need that drawstring bag that was in your welcome packet. Put your paperwork and phone in it. Your watch is your ID, money, and door passes." Cana held the door open for her. "Everyone gets newbies on orientation week until they're the team all-stars. You're my third one. The first two didn't make it out of small time on their city teams. You've got to be exceptional at *futbol* to make it here past one year." Her brown eyes leveled at Daniela. "Are you exceptional, Daniela Gomes?"

How did she answer that? Wasn't that what she was here to determine? "I plan to be."

Cana grunted. "Good. Let's get a snack and get you to the salon. You need to get pampered before you meet the coaches."

"Uh, I don't know that I have the money for that." Daniela followed her down the hall and stopped at the stairs. "Don't you want to take the stairs?"

"The elevator is right here. It's faster. We'll be working our legs off the rest of the week so take it easy." Cana led her onto the elevator. The door closed and jolted into motion. Daniela yelped, grabbing the handles.

Cana smirked. "You're really new to this, aren't you? This should be fun." They walked into the lobby then out into the street.

Five doors down they picked up pastries and drinks at a bakery. They found a table outside in a cute alleyway.

"The truth is, Daniela, that you have to look a certain way in order to make the national team. You're expected to be an icon of femininity and beauty. The country leaders want long, well-kept natural hair, thin but strong bodies, and cleanliness." She leaned forward so other tables wouldn't hear her. "One of the only reasons they lifted the women's *futbol* ban in '79 was because the

In the Shadows

Federation agreed to keep a really firm grasp on the players acting and looking like women. You'd think the starting lineup stepped out of a Miss Universe contest."

"So if you don't fit in with their idea of beauty, they…"

Cana shrugged. "If you're new, they don't invite you back. If you're so good they can't live without you, they force you into it with stern talks about representing the country well and being an icon of what a woman should be to all the young girls out there. Never mind that they barely pay women athletes, but expect us to look like we're swimming in money."

Daniela ran a hand down her long ponytail. She'd never gotten a proper haircut. In fact, she'd never had any beauty treatments. "I'll do whatever is required to have a shot at the national team. That's why I'm here."

"Us, too. And they know that. They dangle your eligibility over your head so they can get you to do what they want." Cana stood up abruptly. "Let's get you an appointment at the salon for this afternoon. We'll stop by the nutritionist and physical therapist before lunch. I'm meeting a group of team members for lunch at one of the best food halls here. You can join us."

Daniela fought hard to make mental notes of where she was and how she got there. Cana finally grabbed a map. They made circles around where everything was. At her salon appointment, a team of people scrubbed, pulled, pinched, and waxed. She ached everywhere when they finally finished with her, but her skin was shiny, her hair cut, her eyebrows matched, and all of her nails were sanded down with clear polish on them.

It was possible Cana lied to her because she didn't think Daniela looked nice, but Daniela didn't care. Despite the pain involved in the hair removal, the pampering felt strangely wonderful. Her nails didn't have dirt under them for the first time that she could remember.

"Whoa. Total upgrade," Cana said with a huge smile when Daniela met up with her in the lobby of the salon. Cana had opted for the full treatment, too, but didn't look much different except her skin glowed.

They headed to dinner together to meet the team. Daniela let Cana do the talking about her life in Sao Paulo where her father ran the zoo and tended the large, exotic cats. She was deep into a story about her father trying to safely extract a flock of geese that landed in a tiger pen, when Daniela spotted a familiar handsome face, smiling and animatedly talking to a group of girls. Those long, dark eyelashes and his short, black hair made her pay attention in a way she'd never considered a man before.

Mac.

The man she'd hoped to forget.

Chapter 20

Alfonso, Ronaldo's incredibly insightful driver, hadn't put a newspaper on his seat in the car for the last week. The man was clearly putting the pieces together that—if he was driving Ronaldo to the courthouse for hearings—Ronaldo under no circumstances wanted to see his face next to fallacious speculation. And Lenz and his lawyer were professional liars so there was plenty of nonsense flying about.

"Senhor Cevere, thank you for coming today. Are you familiar with the accusations against Senhor Pereira?"

Ronaldo gave a slight bow. "Your Honor and Honorable Counsel Members, I am familiar with the accusations. The board and I were aware of Senhor Pereira's proceedings for months and we were collecting the data you have as evidence in front of you now."

"Would you as the head of the FCC tell the counsel the accusations, please?"

"Senhor Pereira paid sizable amounts to referees dating back six years to call games in Brazil's favor. In addition, he promised and delivered favors and gifts to key decision makers in organizations that affected Brazil's men's tournament placement in regional and world competitions, not excluding the World Cup and the Olympics. Senhor Pereira did not act alone, however. He

In the Shadows

reimbursed his assistant Mara handsomely in off-the-books payments from an account he didn't think anyone was monitoring and then relinquished all accessibility to it except him and Mara. He—"

Lenz jumped to his feet. "Those payoffs were all Cevere's idea. Not mine."

The counsel silenced him and motioned for Ronaldo to continue.

"Your Honor, I thought that Lenz might try something like shifting the blame, although foolishly, on me or another assistant or on the accounting department. So as soon as these indiscretions were brought to my attention, I called the board and all of the departments into accountability. They checked my work. They checked each other's work. And I checked their work." Ronaldo looked behind him at Katrina and motioned for her to stand. "I have brought my assistant here today as well as all of the documentation of Lenz's actions and our proceedings since discovering his misdeeds. The truth is sadly often very blurry in cases against powerful people who have the ability to sway votes and opinions, but I assure Your Honor that all the accountability needed for this case are here in these boxes my assistant and I brought today. And lest anyone think that these are the only copies, be assured that we have backups of backups of all this information so nothing will coincidentally go missing."

The room erupted in a wave of murmurs. Several men on the counsel carried and wheeled the boxes of papers to safety behind the desk. Lenz's face was bright red as he spoke in a furious whisper with his lawyer. When he saw Ronaldo watching him, he made a rude gesture and mouthed, "You'll pay for this."

Ronaldo had no doubt that Lenz actually believed that. How he would do that from prison would be interesting to find out.

The counsel dismissed him and called Katrina to speak. He held out her chair for her as she sat and then retreated to the back where the cameras no longer had a view of the back of his head, eager as they were to read volumes into the slightest shift of his body or face. No, he wasn't there to provide anything more than the absolute truth. No commentary. No character assassination above what the facts provided.

Morals and ethics weren't a subjective game to him as so many in leadership these days made them. He knew right from wrong. And if the day came that he got kicked to the curb, it'd be for telling the truth and doing the right thing. No less.

The rest of the day he sat in the back of the courtroom listening to testimony after testimony from his staff tell about the measures they took to stay accountable, many to their great inconvenience. And he was proud of every single one of them. Not one in the group let down their guard, or complained about the precautions they'd put in place.

They had their honor and good name to take away from the whole scandal. Not something many could do. After today, he'd only be brought back in if absolutely necessary. With all that documentation, it shouldn't be necessary.

As he walked down the stairs having shook all his staff members hands, a peace settled over him. Bringing about real change was why he'd put his life aside for so long. Flying those untouchables back down to earth gave him hope that he'd made at least a small difference and gave the underdogs more of a fighting chance.

Now, putting his life on hold couldn't wait any longer. He'd always figured that if he wasn't married by fifty, it wasn't for him and he wouldn't waste the time chasing after it. At age forty-seven with Isadora's name across from his on the paperwork, nothing felt better. He hadn't told Isadora that he'd paid the registry's rush fee to get their paperwork processed faster.

Her impatient plea embedded in his chest, reproducing itself in him. He was ready.

For this surprise, he had done his own legwork. Katrina's plate couldn't fit any more on it anyway. Calling Isadora's schedulers to get her a day off without her knowing equated to running boulders uphill in a snowstorm, but he'd managed. Their wedding day was going to be perfect.

In the morning when she came out of her place in blue scrubs, a ponytail, and tennis shoes, he stood against the railing at bottom of her steps holding their marriage license in his hand. She made it all the way to the sidewalk before she noticed him standing there in his brand-new suit. A loud squeak escaped her perfect pink lips.

"Ronaldo! Wow, you look fantastic." She kissed him, then glanced at her watch. "Why are you here so early?"

He lifted the license to her eye level. "Today's the day."

Her hand pressed against her chest. "It came already. That was fast. But I have to…" Her sentence trailed off. "I don't have to work today, do I?"

With a shake of his head, he grinned.

Her body leaned into the railing. "Thank God." She motioned him in. "Come inside."

Perhaps today is not the day. He followed her in. Rarely did he question his decisions, but her mood seemed off today. Shrugging off his suit coat, he hung it on the coat tree in the front hall and followed her into the kitchen where she placed her things.

When she turned into his arms, her whole body relaxed. Her head against his chest felt like the most natural thing in the world. And it should, as she was his almost wife.

He swung her into his arms, carrying her thin frame to the couch to sit. Her form fit against him perfectly. "Tell me what's going on." His fingers swiped at the tears now dripping silently down her cheeks.

"No one in leadership is taking my Zika warnings seriously. They don't care what's happening in the *favelas*. They tell me to 'monitor' it, because they need statistics. Meanwhile, these people are being crushed with grief and fear because something is very wrong with their babies and they can't do anything about it and no one seems to care." She took a deep breath, as he absorbed her words. "I guarantee you if it affected the politicians' babies or grandbabies, there'd be a vaccine and a campaign about it instantly. What are the poor people worth to the politicians these days? Nothing unless it's an election year."

He stayed quiet. It felt like there was more.

"And a pregnant teen mom died yesterday in my clinic, because she tried to abort her baby on her own. We're seeing as many patients as we can every day in these clinics, but we can't see them all." A sob hiccuped from her throat. "It's too much."

Ronaldo's throat tightened as emotion rose unchecked in his chest. Wasn't life one long war against one thing or another? If you weren't battling people's corruption, you were battling illness, fighting for a chance at a better life, or working for your sanity and your place in the world. Did it ever really end for people who wanted lasting change?

His arms squeezed her closer. Her battles wouldn't end and he couldn't fight them for her. There would always be a new illness to identify and eliminate. He pressed his lips to her forehead, her perfume tantalizing.

"I had planned for us to use today to get married and spend a long weekend celebrating. But we can move it to another day and use today together to plan out what our life might be like together."

She shifted in his lap so she straddled him, her tears gone. In its place blazed desire. "I can't think of anything that will make me feel better about my life than marrying you and celebrating alone for four days." Her lips met his with need.

"Don't start that yet or we'll not make it to our vows," he murmured to her between kisses. "And you're not stealing my virtue without saying your vows first."

She laughed as he plopped her on her feet and gave her a swat to go get dressed. He shoved his hands in his pockets and examined the room. The space was far more modern than his parents' house and another universe from his former apartment as far as inviting went.

"Isadora," he said abruptly. She popped her head back into the room. "I'm embarrassed to say it didn't occur to me before, but I have no place to bring you home to except here." Mark that as a husband fail. "Do you mind if I move in with you here?"

Her smirk pumped his heart rate a little faster. "Only until we can afford our bungalow on the water, okay?"

They laughed together as she disappeared to get ready. He stored the idea away to capitalize on if the chance arose. She deserved a mansion on the water. A palace. But she'd never agree to live in one unless she could fill it with as many orphans as could comfortably fit.

Now, there was an idea.

They hadn't talked about a family but he didn't mind the idea. Isadora might have more to say on the matter as a doctor. But if they did, he'd hope for a bond like his and Mariana's. Similar to what he saw in Davi and Daniela. A tight-knit friendship bonded by the sacred tie of family.

Mariana would have loved Isadora although, truth be told, she probably would have had him married off before now. But that wasn't how life happened for him and he had no regrets.

His whole body hummed in appreciate when Isadora came gliding into the room in a knee-length white sundress. Part of her black hair was pinned back, exposing diamond earrings while the rest of her gorgeous hair flowed down her back. Her makeup was light and subtle. Her traditional heeled gold sandals completed the picture.

In a word, stunning.

She handed him a necklace and turned around sweeping her hair off her neck. He kissed her shoulder as he latched the necklace into place.

"I'm speechless," he said, running his hands lightly down her arms.

She grabbed his hand. "We need a ring for you. Then, let's go get married."

At Isadora's insistence, Ronaldo's town car chauffeured them to the same jewelry store where he'd found her ring. A plain gold band was all he wanted. Nothing ostentatious. As they drove, Isadora called the minister she'd asked to be prepared. He was available right after lunch. Ronaldo texted his parents and Isadora texted her sister and best friend to meet them at the church.

To fill the time, they browsed through stores as if no one else existed. They walked casually through the shops as Isadora quizzed him on his home preferences. Did he prefer fluffy towels or scratchy? Did he eat random meals in the middle of the night on the weekends? Which side of the bed did he sleep on? Did he keep the house cool or warm during the day? Did he sleep with pajamas on or nothing? Was his budget (because she knew he had one) a rule or a guideline?

Her string of questions humored him greatly. None of her answers to those same questions were a deal-breaker for him. They'd learned each other intuitively over the past two years of curating their relationship and helping her navigate away from the last boyfriend she had who was an undeserving, worthless fool.

They strolled hand-in-hand toward the church, stopping for a progressive lunch as they chose their favorite items from different restaurants. At last, they walked into the church exactly on schedule. Ronaldo's parents and Isadora's best friend Eva were already there, dressed up. Papa had donned a tie and coat for the occasion.

Mama grabbed Isadora's hands and kissed her cheeks. "Thank you, beautiful girl, for inviting us. A long time we've waited for someone's love to overcome our son's stubbornness. Thank you for letting us come today. Thank you for loving him."

Isadora brushed away a tear as she wrapped her arms around Mama. He couldn't make out her murmured words, but Mama squeezed her tighter. When they released each other, Mama

In the Shadows

reached into her purse and withdrew her pearl hair comb that she'd worn for her wedding fifty-two years ago.

The tears streaming down Isadora's cheeks moved him to invade their moment. He held her small hand as she bent to let Mama clip the pearls in her dark hair. Mama grabbed Isadora's hand in her right and Ronaldo's in her left, forming a circle.

"May the God of light flood your marriage with peace, bring joy amongst sorrow, fill your home with a hope that looks toward tomorrow. When you are met with darkness, may He soothe your soul and may your love run deep and make you whole."

Ronaldo kissed Isadora's forehead and wiped her cheeks with his thumb pads. Their marriage would bring a fullness to both of their lives he hadn't anticipated.

She'd talked of her parents and their influence often. Isadora's mother had died in a ski accident years ago and her father more recently died of brain cancer. It wasn't fair that she and her brother and sister had to say goodbye so soon as he'd done with Mariana. Her siblings stayed close to each other, though. Her sister Tritessa lived in Rio with her own boutique pet shop. Her brother Keyton lived in Vitoria and worked as a port authority.

Through marriage, Isadora would gain parents and Ronaldo would double his siblings. Love brought them that completeness.

The church door swung open, bumping into the wall as Tessie dodged into the lobby. She held a giant flower bouquet and under her arm was a big bag. She barreled over to Isadora.

"What did I miss? Isa, you look stunning as usual. I promised Keyton I'd video call him so he could see the ceremony and I brought the video camera to record it. Here. It's bad luck to marry without a bouquet." She shoved the bouquet into Isadora's hand and leaned in to fake whisper. "Also, know now that I will shamelessly fight Eva for them in the bouquet toss."

As Eva laughed and issued her own threat, Ronaldo stepped away to greet the minister who walked in from the sanctuary.

"Are you ready, Senhor Cevere?" the minister said, embracing him.

The double meaning wasn't lost on him as he glanced around the lobby. Everyone they'd asked had come. As the minister led them through the blessings, vows, and exchange of rings, Ronaldo memorized every emotion that flickered across Isadora's flawless face. The awe and total rightness surging in his chest the moment he kissed his bride overwhelmed him.

Her love for him made him feel invincible. He'd never had a teammate he trusted more. Now, it was truly them against the world.

Chapter 21

"Cana!" one of the girls from the group called, causing the rest of them and Mac to look in their direction.

Daniela's heart kicked up a notch as she pretended he wasn't there. The rest of the girls looked older than her and effortlessly gorgeous. Maybe there was something to Cana's complaint. Cana greeted the group, then hugged Mac like they were best friends.

"Everyone, this is Daniela Gomes, a newbie out of Rio who thinks she might be up for the task of sticking around. Come say hi." She swung her arm wide. "Daniela, this is everyone worth your time." Peals of laughter and threats about others hearing what she said had her ducking. "I'm kidding. The whole team is awesome. You'll meet the others later."

Names and field positions only partially stuck with her as they descended on the food hall. Daniela's memory was on overload. What a dream to have world-class players know her name and deem her worthy of eating dinner with. At least, they would until Mac spoiled it.

All he'd have to tell them was where she was from and they wouldn't acknowledge her again. Why was he here? She glanced around. He wasn't far behind her, deep in conversation with one of the goalkeepers.

In the Shadows

"Cana, how do you know Mac?" she said when there was a tiny lull in the conversation Cana was having with another defender.

Cana shrugged. "We met here, I think. He covers women's sports for the news network that his grandfather owns, Brazilian News Corporation. Started off as an intern when he was sixteen and now, he's nineteen reporting full-time and doing school part-time. I suppose there aren't too many guys who want the women's sports since everyone thinks men's sports are better."

The question vanished as the conversation segued into the networks covering their sports. Daniela listened intently to the discussion about Brazil's first friendly match of the year against Mexico coming up in a few months. Mexico had gotten a new coach to replace the last one who quit because he and his family received death threats when they lost their game in the World Cup. She was so engrossed in horror stories the other players were trading that she got to the table and noticed quickly the others' plates had a variety of foods on it. The nutritionist had told her something about eating a rainbow, hadn't she?

Her plate was piled high with mostly fruit. Cana looked at Daniela's plate and started laughing. Horror ran from her brain all the way to her stomach where a pain exploded into feeling ill. The other girls giggled at her, too.

"Sorry for the delay. Here's your plate," Mac said, setting a plate of portioned, colorful foods in front of her and sliding her fruit plate toward his seat next to her. "Thanks for splitting the fruit with me, Daniela."

The table got quiet as he sank into his chair next to hers, immediately popping a piece of pineapple in his mouth.

"Sorry for laughing, Daniela. I thought you were planning to eat that whole plate of fruit by yourself and nothing else," Cana said. "You'd be in rough shape for practice tomorrow if you tried that."

Daniela offered her a manufactured smile as she forked some of Mac's food into her mouth. When everyone had gone back to their conversations, she turned to him, letting her hair veil her view of the others.

"Thank you."

His kind brown eyes met hers. A smirk lifted the edge of his lips. "You're pretty and this team is a tight-knit group. Newcomers aren't always welcomed around here."

Daniela choked on a sip of her water. Those were her words to him that night in the *favela*. "Any other pointers I need to know to avoid making an utter fool of myself?"

"Actually, yes," he said, leaning in closer. "The team initiates all the newcomers on a random night by filling the hall with dry ice smoke and setting off a fire alarm. The newbies' roommates pretend to be frantic and send the new girls running out the doors and down the stairs. Then they lock the hall doors so no one can get back in until just before dawn."

"That's horrible." Daniela wrinkled her nose.

Mac laughed, a deep resonating sound that made her laugh with him. "It weeds out the ones with no endurance, too. They might not do it this year, but chances are high. It's an old tradition that started because the team got sick of the newcomers not respecting the sleep rules the coaches put in place. The newcomers would often stay up late since they weren't played during games anyway, causing the more senior members of the team to lose sleep and not do well in practice. And that is also why the senior team members don't room with the new kids anymore."

No wonder the new recruits didn't stick around. "You're not faking me out, are you?"

"Look me in the eyes when I say this, Daniela." Mac lowered his chin, his expression very serious. "You don't know me well yet, but understand that I'm not a liar."

In the Shadows

He seemed trustworthy, but— "Why didn't you tell me who you were when I met you?"

"I didn't lie to you. I told you I was there on business." He reached his fork past her and grabbed a piece of meat she'd left on the plate, the one he'd made for himself.

She pushed the plate in front of him and pulled the fruit over. "It felt a little bit like a lie when it came out that you wrote the story we were celebrating."

"I wanted to talk to you as a normal person. Some people act strangely around me when they find out I'm a reporter." He pinned her with a look that said she of all people should understand about being treated differently.

She'd been in danger of violating what she promised herself she'd never do—judge someone without knowing all the facts. "Well, thanks again for rescuing me from my mortification. I'd completely forgotten what my nutritionist said, but I won't make that mistake again."

Gathering the plates, she stacked them on her tray and walked toward the tray deposit line. She should offer to get him more food. She should stay and get to know her teammates. She should find out Mac's take on the news story. Instead, she dropped her tray on the conveyor belt, fished her mobile phone from her purse, and called Davi.

It rang as she walked outside where it now was dark. She didn't really know her way back, so she found a bench to wait for Cana. As soon as Davi answered, she let out the breath she'd been holding.

"Davi, I miss you." The words tumbled out of her mouth before she could instruct herself to sound as if her new experiences hadn't shaken her.

He smiled. "I miss you, too. It's only been half a day, but it feels longer. Tell me everything."

She must have sat there for an hour describing the village, the dormitories, Cana, the food. "It's another world here and I took pictures to show you when I get back."

"You can send them to my mobile phone like you do an ordinary text." He walked her through the process of sending him pictures.

She was laughing at the ones he sent her when she spotted Cana coming out with the others. "Davi, I need to get going. My roommate came out of the food hall and I don't know my way back to the room yet."

"I'll talk to you later. Have a great time." He cleared his throat. "Daniela, you deserve to be there. Show them what you've got."

She smiled, told him she loved him, and hung up. How'd she get so lucky with a brother like him?

"That your boyfriend, Daniela?" Cana called over to her.

Mac looked at his feet, seemingly uninterested in her answer.

Her grin widened at the thought of having a boyfriend. "Brother who is too good for the likes of you, Cana."

Cana feigned hurt. "I deserved that."

They followed protocol and got into bed early that night. And the next morning was early. They were up before the sun in workout gear running two miles before breakfast. In the gym, a team of physical therapists and fitness experts monitored their workouts. When they finally trudged onto the field for scrimmaging, Daniela really couldn't fathom playing a full game much less keeping this pace of schedule for a whole week.

But then she met the coaches who said they were thrilled she was here and she saw the amount of people in the stands to watch their first scrimmage, and suddenly the wind came back into her sails. It put life in her bones. This was what she loved doing and here she was playing on the same field as a teammate with the women's national team.

Her dream come true.

In the Shadows

This was the final physical demand of the day. She had more to give and everything to prove. The coaches divided the twenty-eight women into four teams of seven. They mixed the first-year players in with the other non-starters and sent them to another field. It was both disappointing and a relief to not be across from the legendary forwards Cosa, Mayla, and Emily. They stayed on the main fields.

But when the whistle blew, her mind zeroed in on the game. Nothing else existed. The defenders took up more space on the field than they did off it. Some of these women that she'd eaten with last night were brick walls with sharp elbows. They may have seen her age, weight, and training as a disadvantage, but when she went flying because a player on the other team pushed her in the penalty box, it was pure good fortune.

The whistle blew, giving her a penalty kick that she sent straight into the back of the net. From then on, Daniela became the target of holding, jersey pulling, tripping, and elbows to the mid-section. Flopping down and crying wouldn't earn her a place on anyone's starting lineup, so she powered through and scored twice more.

A coach ended the game and sent Daniela's team to the main field while one of the teams came to play the team that had just lost. She grabbed a snack bar from the nutritionist. It had no flavor despite being packed with nutrients.

This time she was lined up against the starters. She had just enough time to say "my brother is your biggest fan" to Mayla before the whistle blew, starting their game. Her objective in this match was for the defenders to not even know she was there until too late. Halfway through a sprint to the ball, she remembered Aline's advice to make herself smaller when she ran and it got her there first.

She crossed it in to her teammate who placed it in the left corner, but the goalkeeper snagged it. That put her on the defenders' radars immediately. These women didn't mess around with elbows and kicks to the shins. They went straight for the hip check and slide tackle. She managed to barely avoid a broken ankle by jumping over an incoming slide, kept the ball, and sent it toward the goal with her left foot. It sailed toward the outside of the goal, but curved inward a fraction to put it inside the top middle of the net.

Her teammates jumped her in the celebration. That made the starters mad enough that they came on full force to beat Daniela's team three to one. But that didn't bring her off her high of scoring the first goal against the women's national team startup. Davi would be thrilled about it.

They circled around the coaches in midfield. Head Coach Rocha. "Great start today, ladies. Those were some fun scrimmages to watch. We've got a lot of great talent to work with and develop this year. We'll start delving deep on weaknesses and strengths tomorrow. But for tonight, we've reserved the game room after dinner, so we can all get to know each other over some intense card games. See you there."

After the day of physical work they'd done, there wasn't the same fun banter around the table as last night. Everyone focused on refueling to survive tomorrow's sessions. Daniela tried not to take it personally that these girls she was supposed to be bonding with tossed her around the field like a toy. She'd been treated like that when she first started playing against the guys every night. Davi had always encouraged her to leave grudges on the field and deal with there.

So she did.

Every day for the next four days, Daniela learned her teammates as friend and foe. The coaches and staff treated her like every other team member. And she'd shut Cana down the night they pulled the fire alarm trick on her as Mac had warned her. Every day was harder, but she loved putting in the work. Learning breathed life into her veins.

In the Shadows

The fifth night, Daniela's phone rang during team bonding time after dinner. She was about to win a hand in poker finally. Regardless, she answered.

"Daniela, it's Gia." Gia's tone sent her stomach straight into her throat. "Davi's been seriously injured and is in the hospital here in Rio."

She dropped her cards and left the table despite her teammates' protests. "The hospital? What happened?" She sank into a couch on the far side of the game room.

"I wish we knew details. Two mornings ago, he didn't show up for work with Xander. Xander thought he might be out sick for the day, so he tried calling him but he didn't answer. We checked the apartment. No luck. We finally reached Cambridge who hadn't seen him either. We spent today talking to people in the area to find out if anyone had seen him. Someone said they'd seen a guy matching Davi's description being loaded into an ambulance yesterday, so we called all the hospitals in the area and found him. He's not in good shape, Daniela, but he's going to be okay. He's heavily sedated right now."

Daniela sank into a ball on the floor. "Can you come pick me up right now?" Her voice came out in a whisper. "Please."

"Talk to your coaches to get the all clear. I can at least take you to the hospital and bring you back tonight."

It took thirty-six minutes for Daniela to get permission from Coach Rocha to leave and into Gia's car to head to the hospital. Cana, Mia, and Emily stood waiting with her until Gia picked her up. The drive took impossibly long. Twice, Daniela thought she might need to ask Gia to pull over so she could avoid throwing up in the car.

She knew she shouldn't have left him for a week. How could she be so selfish? There she was pretending like her former life didn't exist, that she could be numbered among the stars one day. She'd been laughing and having the time of her life while her brother's broken body lay in a hospital bed alone. Her stomach roiled again.

If Xander and Cambridge hadn't noticed his absence, Davi could have been lying dead somewhere. Sweet, selfless Davi who only wanted the best for her and always protected her. She couldn't bear the thought.

And she knew as soon as she saw his bruised face and bandaged limbs that she had to give up *futbol*. Davi needed her. He'd been by her side every day of her life. She wouldn't abandon him now, not even for training with the national team.

Chapter 22

Three days into the most blissful, refreshing staycation honeymoon Ronaldo had ever taken, Gia texted him. Isadora lay draped over his chest as they mindlessly watched TV on the couch. Their high-stress careers didn't allow for this kind of evening luxury usually, so they indulged after full days of doing whatever they wanted together in addition to a sprinkling of midnight treats, since they weren't getting up for work in the morning.

At his grunt, Isadora muted the show. "Work?"

"One of my players' brother is in the hospital after getting jumped in the street."

Isadora pushed to her feet. "Would I know her?"

Ronaldo stood right after. He jammed his feet into his shoes and checked his hair in the hall mirror. "Daniela. Her mom came into the clinic with hep B."

They were out the door and into Isadora's car in minutes. Ronaldo took the passenger's side as he texted Gia for the room information. Isadora knew the hospitals in the area like they were second homes. She had doctors' permissions in all of them including the tiny clinics around town that could hardly be classified as health facilities.

In the Shadows

She found a spot in the doctors' parking area close to the trauma wing. Using her badge, they went in a side door and up to the third floor. Xander waited outside the room for them, pacing the hall.

"Gia's on her way from the training center with Daniela and Cambridge just left for the evening," Xander said, motioning into the room.

Ronaldo glanced over the bandaged body, swollen eyes, and a face bruised past the point of recognition. "You're sure it's Davi."

Xander nodded. "The cell phone we gave him was in his personal items and he had his *Registro Geral* on him. They left some money in his wallet, so whoever was after him didn't do it for the money."

Ronaldo took the seat next to the bed, and laid his hand on the part of Davi's arm that wasn't covered in a cast. Isadora glanced over and smiled approvingly. She'd told him before that a comforting touch could sometimes register through the fog of pain.

Isadora brought over his chart. "He's heavily sedated. Broken ribs, punctured lung, sprained shoulder, and broken wrists probably from defending himself. His kidneys sustained some damage from blows to the back." She sighed. "Recovery will take a while so long as he takes it easy. I'm going to talk to the nurses about what they're giving him." Ronaldo watched Isadora leave the room, her confidence stirring up the desire in him. Admittedly, it didn't take much these days. He focused back on Davi's still form, the up and down of his chest.

"Cambridge said one of the women that witnessed the attack reported two men attacking Davi. It happened right outside a bar, so Cambridge will go back tomorrow to talk to the bartender who was working that night to see if he saw anything." Xander ran his hands through his short hair, exhaling. "I hope it's not because he's working with me now and no longer working in the recycling center. Davi has real potential. He's the hardest worker I've ever met, insists on learning the why and how, and he wants better for himself and Daniela. I worry that I'm putting him in a bad place."

"There will always be those who view paying it forward as saviorism or investing in others as a means to an end. The cynics refuse to believe that others could do good with a pure motivation. Don't let their jaded views stop you from helping others." As Ronaldo said the words, he knew they were for him. How many times had he felt he wasn't ever going to get to the point where he could make a difference? And that change would never be enough.

Xander scrubbed a hand down his face. "Gia spent her summers here, so she can step right back in and fit in. I need a translator, culture lessons over breakfast, and a GPS to get anywhere. It's going to take time, but I believe in our mission of being a launch point for those who need it, like Gia was for me." He glanced at the bed at Davi. "He has an eye for business and an unrelenting work ethic. From what he says, his friend Cambridge taught him everything he knows." His phone dinged. "Gia's on her way up with Daniela."

Isadora came back in with a nurse chatting about taking Davi to get more scans to check for more internal damage. Ronaldo left the room as they talked about urine output and skin coloring. Daniela jogged past him into the room, her face pinched with fear.

Gia wasn't far behind. She blew out a breath and pushed back the curls from her face. "She barely said anything on the way here. She's worried sick."

They stood outside the room, looking in. Isadora stood with her hand on Daniela's shoulder while Daniela sat next to Davi on the bed clasping his fingertips in between her hands.

Xander came to the door and slid his arm around Gia's waist. "Think she'll be able to finish orientation week?"

Ronaldo shrugged. Mariana's death had rendered him useless for at least a month until he learned to channel his grief into his playing. "Rocha will know whether to push her or not. He's got really good instincts when it comes to reading his players."

At last, Isadora joined them in the hall. Instinctively, Ronaldo reached for her hand. "Poor Daniela is in shock. The nurse is going to ease up on his medication so she can talk to him while he is coherent. They'll do a couple more scans and watch his kidneys for any signs of failure before they release him to go home. It'll be a few days." She looked up at Ronaldo with a sad smile. "Let's go home. We can check on him tomorrow during the day."

They had one more day of their long weekend before they both went back to work. And Ronaldo planned to make the most of it.

Monday morning, Ronaldo walked into the office more at peace than he'd ever felt. Katrina met him in his office.

"Welcome back, *Senhor*. You seem well-rested and…married?" Her eyes widened as she looked at the ring on his finger.

Ronaldo laughed. "Yes, Isadora and I are happily married now. We kept it low-key so the press wouldn't find a way to distort the story and bring Lenz into it. Let's jump right in and put out the worst fires first."

Katrina hesitated. "I guess you've been at this organization long enough to know that there will always be something going on, especially while you're gone." He nodded. "Some board members will be stopping by this morning to talk to you." She handed him a few release papers to sign.

A knock sounded at his door as he looked over the papers. He signed them and handed them back to Katrina. The board was already here.

Three men and two women followed him to the conference room down the hall. They exchanged pleasantries, but Ronaldo could sense the unrest in the air.

"Let's get to it," Idal said. He was the oldest and had been on the board the longest as the board president. He had a long-standing reputation of being old-fashioned. "Ronaldo, we've loved what you've done with the girls' league funneling into the women's team. It was just what this office needed to shake the negative image that Lenz brought on it. But we feel strongly that it is time to put that project aside and focus on what really matters which is seeing our national team qualify and win world championships."

Ronaldo raised an eyebrow. "And by national team, you mean the men's team?"

The board nodded.

Justina jumped in. "We can all agree that the numbers state the obvious. Men's *futbol* has always brought in more income than women's. It's time we see our team step up, perform well, and inspire national pride. Brazil is known for producing quality *futbol* teams and lately our standards have been amiss."

He breathed deeply to suppress the burning in his chest. They thought the changes he'd made were merely a redirection of the negative attention, in short—a publicity stunt.

"We approached Lenz about this which is what led to his unfortunate decisions," Idal said. "I think if we can entice the players to put in more effort on international games, reward them for their efforts, we'll see a team pull together to make our nation proud."

"Pay them more?" Ronaldo shook his head. "We're thin on margin. They're hardly earning the money they make already."

"We'd like you to create more margin," Faron, a quiet mousy man, cleared his throat. "We looked into the books. The money you redirected for getting the girls' league going can be brought back toward the men's team. We can invest that into more perks for the players, better goal line technology for games, and bigger bonuses for winning. All these things would boost morale and take our team to the top."

No way were they pulling his funding for his league. "Nicer stuff and more money don't make better players. It breeds

In the Shadows

entitlement. It produces lazy players that will fall all over the field if the opponent gets near them to get a call in their favor. I know firsthand. I played with guys like that for years."

Idal gave him a hard look. "We've made up our minds, Ronaldo. The funds you redirected to this girls' league have to be given back. We'll not be a laughingstock to the world, because you want to play around with young co-eds from the slums. You've made it to the big leagues as president of this organization. Time to start acting like it. We'll give you a week to come up with a new proposed budget to show us where the money will be spent and when or we'll need to go our separate ways."

The anger swelled inside him. They'd been on his side just two months ago. Obviously, their enthusiasm had been a ploy. They only saw the bottom line, not the lives affected by their investment into these girls. Now, defending his position would cost him his chance at changing their minds someday in the future.

He clenched his jaw. "Then I'll have that proposal ready for you next week."

He shook all their hands, played nice, and saw them out of the office. When the door closed, he turned to Katrina at her desk. "Let the national team coaches know I want them in my office this afternoon, non-negotiable."

If the board only saw progress measured by the men's team, then all the work he and his team had done to bring the women's leagues up to speed had been a nicety, but unnecessary. Idal made it sound as if the women weren't even included on their measuring stick of success. He wanted to scream and hit something. The board members were fools trying to throw money at the problem, but he'd make it happen without them getting a *real* of the donations meant for the girls.

That afternoon, the coaches could not have made it clearer that they'd become too comfortable with their ways of doing things. They had excuses for every failure and shifted blame for all the losses. He made notes as they answered his questions, treating him like one of the good old boys who was in on their schemes.

They had no idea what was coming for them. This coach had seen marginal success over the last few years. They played well in the tournaments but choked at the finish. The coach had been given a chance to follow through on change and really make a difference. But one more loss and Ronaldo planned to clean house.

When they left, he called Katrina in. "The board has demanded we shut the girls' league down. Tell Coach Habus that he's running the show for my team for their first game tomorrow. The most information he can get is that I'll be tied up with FCC business. After the game, we'll send out a note saying we need to suspend all practices and games for the time being." He slammed his fist on his desk, making Katrina flinch. That was his team. He shouldn't have to let another coach lead them to victory. Imagining their disappointment when they heard the news of shutting down gutted him. "I have to find a way around this. I'm not going to stop until I do. Don't let anything with our new girls' league slip through the cracks. All the money stays where we have it unless I say otherwise. Understand?"

Time for the men's team to earn their keep. And he'd make all the changes he could without the board's input, but then he'd have to pitch to the board his ideas of holding their feet to the fire in a way they couldn't refuse. Lenz had taken the easy way out to get results. Cleaning up this mess was going to require a lot more effort.

Night and day for the next three days, he put his life on hold to find a way to keep the funding for the girls' league. He looked at every contract, every performance record, every pay stub of the players for the last four years. Then he consulted with the lawyers.

He was stuck.

In the Shadows

There had to be a way to keep his dream alive, except there was no breathing room in the budget and the oxygen left was running out quickly.

Chapter 23

A day after she completed orientation week, Daniela pushed Davi's wheelchair through the halls of the hospital. Today was his discharge day. His facial swelling had lessened, and his bruises gave his face a very colorful look. His bones showed signs of mending well, and his pain medication was as needed.

The relief coursing through her overwhelmed the disgust she felt at herself for leaving him, but couldn't touch the hatred and anger at whoever did this to him. Though she'd never condone it, she understood murder a little better now.

Davi moaned as they went over the threshold to the outside and waited for Gia to pick them up. "Take it easy on the bumps, D."

"I'm sorry." She sighed. "I'm just happy to be getting you out, like if we leave, they can't tell us any more bad news."

Most of his classic smile was back. "That's completely illogical, but no surprise coming from you. I missed you last week."

"Davi, I never should have—"

"Don't you finish that sentence, Daniela Gomes. If you'd been home, you'd have been in a hospital bed beside me or worse." He looked out past the parking lot as if he could see the scene play out in his mind. "I wish I could remember anything from that night."

She rubbed a hand across his back. "Doctor Rey said your memory might come back over time. Anyway, I'm not going away again any time soon. We've got to get you well."

Not to mention the bills they'd need to pay for his visit.

A car pulled up beside where they sat on the bench. Gia hopped out and jogged around the car. "Let me get the door."

Daniela took the brunt of Davi's weight as he struggled to stand from the wheelchair. The doctor said any more force would have shattered his hips. He'd have trouble sitting without pain for weeks. She eased him into the front seat, buckled his seatbelt, and got into the back seat.

Gia had been a godsend in offering rides and making sure Daniela could visit Davi in the hospital. Daniela blinked back the tears.

"Xander's excited to have you working with them tomorrow, Daniela. The team so far is Cambridge, two women, and another guy. They've already partnered with three other stores in addition to Gabi's to put their items for sale." Gia drove them to their new apartment. The place felt borrowed, like her room at the training center.

"I'd like to get back to work as soon as I can," Davi said. "I'll be bored sitting at home by myself."

"Xander and Cambridge figured you'd say that. Xander is working on setting up a sourcing role for you until you can get back to making the products. Something about finding new stores to partner with and calling around to manufacturing plants to source supplies for products."

By the time Daniela got Davi comfortable in his bed in the new apartment, he couldn't keep his eyes open. She glanced at the clock.

An hour until she needed to be at their first *Guerreiras* game. She left Davi a note, locked the door, and made it to the fields early. She had emotions to burn off.

Aline and Noemia beat her there. Gilma, their goalkeeper, showed up after a little bit giving them the chance to shoot on goal. As they warmed up, she told them all about Davi's accident and his injuries. Lecia, Pedrina, Valiana, Andressa, Branca, Lia, Alice, Jaenette, Unna, Wandy, and Nan trickled on to the field.

"You get an invite back to training?" Aline asked as they stretched in a circle.

Daniela shook her head. "Not that I heard of. I'm too young anyway."

Andressa snorted. "That team could use some young legs. Most of them are in their twenties and thirties. When's your birthday?"

"Next week, actually." She'd forgotten about it in the midst of everything going on. "I turn sixteen."

Valiana whooped. "Hear that, girls? We're going to celebrate Daniela's sixteenth birthday next week with a party. I know a place." The other girls cheered as Valiana danced in a circle. She winked. "Can't let that day pass without at least meeting up with your friends."

Daniela smiled. They were her friends. She'd spent her whole life on the fringe of society surrounded by males and wishing for what was right in front of her today—sisters. The thought stuck with her through the game, as she saw her teammates through different eyes. They were hers to protect, to celebrate with, to love. They didn't care where she came from. They cared that she showed up.

And that's just what the *Guerreiras* did, despite Coach Cevere's absence. They won the game four to two to really make him proud. It was the first time they felt like a unit, a team.

The next day, she took the bus to meet Cambridge and walk to work with him. She recounted the game in detail like he'd

In the Shadows

asked. She'd rehashed the events with Davi the evening before when he woke up. Her excitement this morning dimmed minutely, but she still felt the rush when she thought about that final whistle blowing. They'd done it. Cambridge laughed at her enthusiasm.

She couldn't wait to win again. It made her feel unstoppable.

Cambridge touched her shoulder as he stopped in front of a store. "Wait here by the window. I need to ask the owner something quickly."

Daniela pulled out her mobile phone. A group text between her teammates had twenty-seven texts she had to catch up on.

Aline texted: *You guys hear the news? Our league, games, practices, and after practice schooling are getting shut down. Coach Habus just called to tell me not to come to practice today.*

A host of other girls chimed in, saying they'd just gotten a call from Habus, too.

Do you think we did something wrong? Valiana said.

Maybe that's why Coach Cevere missed the game. Lecia texted.

Coach Habus said he just heard the news today from the higher ups and didn't get any explanation, Aline said.

Andressa sent a host of emojis interspersed with curse words. *Does that mean I'm not going to see you fools anymore? That's not okay.*

Shut down? The news came as a swift punch in the gut. She could feel her throat tightening. Her breath came in short bursts. They couldn't close everything down. Maybe they didn't get enough donations? She'd seen Coach Cevere at the hospital outside Davi's room. He hadn't said anything.

She was just about to respond when the smell of rancid alcohol hit her at the same time as a brown hand smacked her phone to the ground, the force sending pieces in different directions.

"No!"

"Daniela, my daughter. So good to see you." Gerson slurred as he dropped his heavy hands onto her shoulders and pinned her against the window with a thump.

Her breath left her lungs in a wheeze. When she got the air back in, she pushed at him. "Papa, you're hurting me." She squirmed under his firm hold. "Let go."

"I was wondering when I'd have the chance to talk to you like I did Davi." He snorted out a laugh. "When I saw you out here, I thought I'd take the chance to express my displeasure. He might not have relayed my message accurately to you with that bad memory of his." His breath in her face made her gag. "Now imagine how your poor papa felt showing up to his apartment a few days ago and finding out it has new tenants."

His grip on her neck tightened. She sputtered.

"Do you know what I did?"

She shook her head.

"I had to ask the neighbors where my family went. And picture my surprise when they said you had moved out. I think they actually enjoyed seeing my shock. I don't appreciate being made a fool of, Daniela."

Her fingers ripped at his hand, trying to dislodge him from her throat. Why was no one else on the street helping her? Couldn't they see what he was doing?

"You think you can give up my apartment and walk away to another life, like it'd be better than the one I gave you. You're wrong. You're just like your mother. Nothing but a piece of sh—"

His grip loosened as his body fell backwards into the street. Her body came off the window. Cambridge moved between them, his form looming large over Gerson's.

"Gerson, I've been looking for you." His words hissed through his teeth. The anger rolled off him in waves, rendering Daniela immobile as she watched the scene play out in front of her. "I thought you might have been involved in Davi's attack."

In the Shadows

Gerson stumbled to his feet, dusting his trousers off. An ugly smile stole across his face. "Ah, so this is how they can afford to move. Daniela, you got yourself a sugar daddy to care for you. I knew you'd eventually be just like the other girls. It's only a matter of time before they all give themselves over to their best use in life."

Cambridge moved toward him, as if daring him to look at Daniela wrong again. "Daniela and Davi have more character in an eyelash than you've ever had. They're working hard to give themselves a better life. They've gone for years without adequate nutrition or education. Their mother died alone because you couldn't be a real man and care for your family."

Gerson's loud sneer echoed in the street. "You read too many books, old man. That's not how things are done here and you know it. Patricia knew if she wanted a kid with me that she'd have to take care of it herself. She agreed to that. I didn't want noisy, whiny pathetic leeches."

"Well, you don't have any. Patricia's children are far from dependent on anyone, especially not me. And when they achieve their success, you won't have any part in it." Cambridge nodded for Daniela to start walking away.

"Success picking through trash." He barked out a humorless laugh. "They'll never escape who they've always been. There's no way out of being a *catadore*. Even Patricia knew that when she signed up for that life. They'll follow her footsteps right into their early graves."

Daniela rushed forward. "You're the one going to an early grave, Gerson. Alcohol and drugs have destroyed you. Don't you come crying to us when you've got no one at your bedside to hold your hand when you take your last breath. You made your choice when you walked out on your family. That's something you're always going to regret. Don't ever touch me or Davi again."

He muttered something like "I doubt it" as she spun on her heel and walked away. Tears pricked her eyes, and there was no way she'd let him see that he'd gotten to her.

Cambridge said one more thing to Gerson before jogging to catch up to her. "Disgusting animal. I'm so sorry he said those things in front of you, Daniela. Don't take his words to heart. He's a selfish, careless man. I shouldn't have left you alone in the street. I'd stopped in to ask the shop owner if he thought the guy who beat up Davi was Gerson."

She turned her head to swipe at her eyes. "He wasn't wrong though, Cambridge. We have been dependent on you for a long time now and on charity. What happens when that goodwill runs out? We were barely surviving after the trash center shut things down. And now that Davi's out of work, it's going to get worse. I'm not as good at building things as he is and I have no other skills to offer. We're going to get stuck right back into picking recyclables, because that's who we are."

His hand rested on her shoulder. "Focus on your schooling and *futbol*. That's where you're supposed to be right now. You have a bright future ahead of you there."

The tears came loose in a sort of sobbing hiccup. "Except I just got word that the girls league is shut down which means no *futbol* or schooling. And the national coach said he wants to watch me until I'm old enough to join the team."

It was over. She'd never be good enough for the national team now if she didn't play and practice until then.

Cambridge didn't say a word but pulled her to him in a side hug as they walked. She'd known it was too good to be true, didn't she? Dreams like that never came true for people like her. Gerson was right. She'd always be a *catadore*.

The tears had dried by the time they arrived at Xander's office, but the bad news kept coming.

In the Shadows

"We don't have enough materials for you to join the other women. And the work Davi was doing involved sawing and drilling," Xander said through his translator.

Her heart sunk. She had to do something to keep the money coming in. Gabi's store was one block over, so she told Cambridge she'd go there. But she didn't.

She boarded the bus and got off at the stop to go to the garbage heaps. Her heavy boots and bags were still stashed at Cambridge's apartment across the street. They flopped on her feet in that familiar way, so different to the way her *futbol* boots wrapped around her perfectly. No, she wasn't thinking of what could have been.

The fee had been dropped to a few *reals* to get in, not good but not terrible. She paid it, then chose a place with the least amount of people nearby. Her eyes and hands worked together on autopilot. Over and over her mind reassessed the things she could do to get them an income that would keep them alive and at their apartment until Davi could get back to work.

Xander could toss them out in a heartbeat and they'd be back at Cambridge's.

She took a quick break to text her teammates. *Anyone know of job openings? Help a girl stay alive.*

Valiana texted back within a few minutes. *Come waitress with me at Coma Bem!*

As evening approached, she took her boots back to Cambridge's. Her collection sold at their usual buyers despite their displeasure at the small amount she'd brought. She tucked the money into her bra and texted Davi that she was stopping by Valiana's. He thought she'd been at practice.

And he'd insist she come straight back if he knew she was walking around at dusk on her own. But she had to make money to keep them alive. He couldn't babysit her forever.

The outdoor seating of Coma Bem's was full when she arrived. Popular place. The aromas wafting from the restaurant taunted her aching stomach. Such a different world than the one she'd been a part of last week where she'd eaten a specific diet and as much as she wanted.

She waited outside until she saw Valiana back through the door with food on her tray. Valiana saw her and motioned for her to wait. When she'd dropped off the food, she greeted Daniela with a big hug.

"My manager let me pick up extra shifts since *futbol* is on hold." She scrunched up her face, her shoulders slumping slightly. "My mama agreed to watch the baby, if I'd bring home food. Come meet Olavo."

Inside the restaurant, the music blared and everyone tried to take over it. Valiana held her hand as they walked through the maze of chairs. *Futbol* played on large televisions on every wall. When they got halfway through the room, the diners surged to their feet, screaming and knocking over chairs.

The *futbol* players on the screen sprinted the length of the field to celebrate the goal with the one who scored. Her heart twinged. She'd hoped that someday this crowd would be upending tables cheering for her. It sounded insane to think that way.

Glancing around, she slammed the door on those far-fetched dreams for the future she'd had. Ifs and somedays had no place in her life. At least, she knew she had what it took to survive, and that was where her big plans for the future ended.

Chapter 24

Ronaldo reclined in a porch chair on Tia Ana's deck looking out at the sun creeping toward the water. The peace of the evening wildly contrasted the emotional turmoil inside his mind. Gia's parents, Sophia and Burley, came to visit and Sophia's mother Ana insisted on hosting a family get-together, especially since Gia and Xander were staying in her house. He'd arrived early, bringing his parents so Mama could socialize with her sister. Isadora was supposed to arrive after her shift was over. Everyone gathered in the kitchen and in front of the television, so they'd not noticed his escape to the rooftop.

It was Saturday evening. The board wanted him to present his plans on Tuesday. As it stood at the moment, he had done what they asked, on paper. Nothing was official yet though. All his free time had been devoted to finding a way to keep his girls' league alive. But a league required resources and money which the board had now allocated elsewhere.

Isadora texted him: *Coming in now.*

The sight of her name on his mobile phone made his heart jump every time.

He made his way downstairs to meet her at the door. They'd managed to keep their wedding a secret from everyone except his parents until now. When he opened the door, Isadora in a light skirt and sleeveless top stepped into his arms, smelling like heaven. Their kiss lingered.

Family evenings could wait.

"Want to go home now?" he whispered in her ear.

She winked, stepping away to greet his family. He followed her to the space between the kitchen and front room. There was an understanding that tonight's party would be in English as Burley and Xander were not bilingual as the rest of them were.

"Hey, everyone." Ronaldo shouted to be heard above the noise. It quieted quickly. "In case you haven't met her yet, I want to introduce this incredible woman to everyone at once. This is my wife, Doctor Isadora Rey."

The room erupted in screams and laughter followed by a swarm of bodies around them, congratulating them. He had no doubt Isadora would remember everyone without any problem. Tia Ana who had been married to Uncle Ignatius, Sophia and Burley, Sophia's little sister Judita and her husband Mateus and their two adult sons Silva and Ze, Sophia's brother Roberto and his wife Neves and their three adult children Antia, Sara, and Breno traded hugs and well wishes. After the congratulations came the scolding of not telling their family or inviting them to the wedding. Ronaldo ended up promising to give a party (which would likely cost an obscene amount of money thanks to his huge family) so loved ones could celebrate them properly.

He'd like it better if they just donated the money to his league and Isadora would love donations for her clinics. He shelved his work frustrations in lieu of enjoying a feast with Isadora sitting beside him, her hand on his leg. Papa had finished an exhaustingly long spiel framing the government for the current obesity crisis and how it profits from the unhealthy, when he contemplated throwing Isadora over his shoulder and going home.

"Dr. Rey, what most concerns you in the realm of healthcare today?" Sophia said.

It was his turn to squeeze her leg. She hardly needed his support though. "The list is lengthy, Sophia. Mosquito-borne illness, access to healthcare among the poor which could eliminate many of the epidemics, rising cost of medication which reduces the availability to those in a lower income bracket. It's not a problem to be sick if you're rich, but it's frequently a death sentence if you're poor."

"Cure poverty," Tia Ana murmured, raising her glass that had been magically refilled.

Oh no. She wouldn't dismiss her that easily. "Most recently, Isadora collected a wide range of data and presented a study on Zika to the National Medical Crisis Organization. She wanted to bring attention to the number of children being born with microcephaly because their mothers had contracted Zika," Ronaldo said.

No one made a sound.

"Did they listen?" Sophia asked.

Isadora scrunched her nose. "There's a lot of factors that go into whether or not they raise a red flag and declare something a crisis. They didn't think there was enough evidence tying Zika to microcephaly and its ability to be contracted easily, despite scientists publicly verifying it is mosquito-borne. Because it's often asymptomatic, we don't have real-time data on who has contracted it and how it spreads human to human. Unfortunately, they won't pursue the expense of prevention or cures unless a lot of people are dying from it."

"So it needs to threaten their expensive homes first, then," Burley said.

"Exactly." Isadora nodded. "And this won't go away any time soon, but if it's off the news, it's no longer considered a threat."

"Burley, didn't you say that the shipping industry plays a part in diseases being spread more quickly around the world?" Mateus asked.

In the Shadows

Burley set down his fork. "Because so many countries depend on imports and exports of food, we get weekly checks in port to make sure we're not bringing a disease that will wipe out the nation in our containers. Companies have quality control set up as well. No one wants to be ground zero for a nationwide outbreak."

"A country shouldn't be allowed to export food until all its countrymen are aptly fed," Tia Ana said.

"We got two good kids working on helping making the world a better place for those who need a leg up," Burley said, motioning toward the other room where Gia and Xander sat at a big table with all the other cousins.

"Here, here." Ronaldo added his glass to Burley's. The rest of the family followed suit.

Burley's record of donations, volunteer work, and setting up charities far outweighed all of them at the table put together. He'd been a hungry inventor looking for a way to sell his product. And he'd never forgotten those roots.

He met Sophia on a business trip to Brazil in the 80s while he attempted to source a manufacturer to take on his invention of hemp paper. At night, she managed the hotel where he stayed and by day, she brokered investors for startups. He asked her on a date. She agreed and convinced him to invest in a shipping startup which he eventually bought outright and turned into a major import-export shipper around the world. Together their business acumen made them worth a lot of money.

After dinner, Ronaldo and his cousins and all their spouses left the younger ones to play cards with Mama, Papa, and Tia Ana while they took their drinks to the roof to catch up. They took turns telling stories varying from their childhood memories to problems they saw at work to what their kids were doing. They were an eclectic crew.

Mateus sold computer software and Judita designed clothing for a boutique shop in upmarket part of Rio. On the west side of town, Roberto was the dean for a Catholic university where Neves taught music. They were empty-nesters now.

"Ronaldo, Breno, my youngest, started his freshman year at the State University of Rio this year. Got a full scholarship for *futbol*. He's talking about going pro someday like his famous uncle," Roberto said with a grin.

Ronaldo grunted. "Don't let him do it. It's a vile industry. Fame ruins a man."

They laughed.

"I have it on good authority that the new FCC president is turning things around though. He's a good man," Judita said.

The sigh came out before Ronaldo could stop it. "I'm afraid the board is tying my wrists in regards to change. They shut down my girls' league last week. They want to redirect the money in the budget to spoiling the men's national team more."

"What about all those donations to the girls?" Sophia asked.

"They're in danger of being refunded. We can't operate the league on what's left of the donations we received. Even if we could, the board isn't interested in me heading it up. My attention is needed elsewhere to save our country from certain humiliation at international matches."

Mateus whistled through his teeth. "You need money, a board, and a staff. Too bad you can't just hand it off the books to a league already up and running."

Neves spoke up. "Our university recruits from the Catholic academies around the nation. Schools have leagues. Can you scale back on the league and hand your team over to join one of the school leagues?"

"No, it's bigger than that, Nevie," Robert said. "He's looking to start an elite league, like Breno got invited to join."

"We've got a huge untapped population of girls who don't go to school and can't pay to get into a league." Ronaldo propped his ankle on his knee. "I want to run yearly tryouts in those areas to find girls to create teams. And donations and scholarships have allowed for us to provide schooling for the girls after practice with tutors for their varying education levels. One scholarship includes a babysitter."

The more Ronaldo talked about it the more he realized how deeply in love he was with his league. He couldn't give up on this. Giving up on it felt too much like he'd failed Mariana. Besides, it had incredible potential.

"It'd be a huge investment into each player just to maybe get them onto the national team. Millions of *reals* to win a World Cup or Olympics someday," Nevie said.

"There are other streams of income. An established team can pay a fee to join the league and since it's an FCC league, they'd know that the big-time coaches and recruiters would be watching. The country has a lot of separate leagues in place, but there are not enough recruiters out there to sort through all the talent. We need to bring the talent to our doorstep in order to choose the best of the best for our national teams. And the parents in the poor areas have their daughters working or some of the girls have babies already or some of them are selling their bodies on a street corner because they don't see a way out of poverty."

Mateus leaned in. "How would you incentivize the leagues so the parents would let their daughters join? You can't exactly say 'let your daughter play *futbol* in case she becomes a super star someday.'"

"Collaboration," Burley said.

They turned to face him. He'd been so quiet the whole time Ronaldo had assumed he wasn't interested in the conversation.

"If the purpose of the league is to help, it would need to have an infrastructure in place. The league would need to partner with organizations that provide services like a food pantry, job placement, health care, and so on. *Futbol* would have to meet a need for the family to allow it. That would involve a team being dedicated to identifying needs and meeting them," Burley said.

"Sounds like it would need a whole corporate team to run it," Sophia said.

"That's far more than a *futbol* league needs to do. Why not keep it simple and request the outside organizations show up during tryouts to give the girls access to resources they might need then? Why keep them on payroll, so to speak?" Judita asked. "When we have runway shows to reveal our new collections each spring, we invite the other boutique shops to set up tables so the clients coming can get the whole package."

Ronaldo shrugged. "I honestly don't mind how it runs, so long as the league is running to benefit the low-income families, too. We drew up the paperwork as an official FCC league. I'm not sure I can legally just hand that over to someone."

"Sell it," Sophia said. "The board would probably be happy with the financial burden off their backs. You make money from the sale and can still see annual income from the other teams wanting to join the FCC-sanctioned league. The FCC wins."

"Create a for-profit and sell it to yourself," Mateus said. "And you win, too. You have your baby and control."

Ronaldo shook his head, but Isadora beat him to it. "We're newly married. I want to see my husband at least once a day."

Burley nodded, as he wrapped his arms around Sophia's shoulders. "Not a relationship worth sacrificing for work. We learned that the hard way."

They echoed most of the same thoughts he'd had before. "If I sold it, I'd like to stay in an advisory position. But owning it would be a conflict of interest."

"Why don't we buy it?" Sophia asked.

Ronaldo sat back. Sophia and Burley knew business. Their track records with success spoke for themselves. He could see that.

Roberto laughed. "Don't you have enough on your plate with the businesses you already own? Besides you live across the ocean."

In the Shadows

"No, I mean all of us." Sophia's smile broadened like it always did when she got a crazy idea.

"Uh oh. It's that look," Judita said with a laugh.

Ronaldo's heart started racing with his mind, piecing together what that would mean.

Sophia huffed. "No look. We all want to retire well." She glanced around, her eyebrows raised. Everyone nodded slowly as if waiting for their spouse to agree before they did. "Everyone here on this rooftop except Ronaldo can have a piece. Without Ronaldo's buy in, we'd have a majority of women owning the company and might see a tax break, depending on the laws. You guys are here to oversee things in Rio. Ronaldo stays on board as an advisor since this is his project anyway. If we keep it in the family for now, Ronaldo can trust the direction it's going to take."

"Who would run it though? None of us know anything about running a league," Mateus said.

"I already have a staff in place, but we'd need to replace a few of the key roles. My role being the most important to get right," Ronaldo said. There would probably be a host of people who wanted to get in on running it from the ground-level. Some of his former teammates would probably be game to invest.

"We can't just choose anyone to take over. Whoever it is needs to have a good head for business," Roberto said.

"Someone who really loves *futbol*," Neves said. "I'd say Breno, but he's too young."

"Antia, Sara, Silva, or Ze?" Ronaldo asked.

Judita's face glowered in disapproval. "Not our boys. Silva is a dentist and Ze designs video games."

"Antia is a marine biologist. Sara might be interested. She does marketing for a company somewhere," Neves said, with a flutter of her hand.

"I've got plenty of contacts that love *futbol* and business. They need to have passion," Ronaldo said.

Mateus nodded. "The person has to care about setting these girls up for success in their future and helping their families if they want it."

"Someone willing to let Ronaldo lead," Isadora said.

Xander popped his head up from the stairwell. "I've been sent to request that you rejoin us in the front room for an evening nightcap."

That sent them into a fit of laughter. Tia Ana did not request anything. She got her way or else everyone regretted it.

When Xander disappeared, Judita was the first to say what Ronaldo was thinking. "Xander?"

"He was a *futbol* coach and he's now running a business which he is trying to get running here in Brazil as well as in the US. He loves helping others," Burley said.

"He's American. Not a seasoned businessman. Doesn't speak the language. And he'd need to be back in the States for his business there," Roberto said, quietly.

"Whoever takes over will need someone to show him the ropes of what Ronaldo has in mind. You can't expect a twenty-something to get dumped in the deep end and have it altogether. Someone has to take them under their wing. We were mentored in our jobs. They need it, too," Mateus said.

Sophia stepped in with her hands raised. "How about we ask him first to see if he's interested? If he's not interested long-term, maybe he'd step in short-term until we can finalize something with another candidate. Although truth be told, most experienced CEOs would probably want more pay than we can offer and would want to run things their way."

"I second Sophia. We ask first," Judita said.

Ronaldo's chest loosened as he let out the breath he'd been holding. "We'd need to draw up the paperwork for it, talk monetary needs, agree on a price, and I'd make sure I have the board's approval on it. They don't see the league as having any value, so they would probably be delighted to have that off the books."

As they descended to the lower floor, Ronaldo saw a glimmer of light breaking through the clouds. This could work. Or he could kiss his long-awaited dreams goodbye.

Chapter 25

That night, Daniela came home to tell Davi the news that Coma Bem's owner Olavo offered her a waitressing job. His fury had yet to subside. The styrofoam container of food Valiana had sent home with her hadn't placated him like she'd hoped. While he ate, she retold the whole story of her day, knowing she'd regret telling him that Gerson had come after her.

But if she didn't, Cambridge would.

He listened silently as she talked through the news of the league being on hold, the attack, the rejection at Xander's, and then finally an offer of a job that she couldn't turn down.

His head shook almost imperceptibly. "No, you absolutely can't waitress. I'll go back to work tomorrow so you don't have to worry. Please, Daniela."

"It's safe. I don't cross the Linha Amarela into *favela* territory. Valiana works there. I'm five bus stops from here. They wouldn't ask me to do anything illegal."

"I'm not trying to be irrational here, but what happens if Gerson finds you and decides to express his displeasure when Cambridge isn't around?" Davi's eyes plead with her.

"It's a huge city and we don't live near his stomping grounds anyway." She took his hand. "I know you're concerned. I want to do this. I have to. I've lost or nearly lost everything I love in the

In the Shadows

past few months. I need something to keep my mind off of—" she swallowed. "Life and all the disappointment."

They'd ended the discussion with Davi saying he'd think about it, but she was going to do it anyway. She couldn't bear to sit around doing nothing. The next day, he merely nodded as she kissed his cheek and headed out.

With team practices cancelled, as many girls as could met in the mornings to run around the stadium. Daniela used her bus pass and got off one stop later. It felt strange being in a part of town safe enough to walk places without Davi, but she really enjoyed the freedom. They didn't have access to the interior of the stadium anymore, so they jogged laps around the whole stadium.

This morning two men waited for them as they made their second lap. The men started jogging in front of the girls as they caught up.

Coach Cevere and Coach Habus.

The girls called out their greetings. As they jogged, the coaches asked everyone how they were doing and what they kept busy with. When they finished up their final lap, the coaches stayed to talk. Everyone wanted to know when practice would start back up again.

"I don't know the answer to that," Coach Cevere said, shoving his hands into his shorts' pockets. "But I have a big meeting tomorrow to see if we can't get back to it soon. I'll let you girls know. Keep in shape. I've got our stadium security watching out for you each morning. This is the safest place you can be."

Life felt like all the good things had been put on hold right now. If she was honest, she wasn't coping with the disappointment well. Her shift at Coma Bem's started in two hours, so Daniela rode the bus to Gabi's store.

She hadn't been in so long, and if anyone knew about dealing with disappointment, it was Gabi. She pulled the door open, jingling the bells against the glass. A squeal came from the checkout desk that Gabi scrambled to get around.

"I've missed you, Daniela!" Gabi's words muffled in Daniela's shoulder. She smelled of frankincense balm she used on her hands for arthritis and chest for her cough.

A warmth spread from head to toe. "I've missed you, too."

Gabi guided her toward the back. "I've got everything I need to make breakfast for us, if you're hungry."

Her stomach settled into her post-run hunger ache. "Very hungry."

"Having to get news and updates from Cambridge about you is not the same as hearing it straight from you. You talk while I get things prepared."

Daniela told her everything she'd told Davi and Cambridge plus a little more that included how she felt about training, Gerson, the girls' league, moving, Davi getting attacked, her getting attacked. Invariably, Gabi would prompt her for this information if she left it out.

"I guess I'm really disappointed and discouraged." The lump grew in Daniela's throat as she voiced the words. "I thought this could be it."

Gabi nodded as she set the table. "There is one thing in my life that I have been absolutely sure about and it's that I was meant to serve God. As sure as I was about my heart's next beat. I knew when I met Him as a child that I wouldn't be happy doing anything else, but His work. In my teen years, I found out I am one of the very rare cases in the world that has contracted emphysema from a lack of protein that lungs require to stay healthy. Grab those waters, would you?"

They sat down at the table and Gabi prayed over their food.

"I wanted to do mission work, but my doctors said traveling would expose me to elements that could kill me." Gabi shrugged. "The thought of dying on the field didn't bother me one bit. Except there wasn't a mission board out there that agreed to send

In the Shadows

me out with my health being so precarious. So, I went to school to teach children. They would be my mission field. But they gave me so many sicknesses that I was gone more than I was there."

The doorbell jingled. Gabi got up and returned in five minutes.

Her plate was empty, but Gabi's wasn't so she waited at the table.

"What did you do after teaching?" Daniela said.

"I got a job in a small church as a receptionist. But as the church shrank, I lost my job. From there, I applied to every convent I could around the world while I worked odd jobs at shelters, women and children crisis centers, and volunteered at church. When the church I volunteered at needed someone to run this store for a bit, I agreed. Short-term, I told them. I was sure I'd get into one of the convents I applied for."

"But you didn't?"

Gabi gave Daniela a half smile. "My health prevented me once again. I said to God, 'you were the one who gave me this health. How am I supposed to serve you if I can't even do what you asked me to do?' I asked him this with more anger every time I got rejected. But you know what you helped me realize?"

Her? Daniela raised her eyebrows. Nothing came to mind.

"You showed me that my service is right here." Gabi leaned in, her hand resting on Daniela's. "Every time that door opens, another soul finds their way in here. Some need me. I need them. But all those years of disappointment and frustration have finally led me to peace. I had an idea of what I thought I needed to do in life, so I chased it hard. I couldn't see that my mission was right in front of me. I don't regret it. All that brought me here to having you, Cambridge, and Davi in my life, such special gifts."

Daniela grinned. "Especially Cambridge, right?"

Gabi laughed. "What I'm saying is, it's okay to be disappointed that life hasn't looked like you wanted it to, but don't do what I did and miss the bigger picture. Don't give up on *futbol*, but stay open to new things. They may lead you to places you never dreamed." She collected their plates, lapsing into a coughing fit as she did.

Daniela stayed for another half hour to help Gabi before she took the bus to Coma Bem's for her shift. Something had settled within her. Her disappointment lingered, but Gabi's words touched a nerve.

The next morning at dawn, Daniela, Davi, and Cambridge took the bus to the waterfront. This early the beach was coming to life, but not crowded. They trudged through the sand, leaving their footprints to be washed away by the waves. When they reached the edge of the beach, Daniela led them to the edge of the grassy outcropping. There she laid the rough-hewn cross of wood scraps and string. Next to it, Cambridge and Davi placed the flowers they'd picked off some bushes.

"Life has happened really fast recently. And I didn't see the pain in my heart until I sat with Gabi yesterday. Mamãe wasn't perfect. She made bad choices about drugs." Daniela choked. Saying it out loud felt like betrayal. Davi embraced her in a side hug with his good arm. "She held us tight when we were small. She fed us what food she could find, tended our injuries, made sure we had a place to sleep at night. It wasn't fair that she contracted a disease and died. I wanted her to be at my *futbol* games someday. And I suppressed my sadness when she died, but now I'm okay to sit with it. I want to honor her as my mother, the one who sang to us when we were sad and taught us games to keep us out of Gerson's way when he came home drunk, every night."

She stopped. This wasn't going how she wanted it to go.

"We'll always remember you, Mamãe," Davi said in the silence. "And thank you for giving us life and each other."

Cambridge lowered his head. "You giving me Davi and Daniela as friends will forever be a treasure to me. Thank you, Patricia."

In the Shadows

Her hair blew the long strands into her face. She inhaled deeply as if the salty air could cleanse her grief. When she exhaled, the pain remained. The wind gently ruffled the flowers, pulling them toward the water.

"Mamãe, we miss your steady presence. You loved us and we loved you. Goodbye." The words choked from her throat as the breeze took the flowers off the cross and down the side of the slope.

They didn't chase them to put them back. They belonged to wherever the wind wanted to take them. Her life looked like that flower, battered and moved but by pain and fear. All those amazing dreams that she'd imagined as a child on her bed on the floor in their small apartment had been dangled in front of her face only to be taken away.

But without them, she gave unending thanks for the gifts she had and the good change that had come. Daniela pulled away from Davi and began the walk toward the bus station.

"Can I come with you to the stadium for running practice?" Davi asked. "I need to stay out of the apartment. I'm dying of boredom. I've finished the stack of books Cambridge brought me."

It wouldn't hurt anything. Coach Cevere said it was safe and they were running.

Cambridge stopped them short of the bus stop. "Before we go, I wanted to tell you both together that Xander has asked me to consider being the manager of The Upcycled Life here in Rio. He's still going to oversee it, but he wouldn't be as hands on since he has another venture he's going to be heading up for a bit. My job would be to identify people who need help, teach them how to make things, find resources to support them with other needs. I'm not sure of everything it involves yet, but I'm thinking I'd like to take it. He said it would be a salary position with benefits instead of hourly."

"That would be incredible, Cambridge," Davi said with grin.

Daniela threw her arms around him. "You have to take it! You know so many people who could use help."

Cambridge nodded, his half-smile turning on full beam. "We could really see some change in our community. He said we could establish a library for those in need, too. Davi, he said I could appoint you to be our acquisitions director, so you'd be in charge of sourcing all the materials. We work well together. I wouldn't fire you."

Davi laughed. "Yes, Cambridge. I will be your right-hand man. Anything to keep us out of Gerson and Chacal's way. We might eventually be able to afford sending Daniela to the training center for longer with that job."

Daniela's heart swelled. He was always thinking of her. Maybe her team would get shut down for good, but if she could train at the center more, then she'd stay in shape and under the coach's eye. Gabi was right. She couldn't give up on what was in front of her.

They split off from Cambridge at the bus stop as he went back to work with Xander. Davi and Daniela took the bus to the stadium. They were there early so they sat on the benches.

"It was a miracle Gerson didn't do more damage with the way he came after me," Davi said after a few moments of silence.

Daniela sighed. "I'm so grateful we got away from him. He's a really awful person, Davi. How did we end up with a father who hated us so much?"

"I don't know." He shook his head. "I used to think I understood him a little bit. Poverty can destroy a man. Cambridge made it sound that Gerson had let bitterness eat him alive. Maybe that's true. Maybe it was his addiction influences. Chacal seemed to know him pretty well."

"Hey, Daniela," a voice called from behind them.

Up walked Valiana carrying her baby.

Daniela hopped to her feet. "Hi, Val. You brought Domitila today. Hi, sweet girl!"

In the Shadows

Valiana met her at the bench. "Mama backed out on watching her last minute, so I came to enjoy the time near my team though you will have to run without me today."

Davi stood beside her. "Val, this is my brother, Davi."

Valiana's eyes widened a fraction as she said hello, but she didn't look away. Daniela stepped back, glancing between them. What was going on?

Davi's grin was huge. "Nice to meet you, Valiana. Daniela has told me a lot about you. And your beautiful baby girl looks just like her mother."

Valiana laughed, shifting Domi on her hip. "She might look like me, but she is terrible at *futbol* so far. And she does no exercise, just eats and sleeps and sits."

Davi snorted. "Sounds like she and I have the same schedule right now. She and I could hang out together and heckle you girls as you run today, if you actually want to exercise."

Daniela didn't think it was possible, but Valiana stood staring without saying any words.

"I think that is perfect, Davi. You and Domitila can swap stories on all your favorite bedtime stories," Daniela said. She was almost positive they'd forgotten she was there. They had yet to look in her direction.

"That would be so kind, Davi. Thank you. When Daniela said you were the most selfless person she knows, she wasn't kidding." Valiana followed Davi to a small patch of grass and settled Domitila next to Davi's uninjured arm.

As the other girls showed up, Valiana rejoined the group barely able to take her eyes off the two sitting in the grass.

"Dibs on Daniela's brother, Davi, ladies," Valiana said to no one in particular. "He may possibly be the sexiest man alive."

Chapter 26

The nerves churned in Ronaldo's stomach in a way no *futbol* game ever had. He hadn't eaten anything for the last twenty-four hours as he gathered paperwork for the approaching meeting. Isadora watched him with her doctorly eye, but said nothing about his refusal of food and incessant pacing as he reviewed his presentation to the board. He was fairly certain she slipped something into his drink to help him calm down enough to sleep.

The members of the board gathered in the conference room, unaware of his battle against nausea. This wasn't a high stakes game to them. His whole adult life he'd been positioning himself to make a difference for the girls stuck in poverty, like Mariana had. This was his biggest shot at making that dream come true.

At last, the time came to start. He signaled for Katrina to turn off the lights. She looked as worried as he did. They'd pulled out all the stops for this meeting. Would it be enough?

"Good morning, everyone. Please help yourself to the refreshments on the table. I want to thank you for being incredibly supportive of my transition into this role." He clicked on the slides Katrina had put together with bullet points and graphs. "As a former professional player, the perks and incentives are very familiar to me. So I asked myself, what made me push harder in my career? As well, I took a poll amongst our current players.

In the Shadows

While you might anticipate money being the answer, it's not in the way you think. These players are smart. They know their playable years are limited. None of them said they would turn down a pay raise per game, but if they lose early on in tournaments, that pay boost per game is nonexistent. These guys want sponsorships and influencer opportunities beating down their doors. They're in peak physical fitness. They want to be paid for their photos in magazines, to endorse clothing companies, to be brought on for marketing campaigns for food and drink companies. And they want those relationships to last."

"How do we give them what they want?" a male voice asked.

"I'm glad you asked. The FCC holds their future in our hands. We oversee all the dealings with players to make sure our players are being treated fairly as well as the companies are receiving what they want. If we don't call a player up to the international scene, no one will want to sign an endorsement deal. So we rework our contracts. Deals are no longer multi-year in length. Each year, everyone is up for renewal with the exception of those who have notified us they are moving into retirement. We vet the companies and give them our recommendations for sponsoring. If the players aren't performing well, they risk losing their deals the next year."

"Do we earn a fee for brokering the deal?" Idal asked. His relaxed posture was a great sign.

"We do."

He continued through with the changes he'd made on the men's side and called for a lunch break in which he'd strategically brought in a drink cart that included all of their favorite beverages of every kind.

When everyone was happy and loosened up, he dove into the second part of the presentation.

"Now, with the changes we made on the men's side, we're still going to see some margin in our budget. This is good but it's not enough to continue funding the girls' league that funnels into our women's national team."

Someone made a derogatory comment about girls being a sideshow anyway. He gritted his teeth.

"Let me tell you a story. Once upon a time, there was a young girl who grew up in a bad part of town with a family who loved her deeply. This girl and her brother were thirteen months apart and inseparable. As they chose careers, the girl had a heart of gold and could not bear to live in a world where women were treated so horribly. So, she spent her days working to extract women from dangerous situations, place them in secure jobs, and get them away from their abusive relationships.

One night, a woman called this girl to come rescue her. Her boyfriend had found her and was threatening to kill her. She, of course, rushed to the woman's aid. When she arrived, she located the woman in need of rescuing and just as they got into her car, the boyfriend came out of the shadows and gunned them both down by emptying his automatic weapon clips into their bodies.

That angel with a heart of gold was my sister, Mariana. Her body had so many bullet holes in it that it took the coroners hours of stitching so they wouldn't put pieces of her body in the casket we were burying." Pressure built behind his eyes. He breathed deeply in the silence, willing his emotions to stay at bay after all these years. "The day before she was murdered, she vented to me on the phone about the situations of these girls she helped. 'Ronaldo, if they just had something to look forward to, someone to care for them, someone to give them a boost, there wouldn't be such a huge gap between the poor and middle class. If we could identify their need and a find a way to keep them in school and off the streets, they might be able to break the cycle of poverty.'

Mariana believed in giving others opportunities. Her generosity led her to put herself in danger and ultimately be killed at gunpoint. But that doesn't have to happen to everyone. A sports' league will not necessarily save anyone, but it gives us a

In the Shadows

chance to identify needs and match kids with organizations that can help.

The girls' league we started saw over three hundred and twelve girls come to the tryouts across the city. The *Guerreiras* team provides schooling and aid through donations to fifteen girls who live in poverty on a daily basis. These numbers could grow exponentially which is why I'd like you to approve the sale of the girls' league to a private group of buyers. They are passionate about seeing change in our city and especially with the at-risk children in poor communities. They have agreed to paying a fee to the FCC each year for the league still to be considered FCC-sanctioned. And they would be able to provide resources to help these girls that we do not have manpower to do in-house. That said, we do have room in the budget for discretionary use in supporting this league's running." He paused to look around at the group who hadn't so much as rustled paper since he began his story. "Any questions?"

They shook their heads.

It was time to make this official. "All in favor of the sale?" Ronaldo said.

The vote was unanimous.

****

"Happy birthday, Daniela!" her teammates screamed as she approached the park outside the *favela*.

Valiana insisted she bring Davi along to celebrate with them. She'd said something about the importance of including family in big events, but it wasn't lost on Daniela that she'd gotten his phone number "to thank him for his help." Daniela had caught Davi grinning at his phone several times that day.

The girls brought what little food they could muster, but more importantly everyone had brought their *futbol* gear so they could spend the evening playing. They wasted no time separating into teams so they could put that ball in play. Davi volunteered to be the completely impartial referee, although he missed some of the calls because he'd been distracted by Valiana.

As dusk dimmed their ability to see the ball clearly, they called the game and followed Aline through the woods with one light to illuminate their way. They laughed in fits up the path as girls tripped and fell over roots.

Daniela held onto Davi's free hand to keep him from plunging head first and undoing the healing he'd accomplished so far. They moved slower than the rest of the group, but Daniela liked it that way. Gilma stayed with them though, because she said she couldn't see anything in the dark. Daniela had never heard of that.

What if they were taking her out to the woods to mess with her since it was her sixteenth birthday?

"Are you sure you know the way?" Lecia called out again.

"By heart. Stop questioning me or you'll regret it when we get there," Aline yelled into the dark.

The front of the group disappeared around a bend. When Davi, Daniela, and Gilma reached the bend, bodies jumped out at them screaming.

Daniela about peed in her shorts. Davi only flinched slightly.

"I'm never coming out here in the dark with you crazy kids again," Daniela said.

Noemia, Pedrina, and Andressa laughed the rest of the way up the hill. They stopped when they broke through the trees. Just ahead, a million lights glittered beneath them. Beyond that, the pure black of the ocean contrasted it starkly.

"Careful when you sit down. You don't want to go over the edge," Aline said.

They sat with their feet dangling over the edge. A rush of adrenaline surged through Daniela's veins. Here she was with her best friends celebrating her birthday on top of the world. When they got settled next to Valiana, Davi pulled out Daniela's favorite chocolate treat from his bag.

"Happy birthday," he whispered, handing it to her.

In the Shadows

"All right, Daniela. Since you're the birthday girl, you start. Name your biggest dream, something weird about yourself, and your biggest fear," Andressa said.

Daniela popped some chocolate in her mouth. "My biggest dream is to play in the World Cup and win." A chorus of agreement echoed her. "I've never been in a romantic relationship with a guy." Gasps. "Biggest fear is losing everything because I'm not good enough. I nominate Lecia."

Lecia's fear was never finding someone to love.

Aline's was losing her eyesight.

Andressa's was never being able to support all seven of her siblings.

Valiana's was losing Domitila.

Pedrina's was that her family would kick her out for playing *futbol*.

Gilma's was dying from cancer as her mama had.

Noemia's was that she would always live to survive and never get out of Rio.

When Noemia finished, Andressa broke the silence. "I could stay up here with you fools forever, but I have to get up early with the babies tomorrow before running."

"Can I share mine before we leave?" Davi asked, his voice low. "My dream is to be a successful businessman. I have never learned how to swim. And my biggest fear is that I'll not be there to protect Daniela most when she needs it."

Every single girl sighed and told him how precious he was.

"This sixteen-year old is going places," he shouted into the night.

They cheered as they stood and started the descent. When they reached the street, they stopped in a lit parking lot to chat and say goodbye. Andressa and Valiana had to head home to care for the babies. The rest of them were going to get on the bus to go to their sections of town.

But a group of guys approached them before anyone had time to leave.

"Brother, this is far too many women for one man to handle. Do you need some help?" A long-haired, skinny man swaggered over to them. His shoulders and arms were almost bones beneath his large clothing. His teeth were gray when he smiled.

Davi stepped in front of the man's path. "We were all leaving. It's late and time for everyone to go to sleep to get ready to work tomorrow."

The man didn't look at Davi but kept walking. The other guys in the group did the same, but they appeared to be more Daniela's age. Laughing and smoking, they walked closer.

Daniela glanced around. She couldn't see Andressa or Valiana's backs anymore. They were out of the sight. She motioned the girls to start walking with her toward the bus stop.

"We're headed home, guys. If you take a short walk up that path right there, you can see the whole city at night." Davi pointed the group up to where the trail came out of the trees.

But the guys stopped and stood, eyeing the girls. They made polite conversation, trying not to set any of them off.

"I don't see a path. Show me." So Davi pulled out his mobile phone, held it in his hand, and walked the older man toward the path.

The younger boys stayed.

"You girls look nice. Are you sure you're not going out for tonight?" one of them asked.

Aline shook her head. "We're going home like Davi said."

Another boy stepped over to Gilma and sniffed the air. "You smell edible."

Daniela fidgeted with her mobile phone in her pocket. They had to get out of here. Maybe she could distract the guys long enough to send her teammates away.

"Look guys, I'll show you the path your friend is going to see," Daniela said. "It's just a short—"

In the Shadows

The sound of screeching tires drowned out her next words. An explosion of gunshots rang out over the parking lot. Screams pierced her ears. A sharp pain in her arm dropped her to the ground. Beside her, bodies hit the pavement with a dull thud. Her vision was blacking out. She couldn't see who was hit and how bad.

Where was Davi? What if Davi had been hit? She struggled to her knees.

"Davi. Davi!" She screamed. But her screams made her vision black again. She crawled toward the body closest to her. It was the guy she'd been talking to. Another body lay close. Aline.

"No," she whispered. Not her teammates. Her friends. The girls she'd just shared her hopes and dreams with, not forty minutes ago.

She dropped to the ground on her stomach. She just needed to rest for a second. Then she'd find Davi.

Time slowed. As she lay there, she heard a voice screaming her name. Davi. That was Davi's voice.

"I'm here," she said. Or did she say it?

There was a warm puddle flowing past her fingers. Hands grabbed her body and pushed her onto her back.

"Daniela, wake up. Wake up."

She opened her eyes, blinking twice to clear the fog.

"Thank God. What hurts?" Davi said, his hands pulling at her shirt. "Somebody, help." He roared into the night. "Your side and arm are bleeding. It looks your side is bloody but I can't see a hole and your arm was hit. Here hold your shirt to your arm. I'll be right back." He pressed her hand to her arm and she lay there holding it.

He was okay. He was there to help. They were going to be okay.

When he reappeared, he wore no shirt.

"Aline's shoulder is hit, but she's alive. Noemia is unharmed. I can't get Pedrina, Lecia, or Gilma to wake up." Davi's breath came in harsh pants. "I have to try again, but there's so much blood. So much, Daniela. Hold on to your arm. Try to stop the bleeding."

When he left again, the pain doubled. She cried out. Her vision narrowed into the black. It hurt so badly. Why couldn't Davi make the pain go away?

She just needed to close her eyes.

Chapter 27

The shrill ring of his phone jolted Ronaldo from his nap on the couch. The last week of worrying about the board meeting earlier today had left him low on sleep. With the win came a huge exhale of relief.

He debated not answering, but the screen said Isadora so he fumbled the phone to his ear. "Hi, love. How is your shift going?"

"Not good, Ronaldo." Her voice was dangerously calm. "You need to get down here now. Davi and Daniela came in along with eight other gunshot wound victims. Davi says the girls were from your *futbol* team. I'll tell you more when you get here."

Instantly awake, Ronaldo called his town car service for an emergency ride and dressed himself in whatever he could find while he waited.

Not again.

Not another call about gun violence on people he cared about.

He stuffed random food items in a bag along with his laptop. The car arrived and he took off to the hospital. He was out of the vehicle before it stopped rolling.

Inside the emergency room, he stopped at the desk. "Dr. Isadora Rey said to page her when I got here. I'm her husband."

The nurse eyed him suspiciously, but lifted the phone and call Isadora. The nurse's eyes widened as she talked.

In the Shadows

When she hung up, she said, "I'll take you to her." He followed the nurse around the corner and down a corridor. She showed him into a break room.

He opened his contacts to call his cousins, but he had no information yet. Back and forth, he paced. A nurse came in and then a doctor. No one stayed long.

Finally, the door popped open and Isadora stormed in. She wrapped him in a big hug and gave him a tired smile. "Congratulations on your success today. I hate to end your day like this. We got eight gunshot wound victims an hour and a half ago. All four males were dead by the time they got here." She took a deep breath. "Five girls came in. Three were dead on arrival."

Ronaldo covered his mouth with his hand. "No, not again."

Isadora touched her arm. "Daniela and Aline are in surgery. Davi and Noemia are waiting for them in the surgical wing waiting room. Daniela took a bullet to the left arm and broke the bone. The bullet must have gone through someone else first. Otherwise, it would have shattered the bone and caused her way more damage. Another bullet grazed her side, but didn't do any internal damage. Aline took a bullet to her upper thigh and it miraculously missed arteries, but the surgeons are checking to see if it hit her nerve. She may never play *futbol* again. Both girls should survive surgery and make a full recovery unless the surgeons encounter complications."

He scrubbed his hands down his face. "Who were the victims? What were their names?"

Isadora looked at the clipboard. "Pedrina, Gilma, and Lecia all suffered fatal gunshot wounds from a high-velocity automatic to the torso area. Our nurses are tracking down any parents listed on their *registro geral*." She sighed and wrapped her arms around him. "I'm so sorry, Ronaldo. They were all kids, the guys, too."

The trauma wound from Mariana's death reopened, feeling too fresh and too big. Davi had to be feeling at least a portion of his grief.

"I'll go sit with the kids while they wait." He grabbed his bag and followed Isadora into the hall.

She grabbed his hand and held it through the hospital corridors. Her touch settled his heart, as if she transferred her calm through the touch of their skin. They stopped shy of going through the doors.

Her eyes searched his. Love and pain scrolled across her features. "Take tomorrow off. I get off at six. I'll grab a few hours of sleep and we can spend the rest of the day together doing whatever needs to be done for these families. I'm not on again until the day after tomorrow."

He set his bag down at their feet and pulled her to him once more. The agony lessened with her against his heart. He kissed her hard as if she would provide the oxygen to breathe again. Her hands cradled his head. They poured their grief into their connection.

They broke apart and she rested her forehead against his chin. "Thank you, Isadora, for calling me. I'll email Katrina tonight to let her know what happened and that I won't be in."

They said goodbye and Isadora went off to save more lives. And he headed in to the waiting room. Noemia saw him first. She ran to him tears streaming down her face.

"Coach..." she hiccuped.

Ronaldo hugged her, his heart ripping apart again. Her friends were gone. When she let go, he grabbed Davi next. He didn't know him well, but it didn't matter. In his mind, he was hugging the version of himself from twenty years ago he wished he could have been. He longed for her to have been spared. Surgery and recovery far exceeded the years of grief after losing his best friend, his closest confidante.

In the Shadows

"Tell me what happened," Ronaldo said, settling into a chair next to the couch they had been occupying.

That started Noemia's tears afresh. Davi grabbed her hand.

"Daniela and I met with a group of the girls from the team to celebrate Daniela's sixteenth birthday. We met outside the Linha Amarela near the *favelas*. The girls played *futbol* and then we walked up to oversight point. We came down so we could go home, but while we said goodbye in the parking lot, the group of women drew the attention of some guys on drugs.

They approached and we were trying to engage. I distracted the leader by moving him away from the group. We heard tires squeal and a police car came around the corner spraying bullets everywhere. Everybody hit the ground. I couldn't believe what I was seeing. When I realized what had happened, I ran toward the parking lot. The guy next to me split. There was blood everywhere. It took me a bit to find Daniela. Once I knew she was okay, I went to the others. They didn't move. They laid there." His voice cracked.

It wasn't cartel violence. It was police retaliation. He excused himself. His first call was to Rio's chief of police. They had a solid relationship as the FCC required police screening with stadium events.

He went to voicemail. "Leandro, it's Ronaldo Cevere. I apologize for the late-night call. I'm sitting in the hospital waiting room with two of my team members in surgery and three in the morgue. Survivors think it may have been police bullets. It happened tonight around ten. Please, give me a call and let me know if this was your guys."

He hoped with everything in him that it wasn't how it looked. That Davi imagined Police in bold letters across the side of the vehicle in the dark.

"Noemia, have you contacted your family?" Ronaldo asked.

She shook her head. "We don't have mobile phones."

He glanced at his watch. Taking her back to the *favelas* tonight was a huge risk.

"You can stay at our apartment until the morning," Davi said. "I'll be here with Daniela."

They agreed to wait until the girls were safely out of surgery before Ronaldo had his town car drive Noemia to Daniela's apartment for the night. Ronaldo opened his laptop and set to work writing emails to his staff, his family, and the board about what happened.

He wrote out a list of things they would need to do. The families were being contacted. But would they have money for funerals? Ronaldo made a note to check.

He started working on an official statement to let the media know his players had been senselessly murdered. He drew up an email with the details to send to Brazilian News Corporation about it.

The doctors came out after an hour and a half more of waiting. They stood.

"Daniela is out of surgery and awake. Aline will be waking up soon. Would you like to see Daniela?" the surgeon said.

Davi nodded and took Noemia into the room with him. Ronaldo called his town car while they went in. She came out after a couple of minutes, looking beaten down.

"I don't think I can see Aline tonight," Noemia said. "Would you mind if I left for Daniela's soon?"

Ronaldo walked her down to the front entrance and gave the driver strict instructions to make sure she made it inside the building safely before leaving. Davi had given her Daniela's key and mobile phone so she could contact him if she needed anything.

As he walked back in, his phone rang.

"Chief," he said, stepping into a quiet alcove.

In the Shadows

"Cevere," Chief's naturally booming voice was quieter. "I'm sorry to call so late, but I wanted you to have some answers tonight."

"I appreciate the efficiency. Did you find anything?"

Leandro sighed. "Yes, it was retaliation for a couple of our officers being shot down in the *favelas* last week."

He braced himself against the wall. "So they mowed down innocent kids?" His words came through gritted teeth. The heat in his neck rose exponentially.

"I'm sorry that happened. I didn't sanction it. It isn't right or fair, Cevere. It's the world we live in right now. I'm sorry about your team members. I really am." Leandro sounded exhausted.

"They were teenage girls, the same age as your kids." A few years younger than Mariane. His jaw hurt from the tension of gritting his teeth.

"Do what you need to do, Cevere. I don't blame you. But know our people don't let cop-killing go unanswered. If the cartels see us give a pass to our men being ambushed, then we look soft and they take over the city. The girls weren't supposed to be there tonight."

Ronaldo's mind played tug-of-war. He saw both sides, but that didn't bring him any peace. He abhorred the endless violence. Neither side would back down or agree to a ceasefire. Both wanted control and would do anything to keep what they had and get more.

In the waiting room, he revised his official statement, condemning both sides for their senseless murders and their need to even the score regardless of who lost their life because of it. He called for more accountability and harsher punishments for murderers.

Davi joined him in the waiting room. "Daniela and Aline are sharing a room. Both are awake and would love to see you."

He closed his laptop and moved into their room. Aline, once known for her speed on the field, now lay under blankets, pale and obviously fighting the drowsiness of the pain medications she was on.

Daniela's arm lay propped on a pile of pillows, the bandage thick and bulky. She offered him a weak smile as she rolled her head to see his entrance.

"Hi, Coach. Thanks for coming," she said, her voice quiet.

"The surgeon said I may never play *futbol* again," Aline slurred, then burst into tears. "Our team is ruined. They're dead, Coach. They didn't deserve to die."

Ronaldo strode to her bedside and gripped her hand. "Listen to me, Aline. You will heal and you will play *futbol* again. Healing takes time and a lot of courage. You have truckloads of courage, Aline. You will do anything you want in life. I believe that."

The tears slipped down Aline's cheeks. "*Futbol* was the best thing I had in my life. And I'm not sure I deserve to ever play again when my teammates can't."

"That's the very reason you play, Aline. When my sister Mariane was murdered, I wasn't sure I would be able to set foot on a field again. But I took it slowly. I made short-term goals for myself to get back to playing, because I knew she was so proud of me. She'd been at every game she could to cheer me on." The lump grew in Ronaldo's throat. "If I had given up, I wouldn't have honored her memory. I would have lost more of who I was and what I loved. Aline, when it comes to get back to playing, you decide for yourself when it's time. And we're going to be right there with you, so you never feel like you're fighting by yourself. That's what you'll be doing every day to heal. You'll be fighting like the warrior you are. I'm going to save a spot for you on the *Guerreiras*, because being a warrior is part of your identity."

Aline closed her eyes. "I'm going to fight."

Within a few minutes, the tears stopped. Her breathing evened out and she slept.

"Coach?" Daniela whispered.

In the Shadows

He carefully extracted his hand from Aline's and moved to Daniela's bedside.

"Why them? Why were we spared?"

How many times had Ronaldo wondered the same thing? Why would someone with such a good heart as Mariane's be sacrificed to evil and the rest of them spared to remind themselves to breathe in and out every day? In twenty years, he still wasn't sure he had the right answer for himself, but he knew in his heart the answer for Daniela.

"Because you have incredible things to achieve. The force of their memory will drive you to soldier on and never waste a moment or an opportunity. Make the most of every day. And when you think of them, you will grieve. For a long time, you'll grieve. You'll mourn what they missed and what you missed getting to do beside them, but then you will find a way to make up for what the world now lacks because they're gone." He squeezed her hand. "And the world desperately needs good right now. A million little girls across this country need to go to sleep with hope, dreaming that someday they will live a life they only can aspire to. You can be that inspiration for them."

Because that was what Mariane had been to him. An inspiration.

Hers was the face he pictured in the crowd the next morning as he gave his speech to the press. Hers was the body he reburied at the funeral and gravesite of his three team members.

Violence had cut her life short, but it hadn't stopped her influence. Ronaldo made sure of that. Because of her, Brazilian girls would have the chance to do more than survive. They had the chance to become warriors and to change history in a way no one dared yet dream.

2 years later...

"Daniela, after this next play you're going in for Ava," Coach Rocha called. His steely gaze focused on the field, as if his words hadn't set her nerve-endings on fire.

Daniela smoothed her hair into place, a deep breath attempting to cleanse the anxiety. It helped a little.

Nothing could dull the life-altering excitement of this moment. This was her debut.

She stood at the center line next to the line referee waiting for the ball to go out of bounds.

Brazil was deadlocked in a one-to-one tie with Norway, fighting for the chance to play in the World Cup in a few months.

The crowd roared as the ball flew over Brazil's goalposts. She glanced over her shoulder to where Davi stood next to a blissfully married Cambridge and a pregnant Gabi. Davi jumped up and down, shouting her name. Valiana couldn't make it today, but normally she was in the seat next to him as often as she could be especially as she was his girlfriend. She had become Daniela's best friend and sister. When they made eye contact, Davi gave her a thumbs up.

Hadn't he told her this day would come despite her serious doubts and the major setbacks?

Ava jogged toward her on the side of the field. Eighteen minutes left on the clock.

Coach Rocha put his hand on her shoulder. "Leave it all out there. Your fresh legs will be just what that front line needs to drive it home." Ava slapped her hand, releasing Daniela to take her position. Coach Rocha took an extra second with her. "Go make history, Daniela."

Chills spread across her skin as the crowd's screams grew deafening. It was as if they knew she was making history as the second youngest *futbol* player in Brazil to play in an international match.

In the Shadows

Brazil's goalkeeper booted the ball to Norway's half of the field. Daniela's instincts kicked in over her nerves.

There was no crowd.

No internationally renowned players.

Just her and the semi-deflated ball on a dusty, pockmarked piece of land outside the *favela* in Rio.

She snagged the ball from a Norwegian defender and jumped over the incoming slide tackle. Off to the left, Emily had an open patch of grass in front of her with a clear shot on the goal.

Daniela picked up her head and crossed the ball in. With one touch, Emily redirected the ball's trajectory toward Norway's goal.

Low. Fast. Bending.

The ball blew past the goalkeeper's outstretched hands and smashed against the back of the net. The stadium erupted into chaos. Emily pointed at Daniela and met her in the box for a crushing hug. The rest of the team ran to meet them midfield.

But the game wasn't over until that final whistle blew. With a new wind, Brazil attempted two more goals which Norway's goalkeeper deflected. Norway made a run that Brazil's defense redirected.

The head referee glanced at his watch, lifted the whistle to his lips, and blew it three times.

They won!

Daniela sprinted toward the middle and dove into the pileup of players. Brazil's women's national team made it into the World Cup.

For the first time in her life, Daniela truly believed that dreams really did come true for girls like her.

Get free novella, Perfectly Designed!

Download from cdgill.com

Review:

If you enjoyed this book, would you leave a review on your favorite online retailer? It helps others take a chance on my books!

Social Media:

Facebook: www.facebook.com/cdgillauthor

Instagram: www.instagram.com/cd_gill

Goodreads: https://www.goodreads.com/author/15014967.C_D_Gill

Bookbub: https://www.bookbub.com/authors/c-d-gill

Also, signed paperbacks are available directly from my website anytime: cdgill.com

Acknowledgements

As with every book I finish, the list of people who contributed to its development is always longer than I anticipate when first starting to write it. My gratefulness is deep and heartfelt to these kind souls continue to allow me to invade their world with questions and needs or freely offer support when I need it most.

I am so thankful for the amazing and sweet Brazilian native Priscilla Shin for answering all my many questions about favelas and life in Brazil. She also willingly read this book for accuracy and sensitivity and that is solid gold.

To Peter Gill, my father-in-law and very tolerant medical adviser both fictionally and in real life, I am ever so grateful for your willingness to entertain my uneducated questions about what it takes to live and die.

Thank you, Kyle McVey, for always redirecting my sports world knowledge. It's been invaluable in the creation of Xander's world and beyond.

Clara, Isla, and Joan— your eagle eyes, love of story, and grammatical prowess are lifesaving. Thank you for using your talents to benefit my novels.

Sherri, you are a gift in so many ways that I cannot possibly write out here. Your encouragement and support have driven me to keep on.

No thank-you section would be complete without thanking the ones in my life who allow me the space to chase this dream of being an author. My husband and girls are my biggest supporters and a big reason I write. I couldn't be more grateful for who they are and how they show me love every day.

And to my amazingly faithful readers, your encouragement, excitement, and voracious reading push me to continue. Your support is a lighthouse in this dark world we navigate. I will always be grateful for you.

Thank you to Jesus, the author of hope.

More Ferra cousin books are coming. Contact me and tell me which cousin you want to read about. If you've gotten this far, thank you for reading my books and asking your libraries to get them! Please stay in touch!

All the best,
C.D. Gill

Made in the USA
Columbia, SC
16 November 2022